PERFECT

D. M. QUINTANO

MACMILLAN CHILDREN'S BOOKS

First published 2005 by Macmillan Children's Books
a division of Macmillan Publishers Limited
20 New Wharf Road, London N1 9RR
Basingstoke and Oxford
www.panmacmillan.com

Associated companies throughout the world

ISBN 0 330 42062 3

Copyright © D. M. Quintano 2005

The right of D. M. Quintano to be identified as the
author of this work has been asserted by her in accordance
with the Copyright, Designs and Patents Act 1988.

1 3 5 7 9 8 6 4 2

A CIP catalogue record for this book is available from
the British Library.

Typeset by Intype Libra Ltd
Printed and bound in Great Britain by Mackays of Chatham plc, Kent

'Are you real?' asks Emiliano. She doesn't look real. Not in the world he comes from.

'Of course I'm real.'

'I mean really real. A human – not an android.'

Lucia doesn't know what an android is.

'You must know,' says Emiliano. 'Robots. Machines that look like people.' The puzzled expression stays on the girl's impossibly perfect face. 'Like everybody else in this hole except you and the doctor.'

Lucia's eyes light up with understanding. 'Oh, you mean the AALFs.' She shakes her head. 'But they're not really machines, they're Almost Artificial Life Forms – modified people. They have human bodies but their minds are controlled by computers.'

Emiliano whistles. Flesh and chips. 'Just when I thought things couldn't get any better.' He crosses over to Lucia. 'Maybe I better introduce myself.' He extends his hand. 'Emiliano Shuh.'

This book is dedicated to the men, women, children and elders of the Zapatista National Army of Liberation of Chiapas, Mexico.

¡Sigue la lucha!

PART ONE

THE INFINITE FUTURE

Man Took Up Where
God Left Off

A Note on the Infinite Future

In the year 1940 AD the great war leader Winston Churchill had this to say: '*Never in the field of human conflict was so much owed by so many to so few.*' Mr Churchill was speaking about the plucky British resistance to the mighty Nazi military machine.

Nearly two millennia later the Corporation paraphrased Winston Churchill in the popular slogan: *Never Before Have So Few Done So Much for So Many.* This slogan referred to the spectacular achievements of human science and ambition that had allowed man to supplant both God and Nature as the ruler of the universe.

Man had never seen any real reason to settle for things the way they were when he could make them the way he wanted them to be, but the coming of the Corporation ended all argument on the subject. The Corporation's attitude, expressed in another of its favourite slogans, was: *If We Can Imagine It, We Can Do It.* And do it man did.

Determined to create a perfect environment for perfect people, man came to control the weather, the lands, the oceans, the sky – and even life itself. He created new species and improved on old ones. He designed his own progeny. He made plants that resisted drought and pestilence, and flawless humans who resisted ageing and disease. He made machines that could transmit an image anywhere in several galaxies in a matter of seconds and machines that could raze an enormous city in far less time than it takes you to boil an egg. He reduced the blue-green planet Earth to a grey wasteland with red seas and an orange sky, and built theme parks in the stars.

If Life on Earth were a car, it is fair to say that God and Nature wound up sitting in the back seat while man recklessly spun the wheel, gunned the engine and shot through every red light in sight. Indeed, at the time of our story, man has just about driven the car straight through a wall and over a cliff. God and Nature have passed out in the back seat, and the universe is now officially run by the Corporation.

The science that made God obsolete has turned against itself with spectacular results.

Or, to paraphrase Mr Churchill *and* the Corporation: *Never in the history of the cosmos have so few done so much to so many.*

CHAPTER ONE

Something to Celebrate

After years of disasters and defeats – of wars and rebellions and things going horribly wrong – the Corporation at last has something to celebrate. And celebrating it is.

The grand reception room of the governmental palace shines and shimmers with what look like tiny, far-away stars, and coloured globes of light drift through the air like bubbles. Images of waterfalls and the birds of jungles that were obliterated centuries ago decorate the room – seeming so real that some of the guests flinch from the spray and brush bird poop from their shoulders. Electronic music, sounding exactly like an old-fashioned philharmonic orchestra, seeps through the walls. There are even lavish banquet tables, laden with food that looks the way food used to be, bedecked with artificial flowers that smell as if they've just been picked and hologram candles that seem to burn and melt.

There are only two sorts of living things on the planet of Henry Kissinger: humans and Almost Artificial Life Forms (AALFs). The AALFs, which of course are in the majority, are sophisticated computers housed in the bodies of *Homo sapiens* and used as servants and soldiers and general workers. The humans are the society's elite, the government officials, high-ranking military officers and leading scientists who rule the Corporation, and they are all here tonight – and all resplendent in their dress uniforms or (just for fun) in the clothes of long-gone centuries and worlds.

In one corner of the room a young officer is talking to a girl a few years younger than he. Though barely more than a boy, the young officer, who is not in costume but has come as himself, is wearing enough medals for an entire regiment. The girl, who has also come as herself, has painted her face purple and black, and wears a long black dress with flowing sleeves, but, despite the old-fashioned clothes and outrageous make-up, she is so astoundingly beautiful that, unlike the waterfalls, the birds and the food, she doesn't look real.

The young soldier is Napoleon Lissi, son and heir of Justice Lissi, the all-powerful president of the Corporation. The beautiful girl is Lucia Hiko, daughter of the legendary geneticist Dr Nasa Hiko.

Although they haven't seen each other since the accident, Napoleon isn't asking Lucia how she is or telling her how he's missed her, he's talking about himself. Napoleon talking about himself is not, of course, one of the many rare or wonderful things still left in the cosmos.

Lucia nods and stifles several yawns. She has known Napoleon her whole life and has, therefore, heard it all before. She would very much prefer not to have to hear it again, but she is a captive as well as an unwilling audience. It's impossible for her to escape from him in her wheelchair without mowing down several people dressed as twentieth-century business-men in the process.

'I've made up my mind that that's the first thing I'm going to do when I get my own army,' Napoleon is saying. His own army is to be one of Napoleon's special presents for his twentieth birthday – now only a few months away. 'We've been soft on these rebels long enough . . . negotiating . . . making deals . . .' A gleam-ing green globe passes through his head but he doesn't miss a breath. 'Napoleon Lissi doesn't make deals with toxic-waste terrorists. We know that their stronghold's on Camelot. I'm going to liberate the planet, kill their leader and have done with all this nonsense once and for all.'

'You mean the Earth,' corrects Lucia. That once green and blue planet that is now more brown than green, more red than blue.

Napoleon isn't used to being corrected. Surprised into a pause in his monologue by the uniqueness of this event, he says, 'What?'

'You're going to liberate the Earth. Camelot's just the name of the Corporation outpost that was left there to guard the archives. The planet's real name is the Earth.' If he's going to finish it off he should at least know what it's called.

'Really? The Earth? The original planet?' Napoleon shakes his head – not in admiration, since he admires nothing but himself, but in amazement. 'How do you know all this old stuff?'

'I read a lot while I was convalescing,' replies Lucia. By now she is something of an expert on the past. It was a long convalescence.

But Napoleon, like most people, is only really interested in the future.

'Well, it doesn't matter a gluon what it's called, does it?' Napoleon laughs, a sound reminiscent of old-fashioned gunfire. 'You know what they say, a lump of rock by any other name . . . What matters is that it's from there that these bastard rebels instigate the uprisings in the rest of the colonies. It used to be the least of our worries, but now it's become an insidious network of insurrection. They've got arms caches and training camps and they're clever. Cleverer than you'd expect.' No trace of laughter is on his face now. 'That's what comes of being soft on this scum . . . letting them thrive instead of hunting them down like the subhuman life forms they are. What we need is zero tolerance. That's what we need.' He pounds his right fist into the palm of his left hand. And he is just the man to provide it.

Lucia stifles another yawn. She isn't the only person alive who might term what Napoleon calls 'soft' something else, something like 'ruthless' or 'psychotic'.

'Once I take care of whatever you want to call it, all other resistance will collapse and we can concentrate on decimating the aliens.' Like many great soldiers before him, Napoleon believes that the only way to peace is war. He puffs himself up like a nuclear cloud. 'I'm already preparing more troops. Sneaking them in bit by bit, so no one knows what's happening.' His smile is as thin as the cut of a scalpel. 'Between your mother's science and my military genius all our problems will soon be over.'

All Lucia wants is for the celebration to be over so she can go home and be left in peace. She stifles another yawn and changes the subject. 'This is quite a party, isn't it?'

'It's no more than Nasa Hiko deserves,' he answers. 'After all, she is going to save our species from extinction.' Napoleon's smile has all the charm of organic decay. 'But if you want to see a party, just wait till our wedding. Our wedding's going to make this look like taking a protein pill in space. I'm thinking of recreating something really spectacular – one of those theme parks or twentieth-century cities right here in the palace. What do you think of that?'

Not all that much, really. The mention of their wedding makes Lucia pale in what anyone less self-absorbed than Napoleon Lissi would recognize as abject horror.

'Ah . . .' says Lucia. 'Our wedding. I wanted to talk to you about that . . .' She takes a deep breath and treats Napoleon to a smile of her own – one he usually sees only in his dreams. 'We haven't really had a chance to talk since the . . . since the accident, but I want you to know that, naturally, I don't expect you to marry me now.'

There is little that is natural left in the cosmos, and Lucia's expectation doesn't seem to be one of them.

'What are you talking about?' Napoleon lets off another round of ammunition. 'This celebration's for us as well as your mother. Didn't she tell you?' He gives her another smile – one she usually sees only in her nightmares. 'My father's going to announce our engagement tonight.' As impossible as it might seem to someone who's known him for so long, Napoleon looks even more pleased with himself than usual. He rocks on his heels so his medals glint. 'Make it official.' Lucia Hiko is his other special present for turning twenty.

'Yes,' says Lucia. 'Yes, she told me.' But only as they were leaving their apartment to come to the party – very much as though it was such a trivial detail that the great Nasa Hiko had forgotten all about it until then, what with the dozens of really important things she has to remember. 'I only thought—'

'Don't think,' Napoleon advises. 'Thinking never did anyone any good. You know what they say,' he says, and quotes a Corporation slogan he has very much taken to heart. '"*Be Superficial.*"'

Lucia has by now stopped smiling, her expression as black as the rings round her eyes. 'But this is your chance to change your mind.' Which is what he's supposed to want to do. Which is what she'd been sure he would want to do. It isn't just Nasa Hiko who makes plans.

Napoleon blinks in confusion. 'And why would I do that?'

'Why?' Lucia's laugh is reminiscent of the sound once made by mountain streams. She gestures to her useless legs. 'Because of *these*.'

Napoleon frowns. 'You're not in pain, are you?'

'No, of course I'm not in pain.' Pain, like forests of trees and rivers of water, is a thing of the past – at least for people like them. 'But I'm not perfect any more.'

Lucia has miscalculated. Unfortunately for her, Napoleon is not as obsessed with perfection as her mother is. He has other obsessions, of which blowing bastard rebels into infinity is only one.

'You're perfect from the waist up,' he replies. 'So what if you can't walk, you can still fulfil your marital duties, can't you?'

And this is another.

It's Lucia's turn to look confused. 'Marital duties?'

'Of course.' Napoleon's medals wink like dozens of eyes. 'You're interested in the past – you must know about them . . . marital duties . . . like they did all those centuries ago . . .'

He means sex. Sex, both for reproduction and recreation, went out of usage even before the collapse of the planet Earth, but Napoleon is clearly keen to bring it back.

'Oh that,' says Lucia. 'I don't really know if I—'

'There's no problem there.' One of his hands

moves towards her. 'My father checked with your mother.'

'But you're the son of the most powerful man who ever lived – you're destined for greatness. You don't want to be tied to a cripple.'

Oh, but he does. Another Corporation slogan that Napoleon has taken very much to heart is: *I Am, Therefore I Should Get What I Want* – and Napoleon wants Lucia.

'You're missing the point,' says Napoleon. 'I may be the son of the president of the Corporation, but you're the daughter of the saviour of the human race. Now that Project Infinite Future's about to get started there's no limit to what we can do together.' His hand falls on her shoulder like a crow. 'We can build a dynasty that will rule the cosmos till the end of time.'

And what a thought that is.

Lucia's eyes are on his fingers, curled around her bones tighter than skin. Although Napoleon wants Lucia, Lucia loathes Napoleon and always has. What does she have to do to be rid of him? Kill herself after all?

'How nice to have something to look forward to,' murmurs Lucia.

Like many things, sarcasm is wasted on Napoleon Lissi. 'Exactly.' He gives her shoulder a squeeze. 'Besides, if it bothers you so much you can always get new legs, can't you? I don't see what the problem is.'

'I don't want someone else's legs,' says Lucia, in a tone of voice she usually reserves for her mother. 'Just the thought of it creeps me out.'

'You're probably still in shock from the accident,' judges Napoleon. 'You'll change your mind in time.'

'No I won't,' says Lucia. She wouldn't give Nasa Hiko the satisfaction.

Napoleon smiles as though he knows better. 'You can't tell . . . You haven't heard the big surprise yet.'

Lucia, who has already had enough surprises for one night, says warily, 'What surprise?'

'Well . . .' Napoleon gives her another squeeze. 'I really shouldn't tell you before my father makes his announcement but . . . since you ask . . .' His fingers move over her shoulder like slugs. 'Tomorrow, after your mother leaves for Saint Mona, you're moving into the palace.'

This news does not win him another heart-melting smile. 'I'm doing what?'

'You're moving in here.' He takes his hand away and starts to fiddle with the medals on his chest. 'With me and my father. We don't want you to be alone.'

Lucia stares into the party throng as though she sees the future and it is indeed infinite – infinite and as inviting as a black hole.

'How thoughtful of you,' she says.

While Napoleon and Lucia discuss their infinite future, Justice Lissi, the most powerful man who ever lived, and Nasa Hiko, the saviour of mankind, are on the other side of the room, sipping a liquid that looks and smells and tastes like wine, though, like them, it has never seen a grape.

Both of them are gazing at the highly decorated young soldier and the beautiful, if bizarre, girl in the wheelchair, but they are thinking very different things.

Before everything started to go so horribly wrong for mankind one of the most influential Corporation slogans of all times was: *Choose Your Children as You Choose Your Lunch*. And generation after generation did just that, with the rather ironic exception of Justice Lissi. Justice Lissi had to take what he could get. And yet, as he gazes through the imaginary birds and waterfalls and ersatz bubbles at his son, Justice Lissi can't help but think of himself as a man who would have been happy to lunch on a sandwich capsule but got a three-course meal instead. There is nothing in the cosmos that he wouldn't do for Napoleon. Arrogant, aggressive, determined and ruthless, Napoleon is everything his father could have hoped for. Justice Lissi sips his drink in a satisfied sort of way. Napoleon couldn't be more what he'd wanted if he had designed him himself.

Nasa Hiko, however, does not feel like that about Lucia. Not even a little. On the contrary, Nasa Hiko sees herself as a woman who ordered the kind of meal that used to be served to presidents and kings, and got a cheap vitamin pill, decades out of date, instead. The only thing Nasa Hiko wants for her child is to get rid of her, the sooner the better. As the great geneticist gazes at her daughter, she is wondering what ever possessed her to make herself a child when AALFs, another of her outstanding achievements, are so much more suitable in every way. AALFs – marketed under the slogan *The*

Biggest Boon to Business Since Slavery – never disobey, or talk back, or argue, or dress as though they're from the dawn of human time, while Lucia does all of these things. Nasa Hiko rubs one finger along the rim of her glass in a dissatisfied sort of way and thinks of a slogan she wishes she'd thought of before: *Children – Who'd Have Them*? Lucia couldn't be less what Nasa Hiko hoped for if she'd come about by chance and not design.

It is Justice Lissi who breaks this uncompanionable parental silence.

'Just look at them!' says Justice Lissi. 'The Great Warrior and the Great Beauty. The perfect couple! Doesn't it just take your breath away?'

The only thing likely to take Nasa Hiko's breath away is the atmosphere outside the dome that surrounds the colony on Henry Kissinger.

'*Nearly* perfect,' says Nasa Hiko, with her hooded-cobra smile.

Justice Lissi has the same rapid-fire laugh as his son. 'You're too hard on yourself, Nasa. You did your best to get her back on her feet – if she won't have the transplant there's nothing even you can do. So she can't walk. Walking's not all that necessary in this day and age, is it?'

There is, after all, no place to go.

Not even Nasa Hiko argues with Justice Lissi. 'No,' she answers, through lips as narrow as the beam of a laser. 'I suppose not.'

Justice Lissi sighs with the contentment only a man who has everything he could want or even imagine wanting can know. 'I didn't think anything would make me as happy as finally having a son of my own, but seeing them together like this comes close. It comes very, very close.'

And this, of course, is the reason Nasa Hiko made herself a daughter. It isn't just soldiers, politicians and businessmen who have a weakness for power. Nasa Hiko knew that if she provided Justice Lissi's son with the perfect partner – a partner she herself controlled – her position in the Corporation would forever be secure. But Nasa Hiko forgot that things often don't turn out the way man plans, and this time was not an exception. Too late she has come to realize that she has less control over Lucia than she has over yesterday.

'And I have you to thank for everything,' Justice Lissi continues. 'Especially for Napoleon. If I live to be a thousand, I'll never be able to thank you enough for giving me a son.'

Nasa Hiko accepts this praise with her usual humility. 'I was only doing my job.'

'No one else could have done it,' says Justice Lissi. 'After all those years . . . It was an old-fashioned miracle, that's what it was. An old-fashioned miracle.'

Nasa Hiko smiles. It was less like an old-fashioned miracle than a modern stroke of genius. Choosing children as if they were burgers was as serious a mistake as nuclear reactors. By selecting only the traits they wanted their children to have people eliminated quite a few that might have proved useful and kept the species vital – and alive. After decades of futile attempts to breed the president a son it was obvious to Nasa Hiko that Justice Lissi's genetic material is even more bankrupt that everyone else's. In a desperate but inspired leap of logic, Nasa Hiko, who has always been fond of the slogan *If at First You Don't Succeed, Try Again Somewhere Else*, did the one thing neither she nor anyone else had ever tried. She used the old to create the new.

'You saved me. Just like you're going to save mankind with Project Infinite Future,' says Justice Lissi.

It was Nasa Hiko's success in creating Napoleon by lifting a few ancient bits of DNA from the vaults of Camelot that gave her the idea for Project Infinite Future. If that could turn Justice Lissi's stagnant puddle of a genetic pool into a lake then surely it was possible to turn the human gene pool into an ocean. But she'd need more than a few strands of hair or flakes of skin. She'd need a supply of new genes. And that, of course, was where the problem lay. The Corporation and its citizens have never been as interested in yesterday as in tomorrow – and happily obliterated most of the past with the inspirational slogan: *Throw It Out and Get a New One.* There is little left of what used to be except what's on computer programmes. Where, then, is this new old blood to come from? There was only one answer to that question, though it took a genius like Nasa Hiko to find it: from the past itself.

Justice Lissi raises his glass. 'A toast!' he cries, and around him the guests fall silent. 'Only a person of staggering intellect could have conceived of something as audacious and courageous as Project Infinite Future – and only the great Nasa Hiko could make it work.'

Of all those assembled, only Justice Lissi and Nasa Hiko have any idea of what Project Infinite Future actually is, but they all raise their glasses as if they do.

The ancient and forgotten Buddhists, who taught that men are no more important than specks of dust and should therefore practise humility, lost nothing when Nasa Hiko decided to dedicate her life to science.

'Thank you,' says Nasa Hiko, 'but you're far too kind.' She raises her own glass high and touches it to Justice Lissi's. 'It's simply what I was put in this universe to do.'

CHAPTER TWO

Lucia Hiko Continues to Give Her Mother a Hard Time

Lucia is used to being lonely. She lives in a world where most people engage more with computers than with each other and rarely have any need to leave their homes. The majority of the Corporation's citizens don't notice this lack of human contact, but, thanks to her mother, Lucia is too smart not to. The party, however, made her feel even lonelier.

Though perhaps it isn't the party that has made her feel as the last member of the Mohican tribe must have felt all those centuries ago when he found himself alone with the white men. Perhaps it's the fact that, as unhappy as she is, last night made Lucia realize just how much unhappier she's going to be.

After the party, Nasa Hiko went to her lab to

finish packing, leaving Lucia to go home on her own, with only the sound of her wheels for company. *This is the last time I'll sleep in my bed* . . . Lucia kept thinking as she made her way through the gleaming corridors. *The last time I'll sit in my room* . . . *The last time I'll be me* . . .

The apartment was dark when she got there. The AALFs who look after it and its occupants were already in sleep mode and humming dully. Lucia didn't need them. She's made sure that, despite her useless legs, she can look after herself.

Too unhappy to go straight to sleep, Lucia went to her room and watched old movies on her personal communications system (PCS). The movies Lucia likes best are restricted and accessible only to high-ranking members of the Corporation, but this is a detail she learned to circumvent years ago. To Lucia, watching these movies is like being visited by ghosts – ghosts with tales to tell of a brighter past. On this night, however, the stories of ancient humans who lived with only the sky above them and grass beneath their feet did nothing to cheer her up.

It was a restless night.

Every time Lucia shut her eyes she was back at the party. She saw her mother standing beside Justice Lissi while he announced the engagement, smiling in triumph, her eyes on Lucia as if to say *I won* . . . *I won* . . . *I told you I would* . . . She saw Napoleon Lissi's handsome, vapid face, grinning at her as though she was a bastard rebel he was planning to disembowel.

When she finally fell asleep her dreams were worse than her memories. It was her wedding day. Napoleon Lissi stood at an altar copied from a photograph of a once famous cathedral, imposing in the uniform of a Corporation commander. 'This is the day I've been waiting for since you came out of the incubator,' Nasa Hiko whispered as she pushed Lucia over a path of red carpet strewn with artificial rose petals. 'The day I finally give you away!' Lucia woke up as Napoleon leaned down to kiss her.

By the time morning comes, Lucia is exhausted from lack of sleep but, surprisingly enough, not from despair. Most citizens of the Corporation believe the famous slogan *I Think, Therefore I Can Do What I Want*, but Lucia, perhaps because of her fascination with the past, believes in destiny. There is more at work in the universe than the laws of quantum mechanics. Nor does Lucia accept that her destiny is to spend the rest of her life listening to Napoleon Lissi talk about himself. Unfairness barely comes into it, it just simply cannot be – she won't let it. Lucia doesn't call Nasa Hiko 'mother' for nothing.

Nasa Hiko walks briskly down the corridor, humming the Corporation's anthem, 'We Are the Ones', under her breath. The humming of the anthem raises Lucia's spirits. It means her mother is in a good mood – an event that, like the passing of a comet, happens quickly and infrequently – which could work in her favour. Lucia doesn't ever want to move into the palace, and she certainly doesn't want to move into it any sooner than she has to. Her only hope is to get away from Henry Kissinger. Who knows what might happen in that time? Another rebel bomb might hit the colony. A shipload of space debris might flatten it. Napoleon might contract one of the super infections that have ravished the galaxies. She just needs to be away long enough to give Fate a chance to intervene.

Lucia swings herself out of bed and into her chair. She dresses quickly but carefully. No long black frock, no heavy black and purple make-up, no dangling earrings or clanging bangles this morning. She puts on the plain and functional leggings and top that everyone wears, in colours as pale as most people's memories of the past. She doesn't want to annoy her mother today. She wants to act as though they get on.

Nasa Hiko is at the food centre taking her breakfast of vitamins as Lucia rolls into the room. Lucia starts to call out an untypically cheerful, 'Good morning,' but gets no further than, 'Good—' before Nasa Hiko cuts her off.

'You did it on purpose, didn't you?' she snaps, turning around with a scowl on her face. There is nothing untypical about this.

Lucia avoids her mother's eyes. 'Did what?' she snaps back. Even at its best (a period that ended when Lucia was two) the relationship between Nasa Hiko and her daughter was never perfect, but things between them started to go really wrong as soon as Lucia was old enough to have a mind of her own – and have been even worse since the accident. 'I didn't do anything.'

Nasa Hiko walks behind her as she crosses to the drinks dispenser. 'No, of course you didn't. It was some other ungrateful cripple who told Napoleon he didn't have to marry her.'

Still not looking at her mother, Lucia reaches up and pushes a button, slowly counting to ten while the plastic cup fills with a synthetic liquid that tastes something like tea used to taste. This is not the time for a show of temper. 'I was just trying to consider his feelings,' she lies.

'Oh, please. He's a soldier – he doesn't have any feelings. You just wanted to make me look bad.'

'Make *you* look bad?' It never ceases to amaze Lucia how nothing she does ever affects her as much as it affects her mother. 'And how could *I* do that?'

'Don't act all innocent with me, young lady. You may be able to get Napoleon to believe anything you want just by smiling at him but you can't work me like that. How do you think it would look for me if you rejected the next president of the Corporation? Did you ever think of that?'

'I—' says Lucia.

'No, of course you didn't,' says Nasa Hiko.

'But Napoleon would never think I was rejecting him,' argues Lucia. 'He's too—'

'Stupid?' suggests her mother, who, unlike Justice Lissi, does not regard Napoleon as one of her finest achievements. He's more violent than an exploding star and far less bright. 'Too aggressive? Too self-obsessed?'

But Lucia is not about to be tricked into the truth. 'Too kind,' says Lucia.

Nasa Hiko's smile holds not daggers but a nuclear warhead. 'Of course he is,' she sneers. 'But his father isn't. If Justice Lissi didn't have so much sympathy for you because of your damn accident he would have realized what your touching demonstration of self-sacrifice really meant.'

It is clear that Justice Lissi's sympathy for Lucia isn't shared by her mother. And why should it be? The accident would never have happened if Lucia hadn't wilfully disobeyed her once again.

'But I wasn't reject—'

'Enough!' Nasa Hiko cuts her off as efficiently as an old-fashioned guillotine detached heads. 'I don't want to hear any more. This is probably the last time I'll see you till the wedding and I'd like it to be as pleasant as possible.'

'And I don't? Why do you think I got up so early?' Lucia is as close to apologetic as she has ever come. 'To tell you the truth, I'm going to miss you.'

Her mother smiles, coolly and unenthusiastically. 'How touching.'

'No, really. I mean, it's always been just you and me, hasn't it? It's going to be hard to get used to being without you.'

In reality, of course, this isn't strictly accurate. It has always been just Nasa Hiko, with Lucia off to one side with her late and much-lamented personal AALF, Mr Ford. But, like many a bad mother before her, Nasa Hiko likes to think that she invented motherhood and is happy to accept this distorted version of the truth with her usual modesty.

'It's about time you showed some appreciation for all I've done for you,' says Nasa Hiko.

'Oh, I do . . .' Lucia pauses, taking a deep breath. 'That's why I was kind of hoping that . . . that I could come with you.'

For once the great brain fails. Nasa Hiko frowns. 'Come with me? Come with me where?'

'To Saint Mona.'

It isn't often that Nasa Hiko laughs, and it's probably just as well – given its similarity to the cry of the tortured. 'To Saint Mona? You think you're going to get out of marrying Napoleon by hiding out at the other end of the universe?'

'Of course not. And I don't mean forever. Just for a while. To help me adjust.'

Nasa Hiko eyes her as if she is a recalcitrant gene. 'Have you lost your mind now as well as your legs?'

'But Napoleon's birthday's not for months and he'll be busy preparing for his war. I'd rather be with you than rattling round the palace by myself.'

'You can spare me the daughterly love routine too. It's out of the question. I have very important work to do. And, believe me, *you* are not it.'

'But I—'

'You'll be a married woman soon.' Nasa Hiko takes her flight bag from the counter. 'You might as well start getting used to it.' The conversation is over.

'Well at least can I go down to the ship to see you off?'

Greatness does demand generosity, of course. 'Gate 99.' Nasa Hiko smiles. 'By the time you get back, the AALFs will have packed all your things.'

After Nasa Hiko leaves, Lucia goes back to her room and changes into one of her funereal dresses, hangs feathers from her ears, draws purple circles around her eyes and colours her lips black. She's not worried about annoying her mother now.

The spaceport is larger than Disneyland used to be and even busier, but Lucia isn't daunted by either its size or the activity. She has been here dozens of times before. Nasa Hiko is always going or coming from somewhere, and Lucia (one of the major props in her mother's public performances) is often waving from the appropriate observation deck when she does.

The security AALFs all nod in recognition as Lucia rolls down the main concourse to the gate from which the ship for Saint Mona will depart. There's no mistaking her, of course; hers is the only wheelchair on the planet.

Lucia would have had no trouble finding her mother's departure gate even if she didn't know the number. Justice Lissi and Napoleon are already on the observation deck, their bodyguards around them like a wall. The ship docked behind gate 99 is the president's personal carrier. It bears the muted gold insignia of the Corporation along one side and, underneath, the motto of the space fleet: *If It Exists It's Ours*. Justice Lissi and

Napoleon have their eyes on the ship being readied for take-off.

Perhaps Lucia is right to believe in Fate after all.

For it is certainly true that if Justice Lissi and his son weren't there Lucia would have rolled on to the observation deck as she'd intended. She would have waved to her mother as she boarded the ship. Once the ship had soared into the air and the protective dome had closed again Lucia would have rolled back home to get ready for her move, albeit like a girl preparing for her death.

But none of those things happen because the sight of the Lissis, father and son, fills Lucia with such panic and revulsion. She doesn't want to talk to them right now. She doesn't want to have to act as though marrying Napoleon is a dream come true. She doesn't want them to see her cry as the ship rises above them, even if they think her tears are for the departing Hiko and not the one left behind. She absolutely doesn't want Napoleon to give her one of his slimy, I-own-you smiles.

So instead of going forward, Lucia backs off and rolls down the walkway that leads to the ground.

The belly of the ship is open and Nasa Hiko's things are still being loaded aboard.

Lucia looks up as she reaches the launch area. Nasa Hiko has reached the entrance to the ship and is smiling over at Justice Lissi and his son. Justice Lissi and Napoleon are smiling back. None of them sees Lucia.

Another important Corporation slogan, coined to convince people that virtual reality is better than the real thing, is this: *You Can Go Where You Like, So Why Stay Here?*

Why indeed? thinks Lucia as she gazes at the presidential carrier, its belly open like an invitation.

No one stops her as she reaches the cargo hold. No one shouts at her to get away as she flips her chair on to the moving ramp. And no one hauls her back as she follows the last of Nasa Hiko's luggage into the ship.

Such is the nature of Fate.

CHAPTER THREE

Why No One Ever Visits Saint Mona

'For the love of Lissi,' bellows Nasa Hiko. 'That's not a box of rocks you've got there, you know! I don't want anything broken.'

It's the familiar sound of her mother shouting that wakes Lucia. She blinks in the light that spreads through the cargo hold, thinking, for a second, that she must have been dreaming, not certain where she is. And then her eyes focus and she sees the crates stacked around her and remembers.

'Gently! Gently!' shrieks the great geneticist. 'If you damage that I'll have you disconnected.'

Lucia peers round the boxes that block her view. At the door of the cargo hold two AALFs are loading crates on to large metal trolleys. The AALFs are dressed in the black uniforms, boots and face helmets of the fearsome Elite Guard, though bent under the stern eye of Nasa Hiko they look more like schoolchildren than the scourge of the outer galaxies. Nasa Hiko herself stands at the entrance, overseeing the transfer as though they are not only schoolchildren but schoolchildren defusing their first bomb.

Not a little overwhelmed by her own daring, Lucia hasn't thought about what happens next, but the matter is taken out of her hands when it simply happens. Nasa Hiko turns from the job at hand and looks into the hold as though someone has called her name. Her eyes come to rest on Lucia.

For a second or two the great geneticist is surprised into silence and simply stares at her daughter as though she's merely the hologram of a girl in a wheelchair hiding behind boxes in the belly of a star ship. The AALFs, following her lead, stare too, but, having no feelings, aren't surprised.

'What the hell are you doing here?' shouts Nasa Hiko, recovering from her momentary lapse of control.

Lucia starts. 'Who me?'

'No, that girl behind you,' her mother sneers. 'Of course I mean you. You're the only one who always disobeys me.' Nasa Hiko leaps into the ship as though she's on springs and strides towards Lucia. 'Well? What the hell are you doing here?'

'N-nothing,' stammers Lucia. 'I just . . . I . . .' There used to be an old saying that inspiration is ninety-nine per cent perspiration, meaning hard work, but in this case it means panic. 'It was an accident. I was looking for you to say good-bye and I—'

'In the cargo hold?' Nasa Hiko's scorn is shrill. 'You were looking for me among the baggage?'

Well, you're in the cargo hold now . . . thinks Lucia. Aloud she says, 'Somebody said they'd seen you—'

'It's not going to work, Lucia.' Nasa Hiko gazes at her as many a mother has gazed at her child, wondering what went wrong. 'You'll be on the first flight back to Henry Kissinger . . .' Nasa Hiko checks the personal communicator strapped to her wrist. 'Which will be in exactly ten days, six hours and thirty-seven minutes. I'll tell Justice Lissi you were frightened of being without me because of the accident so I decided to take you with me till you calmed down.' She gives Lucia another look. 'You'll tell Napoleon how sorry you are and how much you miss him. Is that understood?'

As Lucia nods obediently, if unenthusiastically, one of the guards loses its grip on the box it's unloading and it crashes to the ground.

Nasa Hiko swings round. 'What did I tell you?' she screams. 'Watch what you're doing! Pick those things up!'

'What's that?' Lucia lifts herself up in her chair and cranes her head around her mother for a better look.

'Medical equipment,' snaps Nasa Hiko. She turns back to Lucia. 'I have too much to do right now for this nonsense. I'll deal with you later.' She snaps her fingers at one of the guards as she marches back the way she came, jerking a finger behind her. 'EG542! Get her out of here. Take her to my apartment. And make sure she stays there.'

Lucia watches her mother and the other guard heft the box on to the trolley and start across the landing field. She got only the briefest of glimpses of the contents of the box, but she saw nothing that looked like medical equipment – no metal instruments, no machines, no test tubes or vials. What she saw looked like piles of clothes – very old-fashioned clothes.

Trust Us . . . thinks Lucia as a door across the field closes behind Nasa Hiko. *We Know What's Best* . . .

The first thing Lucia realized when she began to think for herself was that she couldn't trust her mother.

On the occasion of her twelfth birthday, Lucia asked Nasa Hiko a simple question, and her mother answered with a simple lie. The question was: 'Why was I made?' Nasa Hiko's answer was, 'Because I love you.' Although Lucia would have been happy to believe this, she'd been taught to choose logic over emotion, and logic said that this couldn't be true. If Nasa Hiko loved her, why did she spend so little time with her? If Nasa Hiko loved her, why did she do nothing but criticize and nag? If Nasa Hiko loved her, why was it that everything Lucia did had to be what her mother wanted her to do? If Nasa Hiko loved her, why had it been decided even before Lucia came out of the incubator that she would some day marry Napoleon Lissi?

But it's a sad fact that to learn the truth you often

have to search for it. It was then that Lucia got the idea to hack into her mother's computer, looking for the answer to her question, and discovered more than she'd bargained for – as people often do.

The answer to Lucia's question was bad enough, of course. Lucia was made not out of love but because of her mother's obsession with perfection. She was not Nasa Hiko's first child; she was simply the only one that came close enough to the great doctor's standards to be kept.

But Lucia's other discoveries were even worse.

Nasa Hiko, as it turned out, isn't the only one who lies. The only time the Corporation itself tells the truth is on the rare occasion when the truth happens to agree with the lie it was going to tell in the first place.

For Nasa Hiko's computer contained the unofficial and very secret history of the Corporation and its empire. Unlike the official and public history, which specializes in glory and triumph, the unofficial and secret history tells nothing but the truth. The empire, it seemed, is not the man-made paradise Lucia (and everyone else) has been told it is. While the ruling elite and their minions live in hi-tech splendour, their subjects either eke out miserable existences in forgotten colonies scattered among the stars or live vegetal lives imprisoned in their domes, beset by the multiple breakdowns of their technology, their environments and their own bodies; a human buffer between the elite of the Corporation and outside invasion. The 'minor rebellions by fanatics and terrorists' are, in fact, major revolts by conquered species that want their planets back, and citizens of the empire who have nothing left to lose. The constant wars that have wreaked such havoc and destruction throughout the universe have not been fought for freedom and democracy 'and to protect civilization against the barbarian hordes of the outer galaxies, but for power and all that comes with it.

The truth made for pretty grim reading, to put it mildly. Which of course is one of the reasons it is kept secret. To paraphrase an ancient poem, when ignorance is bliss leave it alone – and with this thought the Corporation (like many a government before it) enthusiastically agreed, dedicating itself to ensuring that this ignorance was not just blissful but numbingly complete.

As a species, humans have always prided themselves on their superior intelligence, which is somewhat ironic if you consider how little most people think – and to what they put their minds when they do. Not only have man and his superior intelligence managed to all but destroy a universe that took billions of years to create in only a few millennia, but he is easily led – and the Corporation has made it its business to do just that.

As an example of how easy it is to manipulate people, during the years when the Corporation was taking control of every aspect of human life it used the slogan *Trust Us, We Know What's Best* to convince people that its critics were crackpots and dangerous agitators. You wouldn't think that so empty and arrogant a phrase would win the hearts and minds of a gaggle of geese, but it worked like a drug. People believed it.

One of the things the Corporation asked to be trusted about was Saint Mona.

An official Corporation release described Saint Mona like this:

> *Representing the latest in scientific and technological advancement, the medical colony of Saint Mona is a vital research facility, a highly advanced hospital with an intergalactic reputation, and a state-of-the-art rehabilitation centre. Here patients receive the highest level of care at the same time that the knowledge and abilities of science are pushed ever forward.*

Not much of this is true, of course. For although Saint Mona is engaged in medical research, does function as a hospital of sorts and rehabilitates in the sense that it keeps people who should be dead alive, its primary function is as a breeding farm.

When Justice Lissi took charge of the Corporation over fifty years ago, he faced two major problems.

The first concerned the empire itself. The colonies were so far-flung and difficult to maintain, and the wars to protect them so frequent and so costly, that a docile and expendable workforce and army were a necessity.

What to do? The population had been decimated. First by the endless conflicts, then by its own inability to reproduce and, finally, by the arrival of the new, drug-defying diseases and the unexpected return of diseases forgotten for centuries. Fewer and fewer of the Corporation's ordinary citizens – the ones expected to do all the work – were willing to leave the comparative safety of their homes to colonize new chunks of barren rock in the outer reaches of space. Fewer and fewer people were willing to fight in wars from which they knew they would never return.

The second problem concerned the human longing for immortality – as old as the longing for power and possessions. Nobody wanted to die. Ever since the first successful heart transplant, the demand for organs, bones and limbs to replace faulty ones had steadily increased. Indeed, despite the expense of the replacement procedures, the demand soon far surpassed the supply. There would never be enough donors to go around – not willing ones at any rate. Here were limitless profits to be made, and no way to make them.

But once again the ingenuity of man, in the shape of Dr Nasa Hiko, found the perfect solution to both problems.

She created AALFs, humans with computers for brains, to do most of the work and most of the dying. And she created Replicant Life Forms (REPs), humans with virtually no brains at all, to provide the spare parts to repair the human elite. She began to breed people the way people once bred goats. She began to grow people the way people once grew potatoes. There was no limit to the number of AALFs and REPs she could reproduce.

The Corporation would never be short of a soldier, a ditch digger, a kidney or a hefty profit again.

As a matter of galactic security, the breeding farm is top secret. This is not because some wishy-washy liberal might kick up a fuss, as so often happened in the past – wishy-washy liberals being more rare than chickens in this day and age – but because, in the inspirational words of Nasa Hiko, 'The less people know about what we do, the easier it is to do it.' This is why the farm is on Saint Mona. Saint Mona is both difficult to get to unless you run the Corporation and not worth the trip if you don't.

It is here that Lucia, desperate to get away from Napoleon Lissi, has ended up. Which could be a case of out of the frying pan and into the fire, as the people of the Earth used to say.

PART TWO

THE FINITE PAST

If It Exists It's Ours

A Note on the Finite Past

For nearly two decades now scouting parties from Henry Kissinger have been going back through time to the Earth as it once was, gathering information and data so that Nasa Hiko could choose exactly when and where the human specimens that would save the species from extinction should come. Nasa Hiko didn't want to leave anything to chance. Her previous experiments with the past (otherwise known as Napoleon Lissi and Lucia Hiko) made her wary. She wants control, not surprises. She wants, as many before her have wanted, to create a super race, not end up with throwbacks to a time when people painted themselves blue and stuck bones through their ears.

It soon became apparent that Nasa Hiko's caution was more than justified. Quite a few centuries and civilizations proved to be totally unsuitable for exploitation, to say the least. Indeed, some of the scouting parties sent to pre-Christian Rome, medieval Europe and the Mexico of the Aztecs never returned at all. The parties that did return brought back hair-raising tales of such primitiveness, superstition and stupidity that even the great and optimistic Nasa Hiko became temporarily acquainted with despair. It was sobering to think that a species that had mastered genetic engineering should have evolved from a species that believed that a blood sacrifice would ensure a good harvest and a falling star signified starvation.

And then Nasa Hiko finally got the break she needed. One of the parties came back with a newspaper that had been printed at the very end of the second millennium.

This newspaper was printed in the long-forgotten city of Los Angeles, in the year 1999. Most of the newspaper seemed to be devoted to advertisements for things no one uses any more, or accounts of the boring lives of people who are also long-forgotten and tales of pointless violence, but way at the back in the entertainment section, and against all odds, Nasa Hiko finally found something useful. Indeed, it was more than useful: it was exciting; it was inspirational; it was exactly what she'd been looking for.

And so it is that two days after Nasa Hiko lands on Saint Mona the time probe will return with its precious cargo – with the perfect human specimens that will provide everything necessary to haul the human species back from the brink of extinction.

On such small and chance occurrences is the fate of the universe determined.

CHAPTER FOUR

Back in the Twentieth Century, Mrs Fugosi Has Her One Cup of Coffee and Wishes the Day Was Over

Mrs Fugosi finishes checking that the Top Teens' flights that arrive this afternoon are all on schedule, and then crosses the pearl-grey carpet of her office to the table where the red light of the coffee maker glows. She moves slowly because her arthritis is bothering her today. Mrs Fugosi is an orderly and disciplined person who allows herself only one cup of coffee each morning, but today she makes it a large one. It is only nine forty-two and already she wishes the day was over.

Mrs Fugosi has worked for *Top Teens* for five long years, ever since Mr Fugosi was run over by a Cadillac and went to heaven. Mrs Fugosi never had any children, though not for lack of trying. She and Mr Fugosi were desperate to have a child to love, but, as Mr Fugosi himself always said, God had other plans. And then God's plans turned out to include his untimely death, and Mrs Fugosi, rather than get stuck in the past, started looking for a job to give her something to do so she didn't spend the rest of her life watching talk shows and crying.

After several weeks of discovering that no one was particularly interested in hiring a fifty-five-year-old housewife who had never used a computer, Mrs Fugosi saw the ad in the *Los Angeles Times*:

> *Mom needed for popular TV show. Must be organized, patient, kind and good in emergencies.*

Mrs Fugosi is extremely organized, inhumanly patient, outstandingly kind and beyond a doubt the person you want with you when the elevator gets stuck between floors. She applied for the job. When she discovered that the popular TV show looking for a mom was *Top Teens*, the most popular television show in the history of the cathode ray tube, Mrs Fugosi was sure she didn't stand a chance. After all, the *Top Teens* contestants are special in every conceivable way, and Mrs Fugosi is not. She is short, overweight and, even in her youth, was not what you would call a beauty unless you were judging potatoes. She did badly at school, can't sing, dance or play a musical instrument, and has never won a prize for anything – not even a booby prize. What she lacks in skills and talents she makes up for in ailments. Besides the arthritis, Mrs Fugosi has a bad back, migraines and a jumbo jet of allergies. She went to the interview anyway, since, as she told herself philosophically, she had nothing better to do.

Mrs Fugosi was surprised and delighted to get the job. It was a few months before she wondered if anyone else had been stupid enough to apply.

The format of *Top Teens* is uncomplicated. Each week a group of teenagers from all over the United States of America compete for exciting prizes – and, even more importantly, at least five minutes of excruciating fame. The winners not only get thousands of dollars in merchandise and scholarships, but they are treated as celebrities – fêted by the seriously famous, interviewed by the media, paid fortunes to advertise sneakers and T-shirts, and given the chance at careers as pop stars, models or actors as well. These teenagers, selected after a multitude of interviews and tests, represent the current ideal of what a well-rounded person should be. They are attractive, but not too attractive; get good grades but aren't too intelligent; have several talents but no real passions; are personable but have little true character.

It was, in fact, an article about *Top Teens* in the newspaper brought back to Henry Kissinger by Captain Titanic that Nasa Hiko was reading when she recognized the solution to her problem. From what she gathered, the Top Teens are as perfect as humans get without genetic modification, which makes them the breeding stock she sought.

Mrs Fugosi's job is to make sure that everything

goes smoothly. It is Mrs Fugosi who makes all the arrangements for the guests each week. It is Mrs Fugosi who handles all problems and crises. It is Mrs Fugosi who chaperones the girls, and supervises the male chaperone and the driver. Mrs Fugosi's job could therefore be seen as an important one.

This is not, however, the way Mrs Fugosi sees it. Mrs Fugosi sees her job as working in hell with a good medical plan and an expense account.

There was a time – before she actually started doing it – when Mrs Fugosi thought that working for *Top Teens* would give her the children she'd never have. This hasn't turned out to be the case, either.

For, with few small exceptions, the contestants in the nation's most popular television show of all time have proven to be nothing like the children Mrs Fugosi would never have. Demanding, spoiled, self-centred and constantly complaining, they've proven to be the children no one in her right mind would ever want. It is no exaggeration to say that Mrs Fugosi wouldn't care if she never saw another teenager for as long as she lives. Not even from a distance. Not even on a TV set with bad reception. Especially a Top Teen. In Mrs Fugosi's opinion (and she knows that Mr Fugosi would agree with her if he could), if these are the best the country has to offer she would really hate to see the worst.

As if already aware of just how truly awful this day is going to be, Mrs Fugosi sips her coffee slowly, trying to make it last. She has a bad feeling.

Mrs Fugosi considers herself to be at least slightly

psychic, and has been prone to bad feelings all her life. In fact, as she now remembers it, she had a very bad feeling the day Mr Fugosi was hit by the Cadillac. Though she did nothing about it at the time of course – just as she will do nothing about it now.

If Mrs Fugosi were more than slightly psychic, she might realize that today's bad feeling is caused by the fact that once she meets the six contestants at the airport this afternoon, nothing will go as planned. Neither she nor the contestants will ever reach the hotel. Neither she nor the contestants will remain on the planet Earth in the twentieth century either. It would, therefore, be a very good day for Mrs Fugosi to tell her boss that she has a migraine and to go home.

This possible course of action does occur to her. She stares into her cup, chewing on her bottom lip while she debates with herself whether or not she should go home. Unfortunately, the thought of home doesn't make her feel any better. The thought of home makes her feel lonely.

And so it is that, rather than give up and head for the hills, Mrs Fugosi reaches for the phone to tell the limousine to pick her up at three.

CHAPTER FIVE

Emiliano Shuh Writes a Poem

Emiliano Shuh has been in this cabin three days.

Hidden in the trees across the road, he watched the family that owns this weekend home pack up their late-model SUV with a lot of yelling and bad temper on Sunday afternoon. You'd think they weren't four of the luckiest bastards who ever lived the way they sniped and shrieked at each other. You'd think they were suffering. It was enough to break your heart. Emiliano named them the Grump Family because they did nothing but bicker. The squabbling of the parents and the whining of the two children could still be heard as the vehicle rolled down the road. *Dump the Grumps*, he thought as he watched them go. The undeserving rich.

As soon as they were out of sight, Emiliano let

himself in through an unlocked bedroom window. People like the Grumps think they're so entitled to everything they have that they feel safe enough to be careless. Which is not something ever likely to be said about Emiliano Shuh.

It's pretty cool in the cabin, especially at night. Almost like a real home. At least it's what Emiliano thinks a real home would be like. Cosy. Comforting. Safe. He found some feathers and the skull of a bird on one of his walks through the woods, and he's laid them out by the fireplace like an offering – or maybe like an altar. He can't risk a fire or turning on a light – just in case – but he found over a dozen candles in the kitchen and he's put them in the fireplace in soldier-like rows, which solves both problems and is nearly as good as a real blaze.

Emiliano opens another beer and leans back against the sofa, staring at the flames that flicker just beyond his feet. He is imagining the sun setting over the Grand Canyon. Or maybe the sun rising over the ancient Maya city of Chichén Itzá. Seeing the sun setting over the Grand Canyon and rising over the ancient Maya city of Chichén Itzá are Emiliano Shuh's only real ambitions in life. He saw pictures of the Grand Canyon in a magazine in the hospital once. It wasn't like LA or any other place he's ever seen or even imagined. It was timeless. It was pure beauty. It made him think, for the first time in his life, that there really might be a God – one who knows what He is doing. Chichén Itzá he saw in a book in school. The book was called *Worlds of the Past*. None of those worlds reminded him of the one he seems to be stuck in, either, but it was Chichén Itzá, city of warriors, that he remembers. You might assume that it would have made him think of the Maya – mystic and mythic, fierce and doomed – but, like the Grand Canyon, it made him think of the force that shifts the stars.

The feathers shine in the light and the skull seems almost to be smiling. Emiliano is smiling. This is the life. A nice, warm, dry house to sleep in and beer to drink. A place to think about your dreams. He lights one of the cigarettes he liberated with the beers, and blows several rings of smoke towards the candles.

Emiliano feels no more remorse for his theft of the cigarettes and beer than he feels for breaking into the Grumps' weekend cottage – which is none at all. In his opinion, the people who owned the beer and the cigarettes were asking for it too. What kind of dumb deadhead leaves two six-packs just sitting on the patio where anyone could take it? And not cheap crap, either. Imported beer from Mexico. In bottles. Emiliano thought only wine came in bottles. And, up until he held the first one in his hand, reading the label with interest, he didn't know they made beer in Mexico either. He wondered what else went on south of the border that he didn't know about. He's always been a curious kind of kid.

He is not, however, a particularly happy kind of kid. Indeed, it is also Emiliano's opinion, formed over seventeen years of largely bad experience, that life is a mega bummer and waste of time – something to be endured, like a prison sentence – and that anyone who doesn't believe this is either incredibly stupid, incredibly lucky or (incredibly enough) both. Now that he's on his fourth bottle of imported beer, however, he is feeling what passes for happiness in his world: an alcoholic buzz.

Emiliano's never really had much opportunity to stare into a fire before – not even a pretend one like this – but he likes it.

The combination of the shimmering light and the beer has him surfing through space and time. He feels as though he is both moving and totally still. Emiliano is an old friend of fear, but this is the first time in his seventeen long years that he experiences real excitement – and something close to joy. He feels as if it isn't just spoiled brats like the Grump children who have possibilities: he has them too. He has worlds to explore and things to do – if only he knew what they might be.

Just before alcoholic paralysis sets in halfway through the second six-pack, Emiliano writes a poem. He read a few poems long, long ago during his all too brief academic career – none of which he remembers liking – but he has never written a poem himself before or felt any urge to. He writes it on the back of a piece of the cardboard that once held the beer.

This is Emiliano's poem:

Hope for the best but be prepared – even if you don't know what for.

After he writes the poem, Emiliano crawls up on the couch, pulls the patchwork quilt he found in one of the closets over him, and passes out.

Writing poems is hard work.

CHAPTER
SIX
Ora Sonorious Goes Shopping

Ora Sonorious wakes up this morning in a really bad mood.

Ora often wakes up in a really bad mood, and this mood often continues through the entire day. She wasn't always like this – she used to be just as happy as anyone else she knows – but everything seemed to go wrong last winter.

The first thing that went wrong was her boyfriend, Foster. Foster dumped her on Christmas Eve because he'd decided she was too tall. Ora is tall – in fact, she's very tall, especially for a girl – but she didn't think she was as tall as all that. It could make finding true love a problem.

The second thing that went wrong was Ora's best

friend, Meadow. Meadow turned against her because Ora didn't think that Meadow should have her breasts enlarged. Meadow got a new best friend overnight; wrote Ora a 134kb email telling her how much she loathed her and exactly why; and started going steady with Foster.

In January, still suffering from Foster's rejection because of her skeletal structure and Meadow's betrayal because of her stance on cosmetic surgery, Ora went shopping. Ora's father is a very successful advertising executive and her mother is a very successful consumer, so Ora knew that shopping always makes you feel better no matter what horrible thing has happened or how unhappy you may be.

But this time it didn't work.

Ora ran up hundreds of dollars on her credit card, but it didn't make her feel any less betrayed or more loved – and it certainly didn't make her feel any shorter. Under a cloud even blacker than her new Midnight Magic mascara, Ora trudged out of the mall and across the parking lot, her arms filled with brightly coloured shopping bags filled with all the new things she didn't really want and certainly didn't need. Ora thought of plastic as she trudged back to the car. She read some-where that plastic is indestructible and lasts hundreds, even thousands, of years. A lot longer than friendship or love. Ora was an aisle away from where she parked and still thinking about plastic when she saw someone sitting in her mother's car. She must have forgotten to lock the door. Since her parents always believed in keeping her busy, Ora has taken almost every class the great city of Los Angeles has to offer – from tap dancing, tennis and gymnastics to karate, fencing and qui quong. Although it was impossible to tell whether the person sitting in her mother's Jag was a man or a woman, Ora didn't hesitate. She knew she'd be grounded for the life span of a plastic bag if the car was stolen because she hadn't locked the door again. Ora vaulted over three Fords and an old Volkswagen Beetle, and yanked the thief out from behind the wheel. They rolled on the ground for a few minutes, and then the thief landed a punch that nearly knocked Ora out. The next thing she knew, the thief, her backpack, all of her shopping, a brochure for a resort in the Caribbean, the bag of potato chips she was going to eat on the way home and her mother's favourite Frank Sinatra CD had disappeared – apparently into thin air.

It was only later, when she was giving the police her account of the incident, that Ora realized that she could have been killed. This might not seem like such a big deal in a city where people are regularly killed for a lot less than a bag of potato chips or even a Jaguar, but the fact that she could have died so quickly and for so little reason made Ora start to think. Dumped for having long bones, betrayed because she didn't think silicone implants made you a better person and killed for a car that was going to be traded in at the end of the year. It didn't make any sense.

What was the meaning of life? What was the point of any of it – the parties, the friends, the clothes, the Jag, the shopping, the falling in love? What really mattered?

The only answer Ora could come up with was plastic. The same plastic bags she'd carried today would be waving from the treetops long after everyone alive at the moment was dead. As for people, no matter how tall you were or what your cup size, you did the same things over and over, maybe for decades, and then you died. Ora was no different to Solo, the hamster she had when she was seven, who went round and round his wheel for hours, never getting anywhere, and then dropped dead with his head in his food cup.

Overwhelmed with the meaninglessness of human existence, Ora dyed her hair green and started carrying a hardback copy of a novel entitled *Catch-22* in a small backpack that looked like a coffin. *Catch-22*, in Ora's opinion, did a pretty good job of summing up the human condition, and a coffin did a pretty good job of symbolizing mankind's destiny.

It was at this point that Ora's parents finally noticed the change in her.

Because her parents finally noticed the change in her, Ora has been seeing Dr Ramin since March. Dr Ramin is a psychotherapist to the stars and earns more in an hour than most people on the planet earn in a year. Ora told Dr Ramin that her major problem was that it suddenly occurred to her that life has no meaning, and Dr Ramin laughed. 'Meaning?' howled Dr Ramin. 'You have forests, rivers, stars, mountains, orchids and baby elephants – and still you want meaning? Isn't all this beauty enough?' Apparently not, replied Ora. Ora mentioned plastic bags. Plastic bags, she said, would still be on the planet after they were all dead. Dr Ramin said that the rate things were going the planet wasn't going to last as long as a plastic bag anyway, so why worry?

Ora pulls the covers over her head and performs the exercise Dr Ramin gave her to help her out of her bad moods. It's called Ten Reasons to Be Cheerful. The idea is to think of ten things about your life that you should be thankful for – to put things in perspective.

Ora starts to tick ten things off on her fingers:

> It's Saturday – one.
> My parents are in the Caribbean – two.
> I have green hair – three.
> I wasn't born to a third-world peasant living in a mud hut with no electricity – four.
> I don't have to work sewing T-shirts in a sweatshop in South-east Asia just to survive – five.
> I'm healthy – six.
> I have my own phones – seven.
> My mother's not a drunk like Eliza Jarman's mother – eight.
> My father doesn't beat me like Dougal Marin's father beats him – nine.
> The sushi restaurant delivers – ten.

The Ten Reasons to Be Cheerful don't really buck Ora up. Five of the first seven have obvious downsides – it's almost Monday; she's all alone, as usual; no one but her appreciates the colour of her hair; she could develop some fatal disease or be hit by an asteroid or at least a car at any time; she has no one to call on any of her phones. And the last three were something of a stretch – her parents aren't home enough to beat her or get through a case of vodka in a week, and she doesn't like sushi that much.

Ora gets out of bed with a heavy sigh. She follows Dr Ramin's advice not because she thinks it will work but because she hopes it might since he's being paid so much to give it. So far, however, her hopes have not been fulfilled.

Dr Ramin doesn't think that Ora's trying hard enough. He said that if she *were* the child of a third-world peasant she would then have something real to be depressed about.

Ora sits at the counter in the kitchen, sipping a glass of juice, feeling her black mood envelop her like plastic wrap. Dr Ramin says that the trouble with depression is it makes you lethargic, which means you produce fewer endorphins, which makes you feel more depressed. Dr Ramin recommends vigorous exercise.

Ora decides to go for a swim.

She stands at the edge of the pool, gazing down at the bright blue water, the product of chemicals rather than nature. It isn't the ocean. Ora hasn't been any closer to the ocean than the highway since the pool was built when she was six, but still she finds herself suddenly yearning to stand on the shore with the waves breaking over her toes. The fact that the backyard pool isn't anything like the ocean darkens her mood even more. The emptiness of the house echoes in her bones.

Ora decides to go shopping. She's avoided the mall since the incident with the car thief, but she can't think of any activity likely to raise endorphin levels higher in a shorter amount of time.

Ora is dressed and in her mother's car before you can say, 'Put it on my card.'

Ora, of course, will never get to the mall.

Indeed, Ora Sonorious will never really go shopping again.

CHAPTER
SEVEN

Emiliano Is Woken by a Storm –
Though It Could Be by Fate

Emiliano has a dream.

Emiliano has had this dream before. In fact, he has been having this dream ever since he first saw those pictures of the Grand Canyon in the hospital – almost as though there was something in it that couldn't be seen but that he saw. He used to have it every few months, but in the last week or so he's been having it every night.

In this dream, Emiliano isn't being chased by anyone, or beaten by anyone, or threatened, or moved on or told what to do. He dreams about a young Indian warrior. In Emiliano's dreams the warrior is usually hunting or scouting for signs of his enemies. The warrior is confident as a river, sure as the earth and graceful as air. Emiliano always enjoys the dream. But tonight's dream is different. The village is gone. The woods and mountains have also disappeared. Instead, the warrior moves cautiously through a bleak and alien landscape beneath a luminous, orange sky.

Deep in the dream, Emiliano only wakes up because he thinks he's been shot. He is still dreaming when he hears the gun go off. Bam! Right in the chest. He doesn't think that this is part of the dream. He thinks this is real: *Delinquent youth shot by irate homeowner*.

Emiliano sits up, heart racing, blinking and ready to run. But the cabin is quiet and there is no Mr Grump standing in the doorway with a shotgun in his hand, shouting at him to get the hell out of his house.

And then there is another shot and the window flashes and the living room is washed with a blue-white light.

Jesus Christ. Lightening. Jesus Christ, he thought he was dead.

Emiliano lies back on the sofa, laughing with relief.

But the relief doesn't last for long. His eyes fall on the clock on the mantel. Two o'clock. Shit. He slept through the whole damn morning. Emiliano groans out loud. He had a lot of things to do today, the most important of which was getting the hell out of the cabin. It's one of his rules – learned the hard way like all the others – that he's always out of these weekend homes by Thursday afternoon. Just to be on the safe side.

Despite the fact that he has a real put-your-head-in-the-toilet hangover, Emiliano jumps to his feet and starts to pack up his few belongings. He carefully wraps the skull and feathers in toilet paper, and then wraps that in the patchwork quilt, which he takes because it makes him think of smiling grandmothers and home-cooked Sunday dinners, both things he has only seen on TV. He takes some food, a box of matches and several candles as well. He does a last, quick check for any useful articles he might have overlooked. There's a hammer and a small container of nails on the mantelpiece beside the clock. A hammer and nails could come in handy. He's just jammed them into his bag when he hears something outside that could mean that death hasn't been eliminated as an option just yet.

Emiliano peers around the edge of the window as a metallic green SUV splashes up the driveway. Arms are flying in the back seat and even through the downpour he can see that all four occupants are shouting. So no change there. The Grump Family's back – at least a day early and in a storm. Trust his luck.

But Emiliano is a boy who's survived by his wits for long enough to waste no time on self-pity or panic. By the time the Grumps are out of the car he has put on one of the rain parkas that are hanging in the kitchen. By the time they reach the front door, Emiliano is already out the back. Indeed, he is far enough away by the time the Grumps have taken in the scene of devastation in the living room that he doesn't even hear Mr Grump shout, 'Where's my effin' gun?'

CHAPTER
EIGHT

Following Her New Policy of Not Doing What She's Told, Ora Sonorious Picks up a Hitchhiker

The reason Ora never gets to the mall is because she is still thinking about the ocean and takes the wrong exit.

'Damn!' says Ora, when she realizes her mistake.

She comes off the slip road and follows the signs that will take her back to the freeway in the direction she was going.

Masonville – Francis – Liberty City. The arrow points right.

The mall is just outside of Liberty City. Ora hits the right directional.

Sueño – Querido – Hermosa. The arrow points left.

Sueño, Querido and Hermosa used to be fishing

villages, a long, long time ago. They're off the old coast road that runs parallel to the ocean.

Dr Ramin says that another way of getting out of a depression is to do things you really like to do – eat chocolate . . . watch old movies . . . go white-water rafting – whatever makes you happy. Ora decides that what would make her happy right at this moment would be to see the sea.

She takes the left.

The official beaches are so crowded that they might as well be public swimming pools. Although she can, technically, see the ocean from these beaches, it is not the ocean as she would like to see it.

Ora drives for miles before she hits a deserted stretch of road that is one long scenic overlook – brush-covered hills going inland and steep, dark cliffs hanging over the water. No stairs, no paths, no access – no people.

She drives another ten miles before she finds a place where she can get down to the shore without climbing gear or a parachute.

Even for a girl who has taken classes in abseiling, rock climbing and T'ai Chi, the trail to the ocean is a steep and uncertain one. It takes a lot of huffing and puffing and several small landslides before Ora finally stands at the shoreline with the waves breaking across her toes.

As though the weather has been waiting for this moment, it starts to rain.

Dr Ramin would say that the significant physical

exertion needed to descend the cliff had produced enough endorphins to cheer up Ora – which may or may not be true.

What is true is that, despite the rain, Ora begins to feel better – much better. She sits in the shelter of a boulder to watch the storm.

It is another example of the complexity of human beings that, although they can cheerfully decimate whole populations or devastate the Earth simply because they want oil or gold or land, or are in that kind of mood, natural phenomena tend to fill them with terror. Earthquakes, volcanoes, tornadoes, hurricanes . . . all of these things make people feel powerless and therefore afraid. An endless sky and endless sea make them feel small.

But Ora feels none of these things as she sits all alone in the storm. Instead, the shattering ocean and electric sky make her feel calm. They make her feel part of something larger and more important than herself, even if she couldn't tell you what that something is.

The wind and rain pick up, and Ora decides she'd better leave if she wants to get home in time for her parents' nightly five-minute phone call: *How are you . . . ? What've you been doing . . . ? Don't forget to water the bay tree . . .*

Ora scrabbles back up to the Jag with very little trouble, despite the incline and the rain.

She stops to catch her breath when she reaches the top, and sees a figure in a bright-yellow anorak, a backpack slung over one shoulder, standing next to the driver's door, peering in.

What is it with this damn car? thinks Ora. Every time she turns her back on it for a few minutes someone tries to steal it.

'Hey!' she shouts. 'What the hell do you think you're doing?'

Emiliano has been looking into the Jaguar, wondering if there is something he should do. Like break into it and use the cell phone on the front seat to call the cops. As Emiliano knows only too well, bad things happen everywhere, but especially in places like this, where it's so easy to disappear. He looked but saw no sign of anyone on the beach or over the hill on the other side of the road. Besides, how crazy do you have to be to abandon a car like this in the middle of nowhere in a storm?

At the sound of Ora's voice, he spins around to see how crazy she is. She looks pretty crazy. She's got hair the colour of frozen peas, she's covered with dirt, sand and scratches, and she's a hell of a lot wetter than he is – as well as a good four inches taller. He can tell from the way she's holding herself that she's ready to attack him.

'Jesus Christ,' says Emiliano. 'Is this your car?'

Ora holds up the keys and gives them a shake. 'Of course it's my car.' She waits for him to move out of her way.

He doesn't move. He's so relieved to see her he

could shake her, except, of course, that she's at least fifteen pounds heavier than he is as well as inches taller.

'Where the hell were you?' he demands.

Ora raises one eyebrow. 'Do I know you? What business is it of yours where I was?'

What if something had happened to her? What if he'd gotten involved with the cops and they blamed him? Then what? Life without parole?

'I thought you were dead or something, that's what business it is of mine.'

'Well I'm not dead.' Ora gives the keys another shake. 'I'm perfectly fine, and I'd like to get into my car.'

Emiliano's relief starts to sour. Christ, what a princess. He should've known. Who else would be driving around in a $60,000 car and just leave it on the side of the road?

'That's it?' He still doesn't step aside. 'You don't even say thanks?'

Ora can see the time on the dash panel. The telephone in the kitchen will be ringing in exactly twenty minutes. Her parents never call her on her cell phone. They think it makes them good parents if they know that she's at home.

'Thanks?' If he doesn't move she'll move him herself. He's small; she could lift him if she has to. 'Thanks for what? You didn't do anything!'

Emiliano braces himself against the car, carefully so he doesn't set off the alarm in case she's not as dumb as she looks and actually remembered to turn it on. There may be no one else here now but he knows that, with his luck, which is only bad, if the alarm goes off there will be enough cops to cover a mass demonstration in minutes.

'I was worried about you. Doesn't that count?'

'The only thing you were worried about was how to break in.' Ora takes a step towards him. 'Now, if you don't mind, I really would like to get into my car.'

Emiliano would like to get into her car too. Just for ten minutes, to dry off a little. Even with her in it. He decides to make nice.

'You know, you oughta be more careful.' He smiles. 'Deserted road like this.'

Ora pulls herself up to her full height, which is exactly four-and-a-half inches more than his. 'Are you threatening me?'

'Jesus Christ.' This is an example of his bad luck. As lucky as a guy would have to be to even see a car on this road in this weather, he'd have to be a lot unluckier to get the Unjolly Green Giant here as the driver. 'It's more like I was hoping you'd give me a ride.'

Unblinking, Ora stares back at him for several seconds. This is a rich area, and he's not from it. There aren't that many black kids around here to begin with, and none of them wears earrings or dreads or clothes that obviously once belonged to someone else. He looks like he might be in a gang, or carry a knife – both things that interest her more than frighten her. Ora's ex-best friend Meadow Larkin would have already called the cops on her cell phone by now. Meadow would be aghast that Ora would even consider such a thing as giving him a ride. Meadow would be revolted and repulsed by the thought of standing on the same road as this boy, never mind sitting in the same car with him. What if someone saw you? What would people say? Ora's mother, on the other hand, would be more worried about robbery and rape than committing social suicide. 'I don't care how short he is,' Mrs Sonorious would say. 'You DO NOT give rides to strangers.' Hers is a nervous nature. But Ora's is not.

Another interesting aspect of human behaviour is that although many people will do whatever they're told to do without question – even when several questions are in order – others will do things only because they know that someone else wouldn't want them to do it. Ora didn't used to be like this, but she is now.

'OK,' says Ora. 'Where are you going?'

CHAPTER
NINE

Mrs Fugosi's Bad Day

Mrs Fugosi is having a really bad day.

At the moment, she is standing in the Arrivals lounge, flanked by four of the new batch of six contestants, holding up the sign that says **TOP TEENS** in large, black letters, and smiling hopefully, if grimly, at the entrance. She's been standing here, holding the sign and looking welcoming, for over two hours. The plane from Chicago, which should contain Bethesda Parker and Willis Zoya, is late.

The other four contestants shuffle restlessly and every few minutes check the time. On one side of Mrs Fugosi, Ben Adamanti and Diane Procyz are flirting in a habitual sort of way and discussing their luggage, which, as Ben likes to say, is missing in action. On Mrs Fugosi's other side, Luke Beller, who has already heard all about the three days it took Kylie Mirski to decide what to wear on the flight to LA, is now listening to her explain why she likes airline food even though so many people don't. Kylie thinks it's cute.

'I've flown all over the world and nothing like this has ever happened to me before,' Ben is telling Diane. This is true. Ben usually flies on military transport. 'But it really is some coincidence, isn't it? You know, both of us losing our luggage like this?'

Diane gives him a smile she has practised in front of the mirror since she was eight. 'Maybe it's Fate.'

If only she knew.

'Well, I'll tell you one thing,' says Ben. 'If the General was here it'd be all sorted out by now.' The General is Ben's father. 'The General doesn't stand for incompetence.' No one knows this better than Ben.

Diane turns to Mrs Fugosi. 'I really don't see why we have to wait here doing nothing,' says Diane. 'I mean, it's been a very long day and I'm tired from the flight and I really don't know what I'm supposed to do if I don't have my clothes.' Her voice wobbles as though it is only with effort that she is managing not to cry. 'I mean, why can't Ben and I go see about our bags instead of just standing here wasting all this time?'

Mrs Fugosi sighs. 'I already told you – we'll all go together. I'm not letting you out of my sight. Not after the last time.' The last time was when Kylie went to the ladies' room to repair her make-up and was gone for forty-five minutes.

'This happened to my aunt once when she was coming back from France or Europe, you know, some place foreign like that,' says Kylie. 'I bet by the time we do go to check, your stuff will be there just waiting for you. Don't you think so, Mrs Fugoli? You know, everything always ends.'

'Fugosi,' corrects Mrs Fugosi. This is something she's already said more than once too. Mrs Fugosi, certainly, wishes this day would end – and pretty quickly.

'I think that's them,' says Luke, which is the first time his voice has been heard for quite a while.

Mrs Fugosi follows his pointing hand. A boy in a dark suit and steel-rimmed glasses who looks as though he's going to a masquerade party as his father, and a frighteningly well-groomed girl in a Dior suit or a very good copy of one who carries herself as though she's expecting to be photographed, are coming down the stairs, though you would hardly say that they're together. Mrs Fugosi recognizes them even without referring to the 8x10 glossies in the folder she holds in one hand – Willis Zoya and Bethesda Parker. She waves her sign and resists the impulse to cry with joy.

Mrs Fugosi makes the introductions. 'You poor things,' she says to the new arrivals. 'You must be exhausted. We just have to see if Ben and Diane's bags have turned up and then we can go to the hotel.'

'I'm not going anywhere till I've had a cappuccino,' announces Bethesda. 'The coffee on the plane was total pig's swill.'

Mrs Fugosi keeps smiling. 'You can get a cappuccino at the hotel. Their coffee is really excellent. But right now I'm afraid we have to get going. Dinner with the producers is at eight.'

Bethesda, significantly taller than Mrs Fugosi even without the three-inch heels, stares down at her coolly. 'You don't understand,' says Bethesda. 'I'm going nowhere until I've had my cappuccino. I think that's the least I deserve.'

Mrs Fugosi doesn't ask, 'Deserve for what?' Her head is beginning to ache.

Mrs Fugosi leaves Luke, Willis, Kylie and Bethesda in the coffee bar and goes with Ben and Diane to see if their luggage has indeed turned up.

It hasn't. The customer representative is apologetic, but it seems that they were taken from the plane in New Orleans.

Ben says that things like this never happen in the army and Diane starts to cry.

Still calm, pleasant and cheerful, Mrs Fugosi assures them that they can get what they need for the night in the hotel.

'They won't have my shower gel or my shampoo,' Diane sobs. 'There's only one store that sells them in the whole world.'

'Nonsense,' says Mrs Fugosi. 'This is Hollywood. Jennifer Aniston shops here.'

'Maybe I should call my dad,' says Ben. 'Maybe he could talk to someone.'

'I don't think there's any need to get the United

States Army involved in this,' says Mrs Fugosi, sounding as though she is, nonetheless, grateful for the suggestion. 'I told you, we can get you what you need for tonight in the hotel. Your bags will be here before you wake up. Now let's get the rest of the group and go to the car.'

When they find the others, Bethesda is still sipping at her cappuccino as if she lives outside the demands of time and Luke, given a migraine by the lighting in the airport, is in the men's room throwing up.

It isn't until they come out of the terminal that Mrs Fugosi realizes it's raining.

'I thought this was the Sunshine State,' says Kylie.

'That's Florida,' says Willis. 'A lot of people don't know it, but we only bought Florida from the Spanish in 1819.'

There's no sign of the limo.

'Oh, God . . .' moans Diane, a girl who's been raised to expect the world to run according to her whims and plans. 'What else is going to go wrong?'

'It never pours but it rains,' says Kylie.

'The General's driver always waits, no matter how long,' says Ben.

Mrs Fugosi refuses to be daunted. 'The car must've been moved on. It'll be parked in that lot over there. We'll have to make a run for it.'

'I am not going into the rain.' Bethesda not only expects the world to bow to her will, she never expects to have to bow to its. 'It'll ruin my hair. You go get the car and bring it here.'

'I think I'm going to be sick again,' says Luke.

Still smiling, Mrs Fugosi, who has learned to be prepared for most emergencies, rummages in her handbag and pulls out a plastic rain hat and an airplane sick bag. She hands the hat to Bethesda and the sick bag to Luke.

Bethesda groans but takes the hat, weakened by the long flight and her desire to get to the hotel. 'You just better hope I don't run into anyone I know.'

Or what? wonders Mrs Fugosi. *You'll have my head?* She smiles and strides off the curb.

When the seven of them finally reach the waiting stretch limo the driver, whose name is Mo Shufflebeed, is sound asleep.

Mo Shufflebeed is no more perfect than Mrs Fugosi. His body is too long for his legs and his face looks like the features have been rearranged by force, which they have. Mo Shufflebeed used to be an unsuccessful boxer. He is even more kind and more patient than Mrs Fugosi, but if brains were water Mo Shufflebeed's mind would be a desert. He wakes up with a start from a really good dream about being marooned on a tropical island when Mrs Fugosi bangs on the window. It takes him a few seconds to remember what he's doing at the airport.

'No problem,' he says over and over while his passengers climb in. 'No problem, no problem. We'll be there in no time.'

This will, of course, turn out to be somewhat optimistic.

It takes quite a while for the Top Teens to get

settled. Everyone wants to sit by a window and no one wants to sit next to Luke. Bethesda's feet are wet, which means she needs to change her shoes *right now*. Mo Shufflebeed gets her case from the trunk. Diane informs them all several times that her feet are also wet, but of course she can't change her shoes because she doesn't have another pair. Kylie's feet, protected by thick socks and trainers, are dry. 'I never go barefoot,' says Kylie, 'because your feet are like a door, you know?' Mo Shufflebeed puts Bethesda's case back in the trunk.

At last he starts the engine.

The girls immediately start punching numbers into their cell phones. The boys, except for Luke, who sits huddled in one corner clutching the sick bag, start raiding the refrigerator.

Mrs Fugosi's desire for the evening to be over increases with each passing nano-second.

They can't get on to the freeway because of an accident that has traffic tailed back for miles.

'Don't you worry, Mrs,' Mo Shufflebeed assures her. 'I know a shortcut.'

This announcement does little to improve Mrs Fugosi's mood. Mr Fugosi was also a man who always knew a shortcut. It once took him three hours to get to Mrs Fugosi's sister's house, a journey that takes Mrs Fugosi no more than forty-five minutes on the bus at rush hour.

'I thought this was the Sunshine State,' Kylie tells her mother, 'but you should see the rain. I guess it's like Gran always says, every silver lining has a cloud, right?'

Diane has also called her mother. 'Why me?' she wants to know. 'Why does everything always happen to me? There were hundreds of people on that plane but whose bags do they lose? Mine, of course! I really think you and Daddy should sue.'

Bethesda, whose mother left home when she was three, has called her father. 'You can't imagine how totally awful it's been so far,' she tells him. 'The food on the plane wasn't fit for vagrants, my feet got soaking wet and they don't even have a TV or Pepsi in the car. I mean, can you believe that? This is supposed to be Hollywood, for God's sake, not Texas. I bet they wouldn't expect Catherine Zeta Jones to drink Coke!'

The only sound the boys make is chewing, except for Luke, who moans very softly.

Mrs Fugosi gingerly sits back beside Luke and mentally prepares for a long ride.

It is another point in Mrs Fugosi's favour that she never blames Mo Shufflebeed for what happens next.

Kylie has just called her best friend and is in the middle of saying, 'Hot dog, I really never thought it'd be raining like this. I didn't even bring a raincoat. I thought this was the Sunshine—' when the car seems almost to jump in the air, and lunges off the road like a barracuda after its dinner.

Although it's impossible to see much through the tinted windows, Mrs Fugosi knows they've gone off the road because of the way the car bounces and bucks despite its superb suspension, causing a certain amount of shrieking in the passenger compartment. And also by the way the car suddenly stops, causing cola to spray over the immaculate Top Teens and the less immaculate Mrs Fugosi.

'Oh my God! Now look at me!' wails Diane. 'Are you doing this on purpose or something?'

Bethesda says she hopes the hotel has an on-site dry cleaner.

'Gosh.' Kylie giggles. 'This reminds me of that ride at Disneyland.'

'I thought this was a professional operation,' says Ben. 'The General wouldn't stand for this kind of thing.'

Willis says, 'Did you know that 89 per cent of licenced drivers wouldn't pass the test if they had to take it again?'

Luke's moans get a little louder.

Mrs Fugosi taps on the glass divider and it slides open. 'What happened?' she asks.

Mo Shufflebeed doesn't know.

'It was like something was pulling us off the road.' The knuckles of the hand still wrapped around the steering wheel are almost white.

Mrs Fugosi thinks it may have been an oil slick, deadly in the rain. She tells Mo to get back on the road.

Shaken from his tussle with whatever it was that dragged the limo into the middle of nowhere, Mo would be only too happy to get back on the road. But he can't. The engine starts, but the car won't move.

'Maybe we did something to the transmission,' he suggests.

Mrs Fugosi, who wouldn't recognize the transmission if it sat on her lap, agrees.

She and Mo Shufflebeed both get out of the car. Mrs Fugosi stands in front of the headlights with the rain sheeting down on her, staring at the limo as though this act itself will fix whatever is wrong. Here is an emergency she isn't prepared for. Mo Shufflebeed ducks under the hood and stares at the engine in a similar way. Oh, how Mrs Fugosi wishes she would wake up and find that she really is asleep and that this is just some horrible dream. Though she doesn't wish this as much now as she will later.

After a few seconds of looking at the engine, Mo Shufflebeed straightens up, shaking his head. It beats him what could be wrong. This isn't an emergency he's prepared for either.

'Maybe one of the Top Teens knows something about cars,' suggests Mrs Fugosi with a certain amount of blind hope.

Kylie, Bethesda and Diane can all be considered experts on popular culture, make-up and fashion, Ben knows a lot about how to run an army, and Willis knows a lot of facts, but none of them knows anything about cars except how to start them up and put them in drive. Luke actually does know a good deal about cars, but Luke's parents want him to be a scientist, not a mechanic, and have forbidden him to so much as own a wrench, and so he lies and says he's clueless too. This may be a decision he comes to regret.

'Get back inside,' Mo Shufflebeed orders Mrs Fugosi. 'I've got a phone in the limo. I'll call the office. They'll send someone out.'

But the phone in the car isn't working any more than the car is. Nor is the radio. Nor, when she tries it, is Mrs Fugosi's cell phone. Diane, Kylie and Bethesda's phones are no longer working either.

'Maybe I better take another look at the engine,' says Mo. He doesn't sound particularly hopeful.

'Are we going to be here all night?' moans Bethesda. 'I've been wearing these clothes for *hours*.'

'What about supper?' asks Ben.

'So now what?' wails Diane. 'So now the stores are all going to be shut by the time we get to town, that's what. So then what do you expect me to do?'

Kylie says she's sure that if they just let the car have a rest it'll be fine, after all it's always dark before dawn, and Willis starts telling them about something called The Zone of Silence, though he can't remember where it is.

Only Luke, who, considering the green tinge to his skin and the vice that seems to be squeezing his brain, has a really good reason for wanting to reach the hotel, says nothing. If his parents have taught him anything, it's not to argue.

Mrs Fugosi would rather be sucked up by a tornado than stay shut in the limousine with them.

'I'll come with you,' she says to Mo, and, opening the door, jumps straight into a puddle.

Mrs Fugosi and Mo Shufflebeed are back in position in front of the limo when Mrs Fugosi sees the lights of an oncoming car. She is surprised to realize just how far the limousine is from the road.

CHAPTER TEN

Ora Sonorious Wants to Know if She Looks Like a Girl Scout or Something

Ora Sonorious and Emiliano Shuh hadn't gone two yards when she got a fit of giggles because he told her to call him Em.

'*Em?*' she shrieked. 'You *must* be kidding. Your parents named you after a letter in the alphabet?'

He didn't so much as crack a smile. 'It's short for Emiliano,' he explained coolly.

'*Emiliano?*' This struck her as even funnier. 'You don't look like a Chicano.'

'How would you know?'

'We have a housekeeper,' answered Ora.

She hadn't intended to make a joke, but this made him laugh.

'And I bet you give her all the stuff you don't want

any more for her kids,' said Emiliano. He said it as though this was some sort of crime.

For some reason, the fact that she does pass her old clothes on to the housekeeper for her daughters made Ora defensive.

'Look, I don't have to give you a ride, right? I'm doing you a favour.' She glanced over at him. 'So you can cut the attitude right now.'

Emiliano leaned back, putting his wet and filthy feet up on the pristine dash so she couldn't see the hole in the bottom of his right shoe. 'What attitude?'

'I mean it.' She eased off on the gas. 'I can let you out right here, *amigo*.'

'And what if I won't get out?' He folded his arms across his chest. 'You promised me a ride. A person should honour her promises.'

'It wasn't a promise,' snapped Ora. 'It was a moment of madness.'

Emiliano snorted. 'Tell me about it.'

Relations deteriorated after that.

They haven't spoken since the battle over the radio station, which Ora won by the simple expedient of turning it off so violently that she jammed the switch.

Now they plough on through the storm in an angry silence, the only sounds the swishing of the wind-shield wipers and the rain.

Of course, if Emiliano and Ora liked each other, things wouldn't turn out the way they do. They would be listening to music and talking – maybe even flirting – as they drive, and wouldn't notice anything outside themselves. But they don't like each other and are ready to notice anything slightly larger than a gnat. Such is the nature of Fate again.

Ora, her eyes straight ahead, is thinking of whether or not she's going to tell Dr Ramin about this little adventure. She doubts it. He's always reassuring her about the sanctity of the patient-doctor relationship, but she still doesn't trust him not to tell her parents. If possible, adults lie to children even more than they lie to each other. She wants him to tell them only positive things about her, so she can stop seeing him. On the other hand, she would like to shock Dr Ramin a little. *You should've seen him* . . . Ora would say. *His hair was all matted and his shoes were too big and falling apart* . . .

On the other side of the car, Emiliano stares sullenly out of the passenger window, watching the hills turn to shadows in the growing dark and rain, thinking about the Grand Canyon. He thinks it would be nice to climb down to the very bottom and camp. Emiliano is imagining squatting by a fire with coyotes howling in the distance and stars shooting through the sky when he sees someone sitting on a rock, staring towards the ocean. So deeply familiar is this figure – recognized not so much by his eyes as by his heart – that for a second Emiliano thinks it is himself he sees. But it isn't, of course. As the car passes in front of him the young man's eyes meet Emiliano's and he nods. It's the warrior from his dream. It's this jolt of recognition that makes Emiliano scream.

Ora is so absorbed in her own thoughts that when

Emiliano suddenly shouts out, 'Stop!' she too screams, and automatically jams on the brakes, causing the car to skid on the rain-slicked road. They miss ploughing into the craggy embankment by inches.

'Jesus Christ!' Emiliano's feet are now flat against the floor. 'What are you trying to do? Kill us?'

Her heart pounding, Ora turns off the engine, clinging to the steering wheel for support. 'You're the one who told me to stop.'

She thought he must have seen some danger in front of them. A deer or a cow, something like that. Her uncle once hit a cow. He had to scrap his Porsche.

Emiliano hoots with derision. 'A cow? What'd it do? Swim up from Mexico?'

No, what he saw was an Indian. A young guy, sitting on a rock like it wasn't even raining. Emiliano wants to go back and get the Indian.

'You what?' shrieks Ora. This really is too much. 'Are you on drugs? Do I look like a Girl Scout, or something? It's bad enough I've got *you* in my car. I'm not picking up some smelly old Indian too. Besides, if he's an Indian he's used to being out in the rain.'

'But I know him.' As these words leave Emiliano's mouth, he knows that this is true – somehow. Emiliano is not a boy given to delusions, superstitions or hallucinations, but he feels in his bones that something's going on. The dream is one thing – the dream could have come from a movie he's forgotten – but seeing the same man here, sitting in the rain as though he's been waiting for Emiliano to pass by, is a sign. The warrior is important;

he's trying to tell Emiliano something, and Emiliano feels a desperate need to find out what that something is. 'We can't just leave him here.'

'Yeah, right, you know him.' Ora's voice contains more acid than the Jaguar's battery. '*You* know some Indian who sits on rocks in the middle of nowhere in the rain. In your dreams.'

'Yeah, I do,' says Emiliano, but doesn't mention that she's right about just how he knows him.

'Well, that's a good enough reason for leaving him here forever then.' Ora reaches for the ignition key.

But Emiliano is faster. 'I'm going to get him.' He jams the keys into his pocket, pulls a flashlight out of the backpack slung over his shoulder and gives her a big smile as he opens the door. 'You wait here.'

'Oh, sure! Like I should take orders from *you*!' Ora has no intention of waiting anywhere, which blows one of her last chances to spend the rest of her life as her parents, who have high expectations, have planned. She clambers out after him.

Emiliano marches on, Ora trotting beside him, giving him several pieces of her mind.

'This better be good,' shrieks Ora. 'This better be worth catching pneumonia for.'

Emiliano says nothing. Even before they reach the spot where he saw the warrior he knows that he won't be there. Unlike Mrs Fugosi, Emiliano has never thought of himself as being even slightly psychic. But that doesn't mean that he isn't. All at once he understands that the young man exists as surely as the road, or the ocean or the grumbling girl who strides beside him – but not in this time or place. The question now is: is the warrior a sign of the future or of the past?

Emiliano still goes through the motions of dancing the light slowly along the side of the road, but of course there is no one sitting on a rock.

'What did I say?' Ora would like to hit him. 'Didn't I say you were delusional? Now I'm going to get pneumonia and get in trouble with my parents because you thought you saw Geronimo sitting in the rain.'

Emiliano says, 'What the hell is that?'

Ora turns. Parked in the middle of a plot of brush and rocks across the road is a white stretch limousine, lit up like a spaceship and nearly as large. A man and a woman are standing in front of the car, gazing at the open hood as though in prayer.

Ora's problem has just been solved. She will get the couple praying to the limousine to help her get rid of hell's hitchhiker.

'Thank God,' says Ora, who, like many people, often blames and thanks God for things He has nothing to do with.

And she marches smartly over the asphalt calling, 'Yo!'

CHAPTER
ELEVEN

Things Go from Bad to Really Bad for Mrs Fugosi – and Everyone Else

Hearing new voices outside the limo, Ben, displaying the leadership qualities that he believes will some day make him a great general like his father, cracks open one of the windows enough to see out and squints into the rain.

'Who is it?' asks Kylie. 'Is it the police?'

'It won't be the police way out here.' Willis finishes the potato chips he's been eating and stuffs the bag down the side of the seat. 'The driver must've called the Triple A. Do you know how many millions of call outs they have every year?'

But before he can give them the statistics Bethesda says, 'No, Dr Know-It-All, I don't.' She snaps open her compact to check her make-up. 'And I don't want to know.'

'What did he call them on?' asks Luke. 'The phones are all down.'

Diane squeezes herself next to Ben at the window. 'Good God,' gasps Diane. 'It's two homeless people.'

'I don't suppose they've got a thermos of coffee with them,' says Bethesda. 'Or a working phone would be nice.'

Kylie peers over Ben's shoulder. 'Geez Louise . . . Will you look at them? They look like something that's been dragged by a cat.'

'The hair,' agrees Diane. 'It looks like she's diseased. That's all I need. To catch something from *her*.'

Ben frowns. 'Do you think we should go see what they want?'

Still staring into her compact, Bethesda widens her eyes to check that her mascara isn't smudged. She's a girl who knows it's important to look your best at all times, even times like this – you never know whom you might meet. 'What, and get wet again?'

Willis shakes his head. 'He looks like he could have a gun. Do you know what the statistics are on handguns in this state alone?'

'Oh, I'm sure they wouldn't hurt us,' says Kylie. 'I mean the cover of a book can fool you, can't it?'

'Personally, I'm much more afraid of catching something from them than being shot,' says Diane.

'Anyway, that's what Mrs Fugosi's here for, isn't it? To deal with things like that. Shut the window, Ben.'

A good soldier knows how to take orders. Ben shuts the window.

And so it is that, having introduced themselves in the perfunctory way of people brought together by disaster, it is Mrs Fugosi, Mo Shufflebeed, Ora Sonorious and Emiliano Shuh who stand in the downpour, surrounding the front of the car like a prayer circle – though one whose prayers aren't going to be answered.

Her views of teenagers not withstanding, Mrs Fugosi was glad to see Ora and Emiliano crossing the field to them despite the hair and the coffin backpack and their general bedraggled appearance, and this feeling has been only strengthened by the enthusiasm they're showing for the problem of the stalled limousine.

Besides being an accomplished thief – or perhaps because of this skill – Emiliano turns out to be pretty handy with cars, but he can't figure out what's wrong with this one.

He steps out from under the hood, shaking his head. 'Everything looks OK.'

'Except that it won't go,' says Ora.

Emiliano ignores her, which is far easier to do now that they're not alone. 'What about calling for help?' He glances at the windshield. 'Somebody in there must have a phone.'

'We have enough phones for an apartment building,' replies Mrs Fugosi. 'But none of them is working.'

'Just sounds like bacon fryin',' Mo Shufflebeed elaborates.

'Well, then we're saved.' Ora laughs. 'I left my cell phone in the car.' As everything that's happened is all his fault, she looks expectantly at Emiliano to offer to retrieve the implement of their salvation.

Emiliano doesn't offer. He's peering through the rain with a puzzled expression on his face.

'You know, *you* could go get the phone,' prompts Ora. 'You are the reason we're here, after all.'

But Emiliano still doesn't so much as glance her way. 'How come it looks so *blue*?' he wants to know. He gestures to the haze of light that's wrapped around them like a cloud. 'Are the headlights supposed to be blue like that?'

What with the rain, and the car, and the carping contestants, neither Mrs Fugosi nor Mo Shufflebeed noticed how blue the light around them is, but now they do. It's the colour of an unpolluted tropical sea – very much like the one in the dream that Mo Shufflebeed very much wishes he was still in.

Ora hadn't noticed the blueness of the light before either. 'Wow, that's really cool. I wonder if I could convince my mother to get them for her car. How much do they cost?'

'I . . . I don't know,' says Mo Shufflebeed. 'I—'

'That's not the colour they usually are,' says Mrs Fugosi. She is still demonstrating her usual calmness during emergencies, but there is a slight edge to her voice. Mrs Fugosi is possibly experiencing one of her psychic moments because she certainly has a very bad feeling about the blue light.

'Jesus Christ,' says Emiliano. Shielding his eyes with his hands, he is now gazing at the sky over their heads. 'What the hell is that?'

The others all tilt their heads upwards.

What they see is a thick metallic disc, dark except for the light spreading out from its belly. The light, of course, is blue – and getting brighter and bluer as the disc slides closer and closer without a sound.

'Well, I'll be damned.' Mo Shufflebeed whistles. 'Looks like a spaceship to me.' He looks over at the others. 'What does it look like to you?'

'I don't believe this is happening,' says Mrs Fugosi. She knew she should have called in sick this morning. Why, oh why doesn't she ever listen to that voice in her head? If she listened to that voice more often Mr Fugosi might still be alive and she wouldn't be standing here having a paranormal experience in a bad storm.

Another thing Dr Ramin says is that the more you get out and do different things, the more chance you have of shaking your depression. Which is definitely turning out to be true for Ora. She hasn't felt this good in months.

'Wow, is this cool or what?' Unlike Mo Shufflebeed, Ora is not a believer in the regular visitation of the Earth by alien craft. She once saw a documentary about UFOs that seemed to prove that most people who saw flying saucers or claimed to be abducted by aliens made Alice's Mad Hatter look like a bedrock of sanity. 'It must be some kind of experimental Air Force plane.'

Meanwhile, inside the limousine, Luke says, 'Whatever it is they're doing out there it's sure taking them a long time.'

'You can't make an omelette without eggs,' says Kylie.

Ben opens the refrigerator. 'Anyone want another soda?'

'I want to get out of this car, that's what I want,' says Diane.

Luke looks at his watch, not noticing that, like the limousine, it too has stopped. 'My folks are going to be really mad that I haven't called in yet.'

'We're going to be late for our dinner with the producers,' says Willis. He has a lot of information on the history of television quiz shows that he's been looking forward to sharing with them.

'I'm going to close my eyes,' announces Bethesda, 'and when I open them again I expect to be moving.'

Emiliano, Mrs Fugosi, Mo Shufflebeed and Ora are still watching the mysterious disc. Although they aren't agreed on what it is they think they see, only Ora thinks it's a plane.

Mrs Fugosi, perhaps because this has been such an incredibly bad day and she really wants it to be over, is now hoping that the thing floating over their heads is the Angel of the Lord come to take her to heaven to be with Mr Fugosi.

Emiliano is working on the theory that it's a technologically advanced police helicopter, sent by the Grumps to search for him.

Mo Shufflebeed, who once met a man at a party who had been abducted by aliens while camping in Arizona, knows for sure as shootin' that it's a spaceship.

Mo Shufflebeed's guess is the closest to the truth. Although in this case of course being right isn't going to give him much satisfaction.

'I think we better get out of here,' says Mrs Fugosi.

Which is an excellent suggestion, but one that comes far too late to do them any good.

In the few seconds it took Mrs Fugosi to say *I think we better get out of here*, over a dozen soldiers wearing the dull gold insignia of the Corporation of the Galactic Empire and carrying Corporation of the Galactic Empire weapons have silently materialized around them.

Only Ora, who, as we have seen, is not a girl whose first reaction to the unexpected is fear, notices that all the soldiers have the same face, though she doesn't know that this face once belonged to a general named Custer MacIntosh, who died heroically while slaughtering the last of the inhabitants of the planet Rumsfeld when it was still called something else. What she does know is that this definitely isn't the United States Air Force.

Mo Shufflebeed crosses himself the way people in disaster movies do.

'Jesus Christ,' mutters Emiliano.

'If only,' whispers Mrs Fugosi.

Had she gotten a closer look at the person who tried to steal her mother's car, Ora might now recognize Captain Titanic, who, being human, doesn't look anything like the late Custer MacIntosh. On the other hand, if Captain Titanic, who in fact hadn't been trying to steal Ora's mother's Jaguar but was enjoying a break in the busy but dreary routine of collecting data by eating potato chips, listening to Frank Sinatra and pretending she was going to drive to the country, hadn't been so surprised by Ora's attack, she might recognize *her* and wonder at the improbable coincidence of coming upon the same girl twice.

'What do you think?' Ora whispers. 'Do you think they're time travellers, or something?'

'Or something?' hisses Emiliano. 'What's "or something" supposed to mean?'

Captain Titanic tells them to shut up.

'You will do me the favour of being quiet,' she says loudly and clearly, her voice amplified by a sound chip embedded in the collar of her uniform. 'I'm the only one who needs to speak.'

Mrs Fugosi couldn't disagree more. 'Just who are you?' she demands. Mrs Fugosi is now pretty sure that the Captain and her crew are not from the Lord.

Mo Shufflebeed laughs in considerable relief. The aliens who abducted the man he met at the party were over six feet tall and had the heads of lizards. Next to them these guys don't seem so bad. 'At least they look pretty human,' he whispers.

Emiliano, who has had some remarkably negative

experiences with ordinary, run-of-the-mill humans, never mind ones who suddenly materialize out of flying saucers, doesn't say anything. One lesson life has taught him is that the best thing to do in a really bad situation is to keep your mouth shut and pay attention, and this is definitely a really bad situation.

'I am Captain Indianapolis Titanic,' Captain Titanic informs them. 'And you are to do as I say.' Captain Titanic has spent the last fifteen years trawling through time searching for the perfect specimens for the great Dr Nasa Hiko's most crucial project. She and her troops have been attacked by everything from wild beasts to rampaging armies; they've witnessed every spectacular natural disaster the Earth can dish up, from erupting volcanoes to showers of frogs; they've been hunted, hanged, scalped, tortured and two were burned as witches; and through all of this she has never been thanked, praised or offered any reward. Understandably, Captain Titanic is not in the mood for much argument.

Although the four people gathered near the limousine can't see it from where they stand, Captain Titanic holds a very small computer – her Personal Communications System – in one palm. On the monitor is the image Nasa Hiko first saw in the *Los Angeles Times*. It's a photograph of six model teenagers, all smiling at the camera as though showing off their teeth. Captain Titanic looks from the image on the monitor to the group in front of her. No match there.

'Where are the Top Teens?' demands the Captain.

Emiliano rarely sees TV and has no idea what a Top Teen is. 'Who? The what?'

Ora, who has watched the show and considers it a pretty major example of just how futile, pointless and totally devoid of meaning life is, says, 'Are you serious? You're looking for the Top Teens? What for?'

Mrs Fugosi says nothing. It is her job to protect the Top Teens and she takes that job very seriously. The worst thing that has ever happened while Mrs Fugosi was in charge was the time a seagull pooped on a Top Teen's head during a publicity shoot.

Mo Shufflebeed says nothing either, largely because Mrs Fugosi steps on his foot.

'Didn't you hear me?' Given the efficiency of the technology that produced the sound chip, it's a wonder the whole West Coast didn't hear Captain Titanic. 'You do speak English, don't you?' Captain Titanic raises her voice and speaks painfully slowly. 'Where . . . are . . . the . . . Top . . . Teens?'

Behind the tinted windows of the limousine, the Top Teens still haven't noticed that something both interesting and unusual is happening outside, but they have been in the car a really long time by now. Ben and Willis have emptied the refrigerator some time ago and are getting seriously hungry. Luke is worried about his parents. Kylie has started singing songs from popular musicals under her breath to keep herself from getting worried about anything, which is a trick she actually learned from a musical. Diane is grumbling about her need to go shopping or she might as well just die right now. And Bethesda, her eyes still firmly shut, is repeating her opinion that she probably will die if she doesn't get a shower very soon. When they finally hear Captain Titanic boom, 'Where are the Top Teens?' the second time, they think they're about to be rescued. Once more it is Ben who takes the initiative. He opens the door and sticks his head into the rain.

Despite the fact that the photograph on Captain Titanic's monitor is of a previous group of Top Teens, they all look so much alike in a general sort of way that Captain Titanic immediately knows what he is.

'Get out of the car!' she orders. Following an unheard command, several weapons are suddenly aimed in Ben's direction. 'You and your Top Teen friends all get out of the car! Immediately!'

Ben Adamanti is where he is today – along the coast of California in a torrential downpour on the verge of being abducted by soldiers from the future – precisely because he has always done exactly what he's been told to do. Especially if the person telling him is wearing a military uniform, no matter how unusual it may be. With no thought of refusing or even asking a question, Ben steps out of the car.

'All of you!' Captain Titanic repeats. 'Get out of the car!'

The others buzz like a hive of bees. *Are they soldiers . . . ? Are they terrorists . . . ? What uniform is that . . . ? I think they're armed . . .*

'We better do what they want,' says Willis, who is class president and plans some day to be president of the nation. 'It'll be OK if we stick together. Statistics prove that it's better to present a united front.'

Holding each other's hands as though this will somehow protect them, Kylie, Diane, Luke and Willis follow Ben into the rain. All four of them are smiling. They smile not because they're happy or glad to see the soldiers, of course, but because smiling is what they do, especially when – as now – they have no idea what's expected of them.

Smiling is not, however, what Captain Titanic does. Despite the poor visibility, there is no mistaking the irritated scowl on her flawless face. 'Where's the other one? I know there's one more.'

Through the open door comes the voice of the other one, a girl far more accustomed to giving orders than to taking them. 'Stuff it up your gun!' shouts Bethesda. 'I am not standing in the rain like some tramp. This outfit cost twelve-hundred dollars. I'm not ruining it for you.'

Captain Titanic's response to this announcement is to remove the extremely small pistol at her hip from its holster and lightly touch a button in the handle. The stretch limousine evaporates around Bethesda silently and very quickly. Bethesda drops to the ground like a sack of pebbles.

'Jesus!' Bethesda glances over her shoulder as though she thinks the car has simply moved behind her. When she sees that it hasn't she turns back to the woman with the small but efficient sidearm. 'Are you crazed or something? Look what you've done! You've totally ruined my suit! *And* you could've hurt me!'

'Only if I wanted to,' says Captain Titanic.

Any last frail hopes Mrs Fugosi might have had that things are going to turn out well vanish with the limo. Mrs Fugosi wishes she'd acted sooner, but she didn't, so she acts now. She pulls herself up to her full four feet and seven and a half inches and, with all the dignity and authority at her disposal, marches over to stand in front of her charges.

'That'll be enough of that,' Mrs Fugosi informs the Captain. 'I'm warning you, if you harm any of these young people, you'll have me to answer to.'

The only reason Captain Titanic doesn't laugh at this announcement is that she has no sense of humour. But she clearly isn't impressed. Totally ignoring Mrs Fugosi, she looks over her head and addresses the huddle of perfect teenagers behind her. The evaporation of the stretch limousine seems to have knocked their confidence into Oregon. All of them are wide-eyed with terror, and at least two of them are whimpering. Luke looks as though he may throw up again.

'So, you are the Top Teens?' asks Captain Titanic, though it is far from being a question.

Kylie, Diane, Luke and even Bethesda are momentarily incapable of responding. Ben, blessed with so much leadership potential, manages to nod. Tears start to flow from Willis' eyes.

In the way that things seem to be doing at the moment, a circle of ice-white light has suddenly appeared where the engine of the limousine used to be. Captain Titanic gestures towards it with her evaporator.

'Step inside the transport field,' she orders. 'You are coming with us.' And then, remembering the professional courses she's taken on interfacing with ancient peoples and respecting their customs, adds, 'Please.'

Although there is very little likelihood that the Top Teens are going to stampede towards the ice-white circle, Mrs Fugosi puts her arms out to hold them back.

'No one's going anywhere,' says Mrs Fugosi.

The Captain's eyes stay on the Top Teens. 'I do not want to use force,' she tells them, 'but I will if I have to.' Her mouth smiles. 'You've seen what I can do.'

Mrs Fugosi is a woman with a strong sense of hope. She thinks that the only time you should have no hope at all is when you're dead. This allows Mrs Fugosi to believe that the most important thing is to stay alive.

'Perhaps we should go along with the Captain,' she advises. 'Stay close to me.' Holding her head high, Mrs Fugosi steps towards the circle.

'Not you!' shouts Captain Titanic. 'Just the Top Teens.'

'Oh, but they're not going anywhere without me.' Human nature being as peculiar as it is, in this instant Mrs Fugosi completely forgets that she doesn't actually like any of the Top Teens or want to spend any more time with them than necessary. Instead, such an intense desire to protect them surges through her that, in this instant, they might each have been born from her flesh after sixty-two hours of labour and fed at her breast. 'I'm their chaperone,' she shouts back. 'I'm responsible for them. The only way you're taking them without me is over my dead body.'

Captain Titanic has never encountered primitive maternal instinct before. Primitive maternal instinct, like the tiger and home cooking, is a thing of the far, far past. Captain Titanic lives at a time when you think of yourself not as part of a family but as part of the Corporation. Captain Titanic, like everyone else, would unthinkingly give her life to protect property, power or wealth, but wouldn't risk breaking a fingernail to save another human unless she was ordered to. She is, therefore, understandably taken aback by this incomprehensible outburst.

'Not you,' she says again, this time a little more loudly in case the fat old woman didn't understand her the first time.

Mrs Fugosi couldn't get any taller unless she grew. She too steps up the volume. 'Oh yes, *me*! If you think I'm going to stand idly by while you do God knows what to these innocent children—'

'I have my orders,' answers the well-disciplined Captain Titanic.

The Top Teens are far too traumatized to do anything but hide behind Mrs Fugosi, clinging to each other in some desperation.

Mo Shufflebeed's policy in life has always been to keep as low a profile as possible, and so, now, when being a dust mote wouldn't be low profile enough, he is simply hoping that if he doesn't move or say anything the aliens won't realize he's there.

Emiliano and Ora, both of whom have rather reckless natures, have been watching this exchange with interest, waiting to see what to do.

Ora, who isn't sure that her mother, if she happened to be around, would risk her life to protect her, is impressed by Mrs Fugosi's spirit. It also strikes Ora as perfectly reasonable that Mrs Fugosi would prefer abduction to staying in LA. At least it'll be an adventure.

Mrs Fugosi also impresses Emiliano, who knows only too well that his own mother would happily sell him for a case of gin. The old lady's a hell of a lot feistier than she looks. And, since he can't imagine that anything could be much worse than where he is, he too thinks it's reasonable for her to want to go.

And so it happens that the thing to do is now apparent to both of them. As if they'd discussed it before-hand, Emiliano and Ora move next to Mrs Fugosi at the same time.

'To hell with your orders,' says Emiliano.

'That goes for me too,' says Ora.

Captain Titanic is a good soldier. Although she requires detailed instructions for even the simplest task, she, like Ben, does always do as she is told. She was told to bring back the Top Teens. Under the mistaken impression that the two extra teenagers must be connected to the Top Teens in some way, she assumes that if she has to kill either of them she will be in serious trouble. More trouble than she will be in because she brought the short, fat old lady back to Saint Mona. She can easily be dispensed with later.

'Suit yourselves,' says Captain Titanic. 'You can all get into the circle.'

As it turns out, Mo Shufflebeed's policy of not bringing any attention to himself seems to work. Captain Titanic doesn't tell him to join the others, nor does she evaporate him the way she did the stretch limousine.

Mo watches the others step into the icy circle of light, and he watches them disappear in far less time than it takes a dog to wag its tail once. For a few seconds, he just stands in the rain gazing up at the spaceship, trying to memorize every detail, and then that too vanishes.

Mo waits a few more seconds to see if anything else is going to happen and, happily in this case, it does. The car re-materializes beside him. It is, of course, working again. Mo gets in and drives back to the office without any further incident.

For the rest of his life, Mo Shufflebeed will tell everyone he knows or meets even briefly about the time he was nearly abducted by aliens. And he will end every one of these stories with the same words. 'Say what you want,' Mo Shufflebeed will say, 'but I believe they came in peace. I mean, they didn't have to give me the car back, did they? They could've made me walk back to town.'

PART THREE

the peculiar present

*If You Have Something to
Complain About You Don't
Deserve to Be Here*

PART THREE

A Note on the Peculiar Present

Over the decades, the Corporation has come up with a number of innovative if not particularly meaningful slogans to quell its critics. Besides the highly successful *If You're Not with Us, You're Against Us* and *Dissent Is the Parent of Treason* there was: *If You Have Something to Complain About You Don't Deserve to Be Here.* This one worked too.

It worked because people had left the primitive, old-fashioned concept of a society based on the greatest good for the greatest number as far behind them as the stone axe. People believed that the only measure of a person was how much money and how many possessions that person had. The more things a person acquired the better that person was – or, in the Corporation's own words, *The Person with the Most Things When He Dies Wins.*

It therefore followed that anyone who complained about the system did so because they were bad, or lazy, or just generally inferior.

Interestingly enough, this isn't what's peculiar about the present that Mrs Fugosi, Ora, Emiliano and the Top Teens all find themselves in.

What's peculiar is how similar it is, in so many ways, to the present they used to be in.

CHAPTER TWELVE

Lucia Learns Some Things She Didn't Know

'Wait'll you hear what I thought of this time,' says Napoleon. He grins at Lucia from the screen of her PCS, happy as a soldier who's just nuked every rebel in the universe. 'You want to guess what it is?'

'No,' says Lucia, trying not to sound as bored as she feels. She has been on Saint Mona for two days, and for two days she's seen no one, been nowhere and done nothing because there is no one to see, nowhere to go and nothing to do. As far as she knows, there is no one else here except Nasa Hiko and the AALF who guards the apartment door. The AALF isn't programmed for conversation and Nasa Hiko refuses to speak to Lucia, but Napoleon is only too glad to make up for this loss. He contacts her every day – two and three and even four times – to discuss the arrangements for the wedding with her. How should they dress? What kind of music should they have? What food should they serve? Should there be entertainment? Should they turn the reception hall into a beach or a mountain retreat? Should they have the wedding on a planet with a dozen orange moons and showers of stars? The sophistication of the virtual reality system makes anything possible. 'Tell me.'

'You have to guess.'

'You want to have it in the ice caves and we all have to dress like Aleuts.'

He has no idea what she's talking about. 'Take a real guess,' says Napoleon. 'You're going to love it.'

Lucia very much doubts that she will ever love anything. 'I can't,' she says. 'Just tell me.'

'We're going to copy a twentieth-century wedding. You know, a really big one. Movie stars or royalty – something like that. You know, with the big dress and the church and stuff like that. What do you think? I figured you'd like it. You know, because it's historical.'

The face that stares back at him is as beautiful as sunset over the Grand Canyon.

'Well,' says Lucia. 'It's quite an idea.' She'd rather be got up as an Eskimo, pulled across an ice floe by a team of dogs.

Napoleon's enthusiasm makes him seem more like a child than the mass murderer he hopes soon to be. 'I've already done some research.' This of course is a lie. Napoleon may be about to lead the mindless armies of the Corporation to new and greater wars but he does nothing for himself that he can get an AALF to do. If shoes still had laces he'd have someone else tie his. 'There's megatons of material. There's a prince's wedding that's pretty spectacular, but the horses could be tricky. Anyway I'll transmit what I've got to you. See what appeals.'

'Fine,' says Lucia, with all the enthusiasm of someone asked to choose the electric chair for her execution. 'But I'm not wearing white.'

'Well, I don't know about that.' Napoleon's smile is erased by thought. 'White seems to be the thing. Hey, I know.' The smile returns. 'We can ask the primitives. They'll know.'

Now it's Lucia who doesn't know what he's talking about. 'Who?'

'You know. The twentieth centurions. The ship should be landing soon, shouldn't it?'

'The ship?' repeats Lucia.

'You know. For Project Infinite Future. The ship from the twentieth century.'

Lucia rarely listens to much of what her mother says and, because of this and her obsession with studying the past, she knows less about Project Infinite Future than she might. All she really knows is that the survival of the species depends on it. And although she hasn't thought about it since, she now remembers the morning she arrived on Saint Mona, and remembers the crate full of brightly coloured clothes – and instantly knows a lot more than she did a few seconds before.

'Oh,' says Lucia, 'of course, the ship.' She overheard Nasa Hiko talking to Justice Lissi about meeting a ship, but she assumed it was just more supplies. She smiles at the screen. 'I'll talk to you later. I have to go.'

'Go? Go where?'

'*Go*,' repeats Lucia. 'I have to *go*.' And before Napoleon can say anything more, she touches a button and cuts the connection.

Where Lucia goes is straight to Nasa Hiko's official computer. She links up with the cameras in the spaceport and is just in time to see Captain Titanic's ship, the *Hollywood*, land.

While Nasa Hiko, flanked by the troops of the Elite Guard, stands on one side of the field watching, Lucia watches from home.

Nasa Hiko is thinking about the future and how it belongs to her, but Lucia isn't thinking about the future at all. She is thinking about the past.

She zooms in as the precious cargo is carried from Captain Titanic's ship: nine stretchers, and on each a human who has been dead now for a thousand years. The computer's observation system is so sophisticated that she can see each as though it's right in front of her. Three of the faces are dark. One of the girls has a pimple on her chin and one of the boys has a nose that was broken by a baseball bat. Lucia has never seen any of those things before in the flesh. She feels as though she's stepped into an old film. These people come from a world that is real. A world with grass and trees and rivers and rainbows and snow. They live not beneath environmental domes for protection and breathable air but in houses with lawns and gardens and endless blue skies. They've picked feathers from the ground, held puppies, possibly ridden a horse over sand. They've swum in the sea and walked through forests, they've eaten food that grows in the ground. They know about friendship and kindness and joy; they know how to laugh and to love.

Lucia watches as they are wheeled from the spaceport, watches Nasa Hiko strut and nod and smile while she barks out orders.

Another of the slogans used by the Corporation to justify just about anything was: *The Only Way Is Forward.*

As the doors close behind the last stretcher Lucia sighs.

Oh, how she longs to go back.

CHAPTER THIRTEEN

Welcome to the Hotel Saint Mona

The Top Teens, Ora Sonorious, Emiliano Shuh and Mrs Fugosi all wake up to find themselves lying on a very comfortable bed in a room that is small but tastefully, if blandly, furnished in the style of an expensive hotel, notable only for the enormous television screen that fills up one corner. Sunlight seeps in through the closed curtains and very softly, as though he is trapped in the walls several rooms away, Frank Sinatra can be heard singing.

Jesus . . . thinks Emiliano as his eyes take in the room. *How the hell did I get here?*

And then he remembers the rain, getting a ride with Ora, the limousine full of Top Teens and the spaceship and realizes what must have happened. Like so much in life, it was all just an illusion. He and the Jolly

Green Giant must've stumbled into some sort of publicity stunt for the TV show. Somebody made a mistake and took him along.

Emiliano has never been in a hotel before but there is no time now to savour the moment. He has to get out of here before some honcho figures out that he's not supposed to be here. He knows who will get the blame for the mistake, and it won't be some television executive on a million a year.

Life has also taught Emiliano to make thinking and acting one process. He jumps out of bed and grabs his backpack from the bedside table. Nothing's been taken. He slings it over his shoulder and moves towards the door. Halfway there it occurs to him that he might as well grab what else he can, as he's here, and he makes a detour into the bathroom for towels and soap.

There aren't any. Indeed, there aren't faucets or anything he recognizes as a shower either. Everything, including the soap dispenser, is built into the walls. *More pointless expensive ultra modern crap*, thinks Emiliano.

He turns back to the main room. He knows that something is very wrong.

Cautiously, as though the whole set-up might be no more than an elaborate trap, he goes over to the window and pulls back the curtains. Outside the window is not the city of Los Angeles, as he thought it would be, but a sandy white beach dotted with palm trees and a turquoise sea. It's a beach Ora Sonorious might recognize from her mother's Caribbean brochure.

Emiliano is staring out at the improbable view, his

backpack dangling from his hand, when someone very close to him says, 'Welcome to the Hotel Saint Mona.' The voice is so determinedly pleasant that the words sound to him like a threat.

Emiliano looks around.

Ora Sonorious is already going over the events of the previous day in her mind as she wakes up. She went to the ocean. She picked up a hitchhiker. They stopped because he thought he saw an Indian sitting in the rain. They spotted the broken-down limo. They couldn't get it started. And then a spaceship came overhead and beamed them all up. Which will teach her to believe anything she sees on television.

Ora opens her eyes and sits up, looking around the room. It doesn't look like what she'd imagined the inside of a spaceship would look like – it looks like a hotel room. Indeed, it looks very much like a room in the hotel where her parents are staying in the Caribbean. Ora's mother always shows her pictures of the hotels she's going to so Ora won't feel left out.

Shaking her head, Ora touches the sheet and the pillow and the headboard as though making sure they're real. It doesn't make sense. Unless she hallucinated the whole thing there's no way people from an advanced civilization would go through all the trouble of abducting nine people only to bring them to the Hotel Caribe. And if she did hallucinate the whole thing, she wouldn't be in the Hotel Caribe, either. She'd be in the loony bin.

Ora gets out of bed and picks up her bag. She has

to find the others. Well, maybe not Emiliano or the Top Teens, but certainly Mrs Fugosi.

It is at the moment that Ora discovers that the door to her room is locked that a voice that seems to come from right behind her says, 'Welcome to the Hotel Saint Mona.' It's the kind of voice that features in the television ads her father's company makes.

Now what? thinks Ora.

Kylie, Diane and Bethesda are all sharing a large room.

The first thought in Diane's mind when she wakes up and realizes that she's still in the outfit she wore on the plane is that she never went shopping to replace the things in her missing luggage last night. She moans out loud. 'Oh, why does everything happen to *me*?'

Kylie sits up, rubbing her eyes. 'You wouldn't believe the dream I had,' says Kylie. 'It was totally bizarro.'

'I need coffee,' says Bethesda. 'Someone call room service. I'm not moving till I've had a double espresso.'

Diane's lament stops abruptly. She looks over at Kylie. 'You know, I had a pretty bizarre dream too.'

'Really?' Kylie's eyes meet Diane's. 'What happened in your dream?'

'Coffee,' repeats Bethesda. 'It is really, really important that I get some right away.'

Neither Kylie nor Diane hears her because they are too busy swapping stories from their sleep.

As it happens, Kylie's dream is remarkably similar to Diane's.

'Weird beard,' says Kylie. 'Do you think it was something we ate?'

'But we didn't eat anything,' says Diane. 'We never got to the hotel.'

Kylie laughs. 'Of course we got to the hotel.' She waves a hand at the room. 'We're here!'

'Well . . . yes . . .' Diane laughs too, but her laugh is much smaller and more uncertain than Kylie's. 'I guess so. I mean, yeah, we are in the hotel. But do you remember getting here? Do you remember supper?' She looks from Kylie to Bethesda. 'And why aren't any of us in our pyjamas?'

'For God's sake, you two!' wails Bethesda. 'Will you stop bleating about your freaking dreams and get me some coffee?'

Partly because the answers to her own questions require far more thought than she is used to, and partly because she is used to being told what to do by her mother, Diane gives in. 'All right, all right,' she says. 'I'm calling.' And she reaches for the phone. There is no phone.

Diane is about to burst into tears at this, the final straw – no luggage, no supper and now no phone – when the music that has been playing very softly in the background fades and a voice that could sell snow to a Siberian says, 'Welcome to the Hotel Saint Mona.' In the minds of Kylie, Diane and Bethesda it is the voice of someone in control. They look at one another and smile.

'Thank God!' they all say. And then turn around.

Across the hall, in the room shared by Ben, Willis and Luke, only Luke is puzzled by the events of the day before.

'But what happened after that?' he wants to know. 'After the car broke down? I don't remember anything after that.'

Willis and Ben, busy searching the room for the minibar to get something to tide them over until they go down for breakfast, don't answer.

'I mean, I know I wasn't feeling so hot, but I would've remembered getting to the hotel and meeting the producers and everything.'

'Short-term memory loss is more common than the cold,' says Willis. 'It has something to do with aluminium cans.'

'I'll tell you one thing I do know. We couldn't've had too much to eat for supper,' says Ben. 'I'm hungrier than a platoon that's been marching all day.'

'So you don't remember, either,' says Luke.

'There's no way we went up in a spaceship,' says Ben. 'My father is a general in the United States Army, remember. I think I'd know if spaceships were cruising over California.'

'Then what was it we saw?' demands Luke. 'Why don't we remember how we got here?'

Ben shrugs. 'We had a long day. We must've had

some wine with the meal or something and it went to our heads.'

'But there wasn't any meal,' says Luke. 'As far as I can remember, we never left that field.'

'So what's this?' Ben spreads his arms to encompass the room. 'A mass hallucination?'

'Well . . . no . . .' says Luke. 'But I don't remember—'

'If you ask me you're the one who's hallucinating,' Willis says to Luke. 'Migraines can do that, you know. They distort the brain processes.'

'So you do remember what happened after the car broke down,' insists Luke.

Willis shakes his head. 'Not exactly.'

Ben is also shaking his head. 'Can you believe it? There isn't a minibar. What sort of an outfit is this? If the General was here he'd have the manager on the phone pretty pronto.'

'Now there's a good idea,' says Willis. 'Let's call down for room service.'

'There isn't any phone,' says Luke.

Ben and Willis both look at the place where they expect the phone to be, and when they also fail to see it, they look around the room at all the places where they don't expect it to be.

'Just wait'll I tell the General about this dump,' says Ben. 'Heads are going to roll.'

'I think we should find the old lady,' suggests Willis. 'She's supposed to be in charge.'

'Good thinking,' says Ben.

And that is when a voice that apparently comes from the wall says, 'Welcome to the Hotel Saint Mona.' It is a calm, reasonable and authoritative voice – which makes it both comforting and familiar to all three boys.

'It's about time,' says Ben. He and the others turn their heads.

Mrs Fugosi wakes up with a slight headache and the symptoms of a cold. Knowing where she should be – in the room that was reserved for her at the Beverly Hotel, next to the one the Top Teen girls are in and across from the boys and their chaperone – Mrs Fugosi thinks that's where she is.

Mrs Fugosi reaches out for her handbag on the bedside table, removes a pack of paper tissues and blows her nose. That done, she continues to lie there for some minutes, listening to Frank Sinatra crooning in the distance and thinking about the busy day ahead. The Top Teens, and therefore Mrs Fugosi, have three photo shoots, two magazine interviews, one interview on a local radio station, lunch with the stars of a popular soap opera and, finally, a party in their honour at the home of the chief of the network in the Hollywood Hills. It isn't until she thinks of the party that Mrs Fugosi realizes she doesn't remember last night's dinner with the producers. Her memory isn't empty, but it is hazy from the drug she doesn't know she had.

Mrs Fugosi closes her eyes and tries to recall the events of the day before. *Concentrate . . .* she urges her-self. *You went to the airport . . . Diane and Ben lost their luggage . . . Bethesda and Willis were late . . . Kylie never stopped talking . . . Luke was sick . . . It was pouring when we finally got out to the car . . . There was a traffic jam on the freeway . . . Mo Shufflebeed said he knew a shortcut . . . And then—*

Mrs Fugosi sneezes as her eyes snap open.

And then the car went off the road for apparently no reason – or no reason that Mo Shufflebeed could explain. They couldn't get it moving again. The phones stopped working too. A grungy boy and a girl with outrageous green hair stopped to help them. The two of them never stopped bickering.

And then what? If she can remember all that why can't she remember dinner with the producers? What happened after the boy and the girl showed up?

Mrs Fugosi pops up like a slice of bread in a toaster as the next memory finally staggers to the front of her mind.

After that a spaceship emitting an eerie blue light hovered over their heads and they were surrounded by armed soldiers.

Mrs Fugosi looks around the room, from the window with its champagne-coloured curtains to the recess where her clothes have been hung on hangers fixed to a metal rod; from the small glass and metal table next to the bed to the pale blue lamp on top of it; from the prints of watercolours of flowers on the wall to the unobtrusive beige carpet.

Mrs Fugosi laughs out loud. And then what? The aliens took them to a five-star hotel? Where? On Mars?

Mrs Fugosi has spent enough time driving around with Mo Shufflebeed to know what happens when people are abducted by aliens. Either they're taken into spaceships that look like laboratories and experimented on or they're taken into spaceships that look like the Garden of Eden and taught the meaning of life, that's what happens.

Mrs Fugosi shakes her head and laughs again. No fool like an old fool, as the late Mr Fugosi would have said. She had a bad dream, that's all. The spaceship was part of the dream. After the day she had yesterday it's no wonder her subconscious got a little overheated; no wonder her allergies are kicking up. She blows her nose again, but feels no better.

But if all that's true, why can't she remember getting the car going, or coming to the hotel, or having dinner with the producers?

The reason Mrs Fugosi can't remember any of these incidents is, of course, because they never happened. The reason Mrs Fugosi can't remember anything after they stepped into the white light is because, thanks to the spectacular advances of science – and a plant that once grew in what was called the Amazon Jungle – Mrs Fugosi and her companions from the twentieth century slept through the entire journey.

While Mrs Fugosi is still trying, desperately, to remember anything beyond breaking down in the storm, she has another of her psychic premonitions. Something is very wrong. It is now that Mrs Fugosi finally notices that she isn't wearing her cotton nightgown with the daisies and the lop-eared rabbits on it (a birthday present from Mr Fugosi) but the businesslike beige dress she wore to the airport. Like Diane, Mrs Fugosi has never gone to bed in her street clothes. Not ever.

Mrs Fugosi gasps for air as her heart picks up some serious speed.

What in heaven's name is going on? Where is she? How did she get here? Where are the Top Teens? Why doesn't she remember going to bed? Why didn't she at least remove her jacket and her pantyhose?

Mrs Fugosi has seen enough movies for it to occur to her at this point that she may have been drugged. But because she still very much wants to believe that she is at the Beverly Hotel, or some place very much like the Beverly Hotel – and definitely some place on the planet Earth – and that the unsmiling and heavily armed soldiers she remembers were only a bad dream, she pushes this thought very firmly away.

I really am being ridiculous . . . she tells herself. *It's the stress of the job, that's what it is, the stress of the job . . . There has to be some logical explanation . . .*

It is yet another peculiarity of human psychology that even though a person knows something is true beyond any doubt, she will convince herself that it isn't if it happens to be something she'd rather not believe is true.

Which is what Mrs Fugosi – who is actually fairly certain that the aliens weren't a bad dream and that she was drugged and taken to another planet – does now.

Instead of begging God for help, Mrs Fugosi

throws back the covers and gets out of bed, breathing deeply and trying very hard to stay calm. Her temple is starting to throb.

'You're a sophisticated, modern woman, Juliana,' she says out loud. 'Not a superstitious, medieval peasant. You don't really believe the ship and the soldiers and the vaporizing gun were real, do you? How could they be real?' She works for *Top Teens*, not *Sixty Minutes*.

Mrs Fugosi marches into the bathroom where she should find towels and tiny bars of soap with the name Beverly Hotel on them. But they aren't there, of course.

Still staring at the wall where the towel rack should have been, Mrs Fugosi laughs out loud. How stupid can she be? The phone! All she has to do is pick up the phone on the bedside table and call the desk. She slaps her forehead and laughs again. What a dunce. All she has to do is pick up the phone.

There is no phone on the bedside table.

Mrs Fugosi sits down on the bed with a moan.

Which is when Mrs Fugosi hears someone say, 'Welcome to the Hotel Saint Mona.' Mrs Fugosi hears more than calm and authority in the voice. She hears the arrogance of someone who is never wrong – something working with television executives has taught her to recognize.

Oh hell . . . thinks Mrs Fugosi.

CHAPTER FOURTEEN

Different People React Differently to the Same Situation

Mrs Fugosi, Kylie, Willis, Diane, Luke, Ben, Ora and Bethesda all find themselves looking at the image of a woman that has magically appeared on one wall of their rooms. The visual system is as good as the audio, of course; it doesn't look like an image, it looks like a real person has joined them.

Or it would look like a real person had joined them if it weren't for the fact that the face that belongs to the voice is so breathtakingly perfect that it's impossible to believe that it can be real.

This is, of course, the face of the brilliant geneticist Nasa Hiko, and the sincere and soothing voice is hers as well – which just goes to show how right Kylie was about the covers of books.

The flawless face of Nasa Hiko is not quite smiling at them from behind her desk in Central Control.

Emiliano is the only one who doesn't see the face right away because at that moment he is so busy discovering that what seems to be a window is only an illusion showing a hologramic view of a tropical beach that existed a thousand years in the past that he doesn't bother turning around.

'Welcome to the Hotel Saint Mona, my ass,' says Emiliano, as his hand touches solid wall.

None of the others in their separate rooms says anything.

Nasa Hiko speaks gently but persuasively. She's been rehearsing this speech for fifteen years, which has given her plenty of time to get it right.

'I am Dr Nasa Hiko, Head Scientist of the Corporation of the Galactic Empire. The Corporation is the largest and most powerful government that has ever existed. Its empire stretches across the galaxies and has brought freedom, peace and prosperity even to the farthest reaches of the stars. As well as being its Head Scientist, I am also the chief executive officer of the colony of Saint Mona, where I am delighted to say you are our most honoured guests.'

Although a great deal of what Nasa Hiko has told them is of course untrue, Kylie, Ben, Bethesda, Willis, Diane and Luke all gaze at the face on the wall in their rooms as though it is Oprah Winfrey introducing a show that is all about them, hanging on every word.

From the expressions on the faces of Mrs Fugosi

and Ora, however, you might think that Nasa Hiko is the devil herself.

'The first thing I want to do is assure all of you that the Corporation means you no harm.' Nasa Hiko pauses just for a second to let them absorb this piece of good news. 'I am sure that you are all a little confused and frightened at the moment, but let me stress that we are not inhuman alien monsters from one of your science-fiction movies. We are intelligent people, just like yourselves. In fact, we are very much like you. We are the descendants of galactic colonizers from your own planet, the Earth. We are *your* descendants. We are your future – the future you made.' She stares into the tiny camera, no bigger than a poppy seed once was, which has the effect of making her listeners think that she is staring right into his or her eyes. The Top Teens all smile back. 'And you are the past that made *us*.'

It is at this statement that Emiliano finally looks over. He's heard a lot of crap in his life, but this has to be some of the best – real top-shelf, class-A crap. 'Come back, you Klingons,' he mutters, 'all is forgiven.'

Which more or less expresses what Ora and Mrs Fugosi are thinking.

Though it is not what Diane, Willis, Kylie, Ben, Bethesda or Luke are thinking, of course.

Diane, Bethesda and Kylie are all thinking about Nasa Hiko's teeth and how she gets them so brilliantly white. Diane doesn't believe it can be ordinary bleach. Kylie is wondering if there's somewhere in the hotel where she can buy whatever it is that makes Nasa Hiko's smile one Julia Roberts would die for. Bethesda, whose nose, ears, breasts and buttocks have all been improved on by a plastic surgeon, assumes the teeth must be false and wonders if the hotel has a dentist.

Ben and Willis are each stretched out on his bed, wondering if all the women around here are that beautiful, and even Luke, accustomed as he is to having his parents think for him, is feeling more relaxed now that someone is explaining what's going on.

'But just as you are our past, for now we will be your present,' Nasa Hiko is saying. 'I want you to think of this little experiment of ours as a form of archaeology. We want to get to know you, to observe you – to understand what I believe you would call our roots.' She smiles again and then proceeds to quote the Corporation slogan that justified cloning, nuclear warfare and genetic engineering with such staggeringly horrendous results. 'After all, we have the technology.'

'Where's the remote?' Emiliano asks the wall. 'I want to change the channel.'

Ora groans and puts her pillow over her head.

Mrs Fugosi purses her lips.

The Top Teens, however, all nod as though this makes perfect sense to them.

'But even more than reassuring you that our intentions are good ones,' Nasa Hiko goes on, 'I want you to understand that your presence here is not some sort of accident or chance. You have been especially chosen by us – just as you were especially chosen by the producers of the most popular show in the history of your television programmes.'

It could be because Nasa Hiko seems to know about and appreciate them, or it could be because of the magic words 'especially chosen', but Willis, Kylie, Diane, Luke, Ben and Bethesda all sit up a little straighter at this announcement. This also seems to make perfect sense to them.

As though aware of their increased interest, Nasa Hiko leans a little closer to underline her sincerity and says, 'Yes, especially chosen. We searched through the centuries of human history and selected each of you because you are the acme of our species. You are as high as man can go in your time.' She spreads her hands as if she might reach out and pull them close in a happy embrace. 'Put simply: you are the best!'

This announcement is not greeted with smiles and self-satisfied sighs by everyone.

Ora, who has come out from under her pillow, pretends to vomit. Ora has heard enough of the excuses and justifications of her parents for all their broken promises and benign neglect to be able to recognize a snow job when she hears one. The only thing that Nasa Hiko has said that Ora believes is that they are in the future. Which doesn't seem as attractive as she might have thought were she still in California in the twentieth century.

Emiliano knows that Nasa Hiko doesn't mean him when she talks about being the best, but it wouldn't make him believe her if he did. He knows that they are being given a line with a hook the size of the Grand Canyon attached to it to make it easy for her to reel them all in. *We mean you no harm, my ass*, he thinks. *We come in peace; shoot to kill* . . . There are two reasons for this scepticism. The first is that, like the great Greek philosopher, Socrates, Emiliano believes that nothing should go unquestioned. You should always ask Why? Why is A saying X? Why is A doing Y? And, human nature being what it is, life has taught Emiliano that the answer is almost always: Because A wants something. The second reason is that despite Nasa Hiko's fine and reassuring words Emiliano also knows that, especially chosen or not, what they all are is in jail. He can tell. He is now standing on his bed, tapping the ceiling.

Mrs Fugosi isn't fooled, either. She knows exactly what road is paved with good intentions – the road that leads straight to hell without detours, short cuts or traffic lights. She fingers the small gold crucifix she wears around her neck. 'Oh, dear God,' prays Mrs Fugosi. 'Please get me out of here.'

An expression that could be either earnestness or severe constipation has now settled on Nasa Hiko's astoundingly beautiful face. 'I want you all to consider this your home for the time being,' she says. 'But I'm afraid that for the next few days – until we can be sure that none of you has brought any dangerous infections with you – you will not be allowed out to see the many attractions of our splendid colony, but will have to stay in quarantine in the hotel. Your doors, as some of you may have noticed, have been locked for your own safety, but now they are open and you may go wherever you want. You have my assurance that every effort has been made to make you comfortable and happy. I hope you will find that the Hotel Saint Mona not only has all the amenities that you would expect, and are accustomed to – stores, a beauty parlour, a health club, a gym, etcetera – but some you wouldn't expect as well.' Nasa Hiko's teeth flash against the darkness of her smile. 'Remember, my dear friends, anything you want is yours. You are now in a world where all of your needs and desires will be met – and where you are free of all duties and responsibilities.' She tilts her head forward as though about to whisper in their ears. 'Have a good time,' says Nasa Hiko. 'Trust me – we want you to enjoy yourselves.'

Nasa Hiko, of course, doesn't really give a broken test tube whether the Top Teens enjoy themselves or not. There is no return journey, there is no quarantine and there are no attractions to interest the most bored tourist on this barren hunk of rock in the middle of space. There is no Hotel Saint Mona either. The quarantine has been invented to delay the moment when the time travellers realize that they are prisoners of the Corporation. There's no point upsetting them unnecessarily or prematurely. Primitive types, says Nasa Hiko, tend to be less rational and pawns to their emotions. For when Nasa Hiko said that they will be here for 'the time being' she means, of course, until they die – which may not be that long from now, depending on how things go. Once they have been sufficiently studied and their eggs have been taken from them, the girls will be frozen for future research. The boys, who will continue producing sperm for decades, of course, will be kept alive but barely conscious.

But the Top Teens are too accustomed to being spoiled to have any suspicion of any of this. Indeed, they are all so excited you'd think they'd been hoping something like this would happen. As soon as Nasa Hiko vanishes from the walls of their rooms, all six race to their doors and into the corridor. Everyone talks at once.

'How excellent is this?' asks Ben. 'A free vacation . . . anything we want . . .'

'I've never been on an alien planet before,' gushes Kylie. 'I never thought they'd have shopping.'

'Well, thank God for that,' says Diane. 'Since I don't have any clothes or anything.'

'You really are a hick from the sticks, aren't you?' Bethesda says to Kylie. 'I mean, really. You think we're in the third millennium? And what? And it only took a few hours to get here?' She holds out her hands. 'I mean look at my nails. They'd be inches long by now.'

Ben rubs his chin. 'She's got a point. We haven't grown beards or anything, have we?'

Luke, who would need a lot longer than a few billion light years to grow enough of a beard even to shave, says, 'We don't know what their technology's like. Maybe they can do the trip in hours, not decades.'

Bethesda shrugs. 'Well, if you ask me, we're still in California.'

Kylie's ponytails bob with a certain amount of indignation. 'But that doctor said . . .'

'The doctor.' Bethesda folds her arms in front of her. 'That's another thing. There's no way that woman's a big cheese scientist. I mean look at her! She could be a model!'

'Isn't that a pretty sexist thing to say?' asks Luke.

'But she is a real knockout,' says Ben. 'We don't have any doctors like that in the army, I'll tell you that.'

Willis is nodding his head. 'I'm inclined to agree with Bethesda. If you consider the principles of quantum mechanics it's extremely unlikely that we've travelled through time.'

'So where are we then?' asks Luke.

'Isn't it obvious?' Bethesda tosses her head in a very regal way for a girl whose father is a chiropodist. 'We're on reality TV.'

'Reality TV?' echo the others.

Kylie looks around as though expecting to see a camera pointed at her. 'You really think so?'

Diane smoothes her hair. 'You know, you could have something. I mean, *Top Teens* has been talking for ages about doing something different, isn't that right?'

Willis is nodding again. 'That's right, their ratings have been dropping. Which, of course, is inevitable after so many years. Statistics prove that—'

Ben cuts him off. 'Reality TV makes sense. The General says—'

Diane cuts him off. 'I don't want to hear what the General says. Now that that's settled, I would really like to go shopping. I mean, I've been wearing these clothes for over twenty-four hours now . . .'

'I could use something to eat,' says Ben.

Luke looks up and down the hall. 'I wonder where the old lady and those geeks are. Do you think they left them behind?'

The other Top Teens shrug in a disinterested kind of way.

'As if we care, right?' says Ben, and they all laugh.

But this total lack of interest in Mrs Fugosi, Ora and Emiliano is not shared by everyone.

Even as the boys head off to find a restaurant and the girls go back to their room to make themselves presentable for national TV, the old lady and the geeks are being closely observed by Nasa Hiko and Captain Titanic in Central Control.

Mrs Fugosi is yelling at the now blank wall. 'Just hold on a second!' she shouts. 'I have a couple of questions *I* want to ask *you.*'

Mrs Fugosi would like to know just where and what Saint Mona is. She would like to know just who or what the Corporation is. She's not a little curious about Nasa Hiko herself. Mrs Fugosi doesn't want to have fun. She wants to know why she and the others have been brought here. What is 'archaeological experiment' supposed to mean? She would very much like to go home. Mrs Fugosi stares broodingly at the wall. Mrs Fugosi has lived for over sixty years and takes no comfort from Nasa Hiko's assurance that she and her people are just like them. Mr Fugosi, who was the gentlest of men, was sent to fight in Vietnam when he was still in his teens, because he didn't have the money to go to college and so avoid being drafted. Mr Fugosi saw a lot of horrible things in Vietnam, and not all of those things were done by the enemy. Mrs Fugosi therefore feels she knows enough about human behaviour to distrust the smiling Dr Nasa Hiko and her promises of a good time for one and all.

Ora has just thrown one of her shoes at the wall where Nasa Hiko's image appeared, with quite a lot of force. Ora is shouting as well. 'You can't do this to me! I know my rights! My father plays golf with an adviser to the president!' Ora also knows that, since she is not on the Earth, where being acquainted with someone who advises the president might do her some good, and not even in the same century as her father and his golf buddy, this is a ridiculous thing to say, but she can't help herself. She doesn't want to be here any more than Mrs Fugosi does.

Trust is never an option for Emiliano, of course: he trusts no one. He especially doesn't trust anyone in a position of power. Experience has taught him that having power rarely makes a person behave better. Indeed, although he has never heard of John Emerich Edward Dalberg, famous for pointing out that 'power tends to corrupt and absolute power corrupts absolutely', he would certainly agree with him. It has also occurred to Emiliano that if he can see Nasa Hiko it is more than possible that Nasa Hiko can see him. As if he's an animal in a cage at the zoo. Emiliano has never liked zoos. And so he has taken the hammer and nails he had the foresight to steal from the cabin and is hanging the quilt he brought with him over the spot in the wall where Nasa Hiko's face appeared.

'The little savage is clever, I'll give him that,' says Nasa Hiko, as darkness falls on the monitor showing Emiliano's room. She folds her hands together. 'You know, maybe it's a bonus that you brought them along. They might not be useful for reproduction, but they might be very useful in my research.'

'Um . . .' says Captain Titanic. Captain Titanic is not so sure. All three of them strike her as more trouble than they could ever be worth. If she was used to having opinions – which, as a soldier, she of course isn't – Captain Titanic's opinion would be that the best thing they could have done was dispose of the old lady, the wild-looking boy and the green-haired girl as soon as they landed. Captain Titanic clears her throat. 'Don't you think we should put them in the cells?' she asks. 'At least the boy. Just to be on the safe side.'

Nasa Hiko bases her answer to this question on the fact that the three people in question are their prisoners and, though amusing and educational, so primitive as to be totally powerless against the might and sophistication of the Corporation. And so makes one of her fateful and fatal mistakes.

'I wouldn't worry about those three,' she says. 'We can handle them.'

'Well, do you want me to have that thing taken down so we can watch the boy too?' persists Captain Titanic.

This is when Nasa Hiko makes another fateful and fatal mistake.

'Leave it,' she says. 'Let him have his fun for now.'

Lucia sits at her mother's computer, flicking between the rooms of the time travellers with her eyes wide and her heart beating fast. The Top Teens seem almost familiar, as though they've stepped out from several movies she's forgotten she saw – the noisy group of attractive friends with their nice clothes and bright smiles. Unless you include the computer-generated playmates of her childhood and Mr Ford, her AALF, the only friend Lucia's ever had is Napoleon Lissi – whom she has always seen more as a foe. But it's the unexpected guests who intrigue Lucia the most. Aside from feeling warmly towards Ora because of her hair, she likes them all because they're angry and unaccepting. In Lucia's world no one is angry and everyone accepts everything. Except for her.

What if? thinks Lucia – and for the first time since the asteroid hit Henry Kissinger she wishes she hadn't been injured. *What if I could walk?* If she could walk – if she could sneak past the guard and get out of the apartment – then she would be able to talk to the time travellers herself. They could tell her what it's like to smell flowers or swim in a blue-green sea or hold a kitten against your heart.

What if . . . what if . . . ?

Her mother would say she had only herself to blame. If she had listened to her and stayed in the shelter she would still be perfect, still be able to walk today. But Lucia didn't listen to Nasa Hiko. She went back to save Mr Ford. 'Forget about him,' Nasa Hiko ordered. 'He's just a machine.' But Lucia couldn't forget about him. The only kindness she's ever known came from him. Mr Ford wasn't programmed for bombs, he wouldn't know there was any danger, he wouldn't know that he should leave. And in the end what had she risked her life for? The falling wall that crippled her turned Mr Ford off for the very last time.

Lucia watches as Emiliano nails the quilt to the wall. She knows about the rebel attacks and acts of vandalism throughout the galaxies of course, but this – the simple nailing of an old quilt to the wall – is the single greatest act of defiance she has ever witnessed.

What if . . . ? What if . . . ? What if . . . ?

CHAPTER
FIFTEEN

Some People Are Just Naturally
Socially Adaptable

It is yet another example of the complexity of the human being that despite their superior intelligence some people are as easy to manipulate as clay. The Corporation has always understood this, of course. It knows that you can get people to do anything – go to war, enslave other people, starve children, wear neon-pink hot pants and platform shoes or put pins in their tongues – so long as you make them feel that they are right or special if they do what you want and traitors or, even worse, foolish or stupid, if they don't. And so long as you reward them. This ability to be persuaded easily is not called weak submission by the Corporation. It is called social adaptability.

Bethesda, Luke, Willis, Diane, Ben and Kylie, all

of whom agree with the Corporation's belief that the purpose of life is to achieve and acquire as much as possible, are terrifically socially adaptable.

Since they think they're the stars of a reality TV show, they don't wonder what cosmic marvels lie beyond the walls that surround them. They don't think about the force that drives the planets or the force that drove them out of their time. They worry not about the future or the past. Only Luke is curious about how the audio-visual system works. Instead of wasting time on speculation or thought, they throw themselves into life on Saint Mona like lemmings hurling themselves off a cliff.

As Nasa Hiko herself might say, they are just what the doctor ordered.

Kylie dabbles her toes over the edge of the Olympic-size pool. 'How cool is this?' she burbles. 'No school, no chores, no tennis lessons, no nothing. All we have to do all day is shop and have a good time.' Two activities that have always been favourites of hers. 'It's like being a movie star without ever having to actually make a picture.'

Stretched out beside her, imagining the sides of the pool lined with dozens of deck chairs, each holding a girl that looks very much like Nasa Hiko only substantially younger, Ben says, 'You said it. This is the life.' No orders, no schedules, no unending list of things to live up to. He doesn't have to fold his clothes with a military crease or even pick them up from the floor. 'The twenty-four-hour party.'

'To tell you the truth,' says Willis, 'I don't really

care if we have to stay here for months.' He is so happy that there is no one constantly telling him what to do, or to do it better or expecting him to show off what he knows, that he doesn't even miss his dog.

Luke doesn't care either. His allergies and migraines have all taken a vacation, and for the first time since he was born he feels like a regular person who doesn't have to ask if there are nuts in the sauce or if the water the soup is made from comes from a natural spring. This could be because he's in the luxurious Hotel Saint Mona being treated like a real celebrity, or it could be because this is also the first time in his life he's been out of his parents' reach for more than a few hours. Luke doesn't really care what the reason is, he just wants to enjoy it for as long as he can. He's much more interested in the workings of electrical systems than he is in the workings of the human heart and mind anyway.

Diane too has succumbed to the benefits of being a thousand years and galaxies away from home so completely that she's actually stopped missing her mother. She can choose a blouse or what to have for breakfast without first asking Mrs Procyz what she thinks Diane should have. She sits up and glances at her watch. 'So what should we do this afternoon?' She looks at Kylie and Bethesda. 'Anybody want to go to the mall?'

The shopping mall on the ground floor of the hotel is a perfect replica of the ones back home, down to the trees, the benches, the pleasant water features and the ambient music. As long as a city block, it has boutiques, a sports store, a record store, a food court, a drug store and a virtual reality games arcade that, quite literally, is out of this world – or certainly out of the world they come from.

Even Bethesda is so used to the idea of being in a television show by now that she allows herself a public yawn. It's the yawn of a queen presented with yet another diamond necklace. 'The clothes are all so last winter,' she complains.

'So what?' asks Kylie. 'We don't have to pay for them.'

'*So what?*' Bethesda eyes her from a great distance. She regards Kylie, with her ponytails, her obsession with the colour pink and her Tennessee twang, as a hillbilly, though she tries to keep this opinion private, of course, since she doesn't want to be dumped from the show because she isn't nice enough. 'So I simply do not wear last season's clothes. I'll wait till the new stuff comes in.' She picks up her beach bag. 'I think I'll go to the gym.'

Also on the ground floor of the hotel is a five-star restaurant, a state-of-the-art gym and health club with masseuses, beauticians, a nail salon, a sauna and a Jacuzzi, and basketball and tennis courts.

None of these things is real, of course. The hotel and everything it encompasses has been elaborately and meticulously constructed from the west wing of the hospital, and such a good job has been done that the Top Teens don't suspect a thing. As far as they're concerned, Dr Nasa Hiko is not only beautiful and in possession of teeth more perfect than God could have created, she is also a woman of her word. The Hotel Saint Mona is all that she said that it would be.

Ben looks at the other boys. 'I don't suppose anyone wants a game of basketball?'

No one does. Willis only plays polo and squash, and Luke plays the piano.

'I guess I'll go to the virtual reality arcade.' Willis is revelling in all the free time he has now that he doesn't have to study constantly. 'I didn't finish my trip down the Amazon.'

'Me too,' says Luke, who, because of his delicate constitution and his doting parents, has always been discouraged from any physical activity that might lead to death or an asthma attack. 'I thought I'd try surfing in Hawaii today.'

The Top Teens leave the pool area to go to their rooms and change for the afternoon.

Nasa Hiko leans back in her chair as she watches Kylie, Diane, Willis, Ben, Luke and Bethesda do exactly what she wants them to do. Humility not being part of her nature, she congratulates herself on a job brilliantly done. She really does have to hand it to herself: the Top Teens couldn't be more perfect for her purposes if she'd created them in her lab.

CHAPTER SIXTEEN

And Some People Aren't Socially Adaptable at All

Neither Mrs Fugosi, Ora Sonorious nor Emiliano Shuh has so far joined the Top Teens in taking advantage of all that Hotel Saint Mona has to offer.

Mrs Fugosi wouldn't take advantage of the sauna or the sunbeds or the free shopping, even if she could. Mrs Fugosi doesn't believe that God would go through all the trouble of creating the universe just so, after thousands of years of struggle, suffering and heartbreak, a small number of the billions of people on the Earth could drive expensive cars and wear Rolex watches and clothes with designer labels. She has always expected more from life than a truckload of possessions that will be given to someone else when she dies.

As it happens, however, Mrs Fugosi can't enjoy all

the pointless activities and luxuries the Hotel Saint Mona has to offer because she isn't feeling very well.

Far from taking a vacation, as Luke's various ailments have, Mrs Fugosi's are working overtime. She has a constant, if dull, headache, her nose won't stop running and her joints feel as though someone's been tightening them with a wrench.

Mrs Fugosi snuffles, blows her nose and takes another painkiller from the silver pillbox in the shape of a frog that she always carries in her bag, staring at the phoney window in her room and the phoney scene of a Caribbean beach. Mrs Fugosi sighs.

Besides feeling unwell, Mrs Fugosi is feeling pretty homesick. She misses the sunrise that woke her each morning, and the moonshine and stars beneath which she fell asleep each night. She misses the humming birds that feed at her kitchen window. She misses her garden. She misses clouds and rain. She misses her favourite radio station and the neighbour's dog, an English bull terrier named Frisco, who can say 'sausages' and open the front door. She longs to smell freshly cut grass and hear the ocean. She wouldn't even mind being stuck in traffic. If Mrs Fugosi knew that now, in the future she's in, all those things aren't even memories – that the Caribbean beach that looks so real outside her window is now no more than sludge surrounding a red and broiling soup, she would undoubtedly feel even worse.

Mrs Fugosi once saw a girl in Oakland, California, wearing a T-shirt featuring a photograph of the Earth that was taken from a satellite. You couldn't see the cities or the highways, or the oil fields or the endless miles of factories and stores, or the nuclear plants in this picture. The Earth was blue and white and green and rather perfect looking. If you were wandering through space, looking for a home, this was the place you'd choose. Beneath the picture were the words: **Love It or Leave It**. Mrs Fugosi laughed at the time, but she is not laughing now.

While Kylie, Bethesda and Diane shop and lie by the pool and hang out at the gym, and Ben, Luke and Willis eat and have adventures in the arcade, Mrs Fugosi spends most of her time in worry and prayer.

Mrs Fugosi's worry, of course, is not for herself but for the Top Teens. She hears them in the hallway, laughing and talking as though they're still back on Earth, so she knows they are all right, but that still leaves several questions unanswered. Why have they really been brought here? What's going to happen to them? These questions play over and over in her mind as though they're on a tape loop. Mrs Fugosi feels responsible for their fate. They were, after all, in her charge, and she has let them down. She feels especially guilty that she doesn't actually like them very much.

The guilt and worry might drive Mrs Fugosi crazy, but the prayer keeps her sane, not the least because she believes it will do her some good. The Lord, as Mrs Fugosi knows only too well, works in ways that are puzzling to humans, but she also knows that, despite appearances, He is not without compassion – though sometimes it may be slow in coming.

'Dear Father,' beseeches Mrs Fugosi, 'I know you have a plan here. All I ask is that you show me what it is.'

The Lord, so far, is staying silent.

While the Tops Teens have a good time, and Mrs Fugosi sniffles, frets and prays, Emiliano broods. It is another noteworthy example of the complexities of the human mind that Emiliano, whose first reaction to any situation he doesn't like is to leave it, now refuses to step from his room. When he's hungry he turns down the sound on the entertainment system and shouts out, 'Room service! I want some food!' Eventually a tray is left outside his door. If it weren't it would make no difference. His is a stubborn and unmalleable nature – a fact that has so far saved his life; he is more than prepared to starve to death.

To hell with them, is what Emiliano thinks. *Better to die on your feet than live on your knees*, is what he also thinks. There's no way he's going to give the creepy Dr Death even the tiniest particle of satisfaction. It's bad enough that twice a day he has to listen to her inane pep talks, designed to cheer and reassure her guests, without letting her think that she's winning him over with her smiling lies and empty promises.

Only a week ago if someone had offered Emiliano the chance of being permanently warm, dry, fed and looked after without being behind bars he would have jumped at the chance. No *problema*, Emiliano would have said. A fancy hotel? Clean sheets and a TV as big as a caterer's refrigerator? All the food he can eat? Lead the way. He would have thought it was a dream come true.

It is, however, another of life's more persistent ironies that when you get what you want you often discover that it wasn't what you wanted after all.

This is certainly true for Emiliano Shuh, who spent enough nights sleeping in unlocked cars and doorways to think that a bed of his own would be close enough to paradise to keep him happy for the rest of his life.

But he was wrong. His days on Saint Mona have already taught him another valuable lesson. This is the lesson: everything has its price.

And in this case the price is way too high. Now he will never see sunset over the Grand Canyon or the magical city of Chichén Itzá. What use are a comfortable mattress and all the hamburgers you can eat if you don't have any dreams?

Like Mrs Fugosi, Emiliano stares at the palm trees that so realistically bend in a non-existent wind and, also like Mrs Fugosi, he sighs.

Protected from the prying eyes of the Corporation by his patchwork quilt, Emiliano taps the walls and floors and ceilings. If there is a way into a place, he figures, then there must be a way out. He may be beaten at the moment, but he is far from accepting defeat.

CHAPTER SEVENTEEN

Ora Sonorious Leaves Her Room

Ora Sonorious has also stayed in her room since her arrival, but she hasn't been praying, sneezing or tapping the walls. Residence at the Hotel Saint Mona has brought on a depression that makes all the depressions that came before it laughable. Dr Ramin's Ten Reasons to be Cheerful exercise hasn't made a dent in it. Indeed, Ora has only been able to come up with one reason for being cheerful, and that is that she isn't dead. Unfortunately, given the fact that she is hundreds of years and zillions of miles from where she should be, this simple fact isn't much consolation.

This afternoon, however, grumpy, sulky and danger-ously low on endorphins as she is, Ora has decided to venture forth.

Nasa Hiko, who happens to witness this significant occasion, smiles. 'That's more like it,' Nasa Hiko says to the monitor. 'I knew you'd break down in the end.' They all will. In Nasa Hiko's experience, strength of character is not a predominant human quality.

There are two reasons why Ora has decided to finally leave her room, but, contrary to what Nasa Hiko believes, a weak character isn't one of them.

The first reason is that, unlike Emiliano, Ora is accustomed to brushing her teeth, washing her hair and changing her clothes on a fairly regular basis and, since she left Los Angeles with no chance to pack so much as an overnight bag, she needs toothpaste, shampoo and something else to wear.

The second is that Ora is tired of being on her own. She hasn't heard a peep from Emiliano or Mrs Fugosi, of course, but she hears the Top Teens beyond the walls of her room, and their laughter and apparently carefree babble has made her feel far lonelier than she has ever felt before. Necessity isn't just the mother of invention; she's the mother of compromise as well. Ora's decided it's time to make friends.

And so it is that when the Top Teens come out of their rooms on this afternoon Ora takes a deep breath, swings her backpack over her shoulder and marches out of her door, nearly tripping over a tray of empty dishes in front of the room next to hers.

Willis, Ben, Diane, Luke and Bethesda are waiting by the elevator for Kylie, who is still putting on her make-up.

They turn as Ora approaches, thinking that's who it must be.

'God, it's about time—' begins Diane, but breaks off when she sees Ora and the black vinyl coffin with the bat embossed on the lid. Diane doesn't try to hide her dismay. 'Oh,' she says. 'It's *you*.'

Ora can tell from Diane's tone and the noticeable drop in temperature in the hall that the trip to Top Teen friendship is going to be all uphill in bad weather, but she puts a hopeful smile on her face.

'Hi,' says Ora. 'How're you doing?'

'We thought they must've left you behind,' says Luke.

'No.' Ora shakes her head. She smiles a little harder. 'No, here I am.'

Neither Diane nor Bethesda smiles back.

Ben and Willis glance at the girls, and risk a nod.

'So,' says Ora, 'been doing anything interesting?'

Bethesda and Diane continue to glare at her in the cool, disdainful way Ora became so familiar with after Meadow dumped her.

Ben and Willis look at the floor and grunt.

Luke, who seems to be the only one capable of speech, says, 'Yeah. They've got some pretty cool games in the arcade. You can go anywhere and do anything you want. It's really awesome.'

'Oh,' says Ora. 'That sounds great.'

'And there's a gym and stuff like that,' he goes on, oblivious to the disapproval emanating from Diane and

Bethesda that is thickening around him like a poisonous gas. 'And the restaurant's pretty co—'

'Where the hell is Kylie?' Bethesda looks at her watch as though time still has some meaning. 'I don't actually want to spend the whole afternoon in this hallway, you know.'

'Me neither,' says Diane.

As though summoned, the door to the girls' room opens and Kylie steps out, already talking. 'I'm sorry I took so long,' she's apologizing, 'but you know what it's like when you mix your own col—' She breaks off as her eyes fall on Ora. 'Jumpingeehossapheffer,' gasps Kylie. 'I didn't know *you* were here.'

'Where else would I be?' Ora manages to keep the smile in her voice as well as on her face. She laughs. 'We didn't exactly get return tickets, did we?'

The smooth and constant voice of Frank Sinatra is punctuated by a tiny *bing*. The elevator doors glide open.

Bethesda wants to win the television show she believes that they're in, and so has been making an effort to be as nice as can be – even to Kylie and Willis, both of whom irritate her like a skin rash. She doesn't feel, however, that this gracious behaviour has to include Ora, since she is so blatantly not one of them. 'I didn't think you got any kind of ticket,' says Bethesda as she steps into the elevator. 'I mean, it isn't as if you and that criminal type you're with were *chosen*, is it?'

Diane's thinks this is one of the funniest things she's ever heard. 'Chosen!' she shrieks. 'The only thing they'd be chosen for is the losers' team.'

'I wasn't actually *with* him,' says Ora. 'I was just giving him a—'

The doors close.

'Ride,' finishes Ora. She's still in the hall.

By the time Ora gets downstairs, the plush and modern foyer of the Hotel Saint Mona is empty of Top Teens.

To her right is the restaurant. Ora goes to the sparkling glass doors and looks in. The tables are covered in bright yellow cloths and set with plates and cutlery and glasses and candles in holders made of bamboo, very much, if Ora thought about it, like the restaurant in the brochure from the Hotel Caribe. But Ora has more pressing things to think about than the faintly familiar decor. Although the restaurant could easily sit a hundred people there is no one in the dining room but the waiters, lined up on one side in an orderly row, placidly waiting for something to do. Ora stares at them with what Mrs Fugosi would recognize as a very bad feeling. Some of the waiters are male and some are female; some are dark and some are fair; some have long hair and some have short hair; some have blue eyes and some have brown. But those are the only differences between them.

'Oh my God . . .' whispers Ora. 'They all have the same face.'

The more Ora studies the waiters, the stronger becomes the very bad feeling. Maybe she should have stayed in her room after all. *Toothpaste*, Ora tells herself. *You're here to get toothpaste. Toothpaste and shampoo and clean underwear* . . . Like a mystic chant, just saying the names of such normal things makes her feel slightly better. Not good, exactly, but better enough to cope. She turns away from the restaurant door and hurries off in the opposite direction.

At first glance, the shopping plaza is as calming as a fistful of tranquillizers. Although it's only one floor and therefore much smaller, it reminds Ora of the Kennedy mall back home – the one she never got to on that fateful day. She stands at the entrance, taking it in. The walkways are spacious and lined with small trees in large pots, just like the Kennedy mall. There are rows of stores on either side of the plaza and wooden benches along the artificial pond – just like the Kennedy mall. There's a food court in the middle of the concourse, and at the other end of the promenade she can see the entrance to the health club. This is also just like the Kennedy mall.

The bad feeling starts to throb.

Slowly and warily, Ora makes her way down the walkway.

She comes to a stop in front of the boutique. The display in the window is also unnervingly familiar. That black skirt . . . that T-shirt with the screaming face on the front . . . those thick-soled, lace-up boots. Ora frowns. She had, if only briefly, that same skirt, T-shirt and boots. She bought them the day her mother's car was almost stolen. They'd been in the window of the boutique in the Kennedy mall, just as they are here. The name of the boutique in the Kennedy mall all those light years away is La Vida Loca. Ora takes a step back and looks up. *La Vida Loca*, shouts the multicoloured sign above the store. Across from La Vida Loca in the Kennedy mall are a shoe store and one that sells underwear. Very slowly, Ora turns around to see what's behind her: Born to Walk and Beneath the Surface.

Well, thinks Ora, *at least I know why everything seems so familiar.*

She hurries on to the food court. Like the one in the Kennedy mall, it has an Italian snack bar, a McDonald's, a Chinese-Vietnamese-Thai snack bar, a Taco Bell and a KFC, a pizza stand and five coffee bars. There are neon signs and bright menus behind the ser-vice counters. There are plastic streamers and miniature flags. The staff behind each counter is dressed according to the cuisine it represents. There is, in fact, only one thing that distinguishes this food court from the one in the Kennedy mall, but it is a significant difference. And this is where the shopping plaza stops having even the slightest calming effect and the bad feeling goes into fifth gear.

Ora lets out a soft bleat of horror. The counter staff all look like each other too.

Robots, Ora tells herself. *You're in the future – they must be robots.* But there is, of course, no real reason why this assurance should give her any comfort – and it doesn't.

It's with some small relief that Ora spots Kylie, Diane and Bethesda sitting at one of the small round tables outside Coffee World, drinking cappuccinos from white china cups. Ora waves in their direction. They act as though they haven't seen her.

Ora strides towards them, calling out, 'There you are!' as if they've been waiting for her.

They don't look up.

Smiling with a determination that even Dr Ramin would be proud of, Ora pulls an empty chair up to their table and sits down.

'What do you guys think of this place?' Ora lowers her voice. It has occurred to her that if the walls have faces they may also have ears. 'Isn't it weird?'

Only Kylie responds. 'Weird? What's weird about it? It's a shopping mall.' She giggles. 'Maybe for someone from your planet it's weird but it seems totally normal to us.'

'But it's an exact copy of the mall I shop at back *home*.'

'Um duh . . .' Diane looks at her blankly. 'In case you never noticed, all malls look the same. They're supposed to.'

'Um duh . . .' returns Ora. 'In case *you* never noticed, everybody who works here's a robot.'

'Yeah, right . . .' says Diane.

'A robot?' Kylie's giggles seem to bounce. 'You mean like R2D2?'

'No,' says Ora, 'not like R2D2. Like in *Bladerunner*.'

'Oh, I've never seen *that*.' Kylie giggles some more. 'It's very dark, from what I hear.'

'It's not as dark as this dump.' Ora leans forward,

insistent. 'Don't you see? They all look exactly the same. The waiters in the restaurant all look the same . . . this crew here . . .' She nods to the row of stores across from them where the same smiling faces look out at the concourse, waiting with inhuman patience for a customer. 'Even the salespeople—'

'You must be blind as well as stupid,' Bethesda cuts in. 'They look nothing alike.' She laughs sharply, as though Ora is, indeed, the most stupid person she's ever met. 'And none of them looks *anything* like a robot.'

'That's right,' says Diane. 'I mean, you may not have noticed, but the girl who waited on us is blonde. And the one over there in the sports store has red hair.'

'And the guy in the pizza place isn't even a girl,' chimes in Kylie.

'But they all have the same face,' points out Ora. 'And they're all the same height, and the same build, and—'

'What is it, drugs?' Bethesda gives Ora a pitying look. 'Or has the dye seeped through your skull? Is that what's destroyed your tiny brain? Because, for your information, the waiter in the restaurant at lunch touched my hand and he was definitely made of flesh.' She smiles an arch and sour smile. 'Not metal. Or plastic. Or tin cans.'

Ora sighs. 'Look,' she says, 'whether you three like it or not, we're all in the same boat, aren't we? Or should I say on the same planet – wherever that may be.'

'*Wherever that may be?*' Diane's laugh is sharp

with contempt. 'Oh, don't tell me you believe all that crap about being in the future? You really are too much.'

'Freaking priceless!' hoots Bethesda.

Ora smiles her sweetest smile. 'And what crap is it that you believe?'

'Well, it's obvious, isn't it?' says Bethesda. 'We're in a reality TV show.'

Ora's smile sets like concrete. 'You what?'

'That's why the staff all look alike. It's part of the game. It's just make-up.' Her eyes look right into Ora's. 'So the dumber among us will believe that we're on another planet.'

'It's true,' agrees Diane. 'It's the only thing that makes sense.' She has learned to duplicate Bethesda's condescending smile. 'And *you* should watch what you say. You're making a fool of yourself on national TV.'

'I think I'll take my chances,' mutters Ora.

'We're all famous.' Kylie eyes her sorrowfully. 'Well, except you and that boy and Mrs Fugoli.'

'Fugosi,' Ora automatically corrects her. She looks from one pretty face to the other. 'Are you serious? You think this is a *TV show*?' She shakes her head. 'Why would you think that?'

'Because it's the only thing that makes sense,' repeats Diane.

'No, it isn't.' Ora's head is still shaking. 'It doesn't make any sense at all. If this is a TV show, why are you all still here? Why haven't any of you been eliminated?'

Bethesda's smile suggests that Ora's stupidity is

almost painful. 'Because they're using a different format, that's why. They'll tell us who won when it's all over.'

'You see?' says Diane. 'It does make sense.'

'Good God!' groans Ora. 'What's wrong with you? What that doctor told us is the only thing that makes sense.'

Bethesda's cup clicks back into its saucer. 'I wouldn't expect *you* to understand. You're not one of us, are you?'

'No,' says Ora with a bit more force than she intended. 'No, I'm not.' And never has she been so happy not to belong.

Bethesda shrugs. 'Well, there you are. We all came to LA to be on television. This is all just part of the show.'

'Right.' Ora sits back, her eyes on Bethesda. 'Well, could you just tell me how you explain the space-ship and the vanishing limousine then?'

'Special effects,' says Bethesda.

'That's right,' Diane agrees. 'Special effects.'

'They can do anything nowadays,' says Kylie.

'In movies.' Ora says this slowly but firmly. 'In movies they can do anything. This isn't a movie.'

'It's a TV show.' Kylie smiles triumphantly. 'It's the same thing.'

Ora is too stunned even to laugh.

Bethesda stands up. 'Well, this has been really lovely, but I have to go.' She tosses her hair, her eyes on everyone but Ora. 'I have to get to the gym.'

Diane and Kylie jump to their feet as though yanked on strings.

'That's right,' says Diane. 'I have to go too.'

'I want to get some postcards.' Kylie turns her back on Ora. 'My mom'll *kill* me if I don't send her a postcard.'

Now Ora does manage to laugh. 'Postcards? Are you crazy? From the future? From outer space?'

None of them looks at her.

'And I thought I'd get one of those cute little bears in the gift shop for my sister,' Kylie goes on. 'She *loves* bears.'

'I should get some postcards too,' says Diane as the three of them walk off. 'Did I tell you my mom collects them? She's got sixteen whole scrapbooks of postcards from all over the world.'

'I bet she doesn't have one from Saint Mona,' mutters Ora, as she watches them go.

Ora Sonorious sits at the small round table outside the coffee bar for a while, fervently wishing that she'd stayed home instead of going to see the ocean, and then she forces herself to do her shopping and heads back to her room, watched by Nasa Hiko in the control room and by Lucia in her mother's study.

Nasa Hiko smiles with satisfaction as Ora retraces her steps over the carpets that make her footsteps soundless and through the hallway that could very well be in a hotel in Los Angeles or the Caribbean. Nasa Hiko has often wondered how different the ancients were from the people of her time. And the answer she now knows is: not very. Their clothes may be foreign, their knowledge of technology primitive, their physical traits not as perfected or as homogenous – but those things aside they are reassuringly the same. The same fears, the same weaknesses, the same pointless desires. It's only a matter of time before Ora falls into line. She may have a little more spunk than the other girls, but this will soon fade. The Corporation didn't get where it is today by not understanding the great human need to belong. Using that need, you can get people to kill anyone, destroy anything, buy whatever you want to sell them. Peer pressure, Nasa Hiko knows, is more effective than torture.

Lucia doesn't smile. Ora's encounter with Diane, Kylie, and Bethesda has damaged Lucia's belief in the perfect world of the past. Lucia too is beginning to understand that the people she's descended from are not so different from the people who live now beneath their domes with their eyes shut tight and their hearts as good as gone. Or some of them are.

But she's just like me, thinks Lucia as Ora, swinging her bags of shopping, strides out of the make-believe mall. *All alone and powerless.* The light on Lucia's communicator flashes, bleepbleepbleep, call coming through – Napoleon Lissi with another idea for the wedding that moves towards Lucia like a tank. She sighs. What in the universe are any of them going to do?

*

Ora sits on her bed in the quiet of her room, trying not to cry. She knows exactly what she's going to do now: she's going to do nothing. What's the point?

Things are even worse than she thought.

One of Dr Ramin's favourite refrains in his conversations with Ora was the You-don't-know-when-you're-well-off refrain. 'You don't know when you're well off,' he told her at every session. 'You've never had a real problem in your entire life.'

Too late to do her much good, Ora finally sees how right Dr Ramin was; she had nothing to be depressed about before. Well, now she does. Now she's a permanent resident of the Hotel Zombie, staffed by robots and inhabited by the living dead. Now she really feels like poor little Solo the hamster on his blue plastic wheel. This is futility with a capital F. Get up, wash, eat, watch television, eat, watch television, eat, watch television, eat, watch television, sleep, get up . . . Over and over and over – possibly for ever. Or possibly for not that long. She doesn't know which would be worse.

At least when she was still on the Earth Ora had a future. Gloomy though she was, there were still things that could happen; still things she might become that could make things better. Now the only thing she can ever become is dead.

With a certain amount of resignation, Ora turns on the TV, clicking through the hundreds of channels in the bored and uninterested way of someone who feels that her situation is without the smallest shred of hope and that she might as well be dead after all.

She finally stops on the movie on channel 109.

It's a very old movie, made decades before Ora was born, and set in the Second World War. It's about a place called Colditz. Colditz was a town in Germany, famous for its cliff-top castle surrounded by a moat. Just like in a fairytale. If you saw that castle now, it would make you think of Disneyland rather than the Holocaust, which is an example of what a great healer time really is. During the second war the world had to end all wars the old castle was used as a high-security prison for soldiers who had already got free from somewhere else. It was supposed to be escape-proof, but British soldiers were always getting out by ingenious if not actually miraculous means. That's what the movie is about: a daring break-out from Colditz. It required a lot of team effort. Dozens of soldiers worked for months to make it possible for a few to escape. The very act of resisting kept them fighting and alive.

Interestingly enough, for all the hours and thousands of dollars Ora has given to Dr Ramin, she has never been as affected by anything he said as she is by the struggles of these doomed and desperate men. They had no reason to hope, and yet they did. They had no reason to keep on, but they refused to give up. And at long last Ora thinks she understands something of what Dr Ramin was trying to tell her. The only meaning in life is the meaning you give it by your actions; by the way you fight to find it.

Ora sits up, paying attention.

If British soldiers, exhausted and battered by years

of war, could get out of a prison where the enemy was ready and waiting for them to try to escape, then surely she can escape from Saint Mona, where, presumably, it hasn't occurred to anyone that an attempt might be made. After all, who would be that crazy?

But Ora knows that she can't do it alone, just as the men of Colditz couldn't do it alone. She needs an ally.

Ora can think of one other person who might be that crazy, which, considering the small human population on Saint Mona, is really pretty good.

Though not, perhaps, quite good enough.

No . . . no . . . no . . . Ora tells herself. *It's out of the question. He's obnoxious, and hostile and a pain in the ass.*

Ora is still telling herself no when she remembers something else that Dr Ramin said. During one of their many conversations about Ora's sense of disappointment in life, Dr Ramin had this to say: 'You're like a person who's been given a house, but isn't happy because it's not as big as she wanted, or there's only one bathroom. You have to make the best of what you have, Ora. There's nothing else you can do.'

Make the best of what you have . . . There's nothing else you can do . . .

All Ora has is Emiliano Shuh.

But I don't like him, thinks Ora. *And he doesn't like me.*

Dr Ramin's voice immediately answers this objection in her head. *You have to make the best of what you have . . . What else can you do?*

Ora sighs. She isn't stupid. There is nothing else she can do.

Ora sighs again. God how she hates it when Dr Ramin is right.

CHAPTER EIGHTEEN

Several People Discuss Their Situation

Nasa Hiko is, of course, as busy as a politician at election time – perhaps even busier. As well as running Project Infinite Future, she is supervising the AALFs who man the monitors, overseeing the production and dispersal of several thousand troops for Napoleon Lissi's Army of Liberation and, now that she is on Saint Mona, managing the supply and maintenance of REPs, as well. So busy is she that the only time she isn't doing at least two things at once is when, as now, she has her daily briefings with Justice Lissi. Justice Lissi doesn't share anything with anyone – not even time.

'So, what's the schedule looking like?' asks Justice Lissi. 'When do you think you'll be able to start the . . .' He hesitates. As head of the Corporation he is so accustomed to using euphemisms ('collateral damage' when he means murdered women and children; 'small disturbance' when he means a massive uprising; 'bit of a decline' when he means economic collapse) that even with Nasa Hiko he finds it hard to speak plainly. '. . . the practical side of the project?'

'A week – maybe a little less, maybe a little more. We've got all the physical data in from the AALFs in the gym and the health and beauty club now.'

'And?'

'And they're just what I said they would be.' Nasa Hiko gives a little laugh, but Justice Lissi doesn't crack the smallest smile. 'No real athletes or brains among them,' Nasa Hiko continues, 'but they're all healthy and of at least average intelligence. The boys' sperm counts are normal and the girls' reproductive systems are all in order.'

'Then what's holding us up?' demands Justice Lissi. 'What more do you need to know?'

Because he can see her, of course, Nasa Hiko doesn't roll her eyes and groan at the inefficiency of the unscientific mind the way she's tempted to do. 'I'm still waiting for the psychological profiles. The computer's analysing the data but it'll take a while.'

Justice Lissi doesn't see the need for this, either. 'Who cares about their psychological profiles? We want to reproduce them, not give them jobs.'

Nasa Hiko, who of course blames her random selection of unknown genetic material for the dense and aggressive nature of Napoleon and the rebelliousness of her own child, doesn't say that she'd rather not take any more shots in the hereditary dark than she has to. She says, 'We want to make the best matches possible, don't we? Think how much it will cost if we have to start all over again.'

If there's one thing Justice Lissi understands completely, that one thing is money.

'No, of course we don't. Good point. It would put us back decades. Especially with our military budget being what it is.' By which he means totally out of control.

'Exactly,' says Nasa Hiko. 'That's what I thought. Wars cost more than just lives, after all.'

This time they do both laugh at her joke.

'And what about the other three?' asks Justice Lissi. 'Anything new with them?'

Nasa Hiko nods. 'We're making progress. The old lady talks to herself, and no one's seen the boy since the first day, but the girl's coming round.' Just as Nasa Hiko said she would. 'You never know – she has strong deviant tendencies, but we might be able to use her too. Which gives us seven for the price of six.'

This does make Justice Lissi smile. 'Now that's what I like to hear.'

Napoleon Lissi finally comes to the end of a very long explanation of his battle plan for liberating Camelot or whatever Lucia wants to call it and says, 'So? Did you ask them? What did they say?'

Having fallen into the stupor listening to Napoleon always causes, Lucia says, 'What? Did I talk to who?'

'The time travellers, you void.' He laughs affectionately. 'About wearing white for the wedding.'

How could she forget something of such universe-shaking importance?

'Oh . . . oh, no . . . I . . . I haven't talked to them yet. You know, because they might have infections.'

'Oh, right.' Napoleon nods with understanding. 'We wouldn't want you catching any of those old diseases.'

Lucia thinks of all the old diseases she might catch and how fatal they might be compared to spending the next hundred or so years with Napoleon. She should be so lucky.

'Well, why don't you ask your mother to find out?'

'There's no hurry,' says Lucia. *It's not as if they're going anywhere, is it?*

'Of course there is.' He smiles at how sweet and naïve she is. It's just as well he wants her as a bride and not a soldier. 'Once the project really gets underway they'll be out for the count, won't they?'

Will they?

'But I thought they were going to be bred,' says Lucia.

'It's no wonder men have always run the big show,' Napoleon chuckles. 'The female mind is so inefficient.' And then, realizing to whom he's talking, adds, 'Except for your mother, of course. There's nothing inefficient about her mind.'

In Lucia's opinion, Nasa Hiko's suitability for running the big show is down more to her lack of a heart than her efficient mind, but all she says is, 'No, there isn't.'

'Anyway,' says Napoleon, 'the point is that once your mother's completed her observations they won't be conscious any more, will they? They'll be like REPs – brain dead but alive. Why waste money feeding them and dressing them and keeping them entertained? I could arm another thousand troops on what it's costing to pretend they're in a hotel.'

Lucia sees Emiliano nailing up the quilt on his wall and Ora trying to convince Diane, Kylie and Bethesda that they really are on a different planet in a different time and not on TV, but stops herself from going on to picture them in a small dark room with tubes running into them and their breathing regulated by a machine.

'All nine of them?' asks Lucia. 'Are you certain?'

'There aren't nine of them,' Napoleon informs her. 'There are only six Top Teens. The other three were taken along by accident.'

'Oh, I didn't realize.' And, trying to sound both casual and calm, Lucia says, 'So what's going to happen to them?'

Napoleon laughs. 'What do you think? They're not good for much, are they?'

'No,' says Lucia. 'I guess they're not.'

*

At night, the lights of the restaurant in the Hotel Saint Mona are dimmed. The fake candles in their bamboo holders are turned on at every table, even though there is only one table being used, because this is the way the restaurant appeared in the brochure Captain Titanic took from Mrs Sonorious's car (except of course that the candles in the brochure were real). The Corporation favours the literal mind.

The Top Teens all sit at the large table in the centre of the room while the waiters go soundlessly to and fro, serving each course with silent precision.

'I mean, really, you should've heard her.' Bethesda's voice is heavy with scorn and her wide, blue eyes and practised smile are facing where she thinks the camera is likely to be. 'She actually believes that we're in the future! Have you ever heard anything so *gullible*?'

Ben, Luke, and Willis all laugh.

Ben shakes his head. 'It's like the General always says, isn't it? Most people are born to be led.'

'And that's not all,' Diane looks to see that there aren't any waiters nearby and leans over the table towards the boys. 'She thinks everybody in the hotel is a robot!'

'Isn't that too much?' Kylie's ponytails bob in astonishment. 'Like in a sci-fi movie!'

Bethesda stabs at her salad with her fork. 'I think *she's* in a sci-fi movie. She's like something that came out of a pod.'

'I think she's really stuck up,' says Kylie. 'She's

one of those people who just think the whole world evolves around them.'

'I don't understand what she's doing here,' says Luke. 'Do you think she's some kind of plant?'

'Yeah,' says Bethesda, 'rag weed.'

Diane chokes on her chicken. 'Rag weed! That's so funny!'

'No, seriously,' says Luke. '*Why* is she here? She can't be part of the show.'

'Luke has a point.' Willis sits up a little straighter. 'She's obviously not a high achiever.'

'And she's not exactly beautiful,' says Diane. 'I mean, her nose is enormous. And her eyebrows are too thick.'

'Plus she's taller than the boys,' adds Kylie. 'She could never wear heels.'

'Can you imagine her in a *dress*?' Bethesda's laugh glides through the quiet of the restaurant like steel over ice. 'She'd look like a basketball player in drag!'

'So why is she here?' repeats Luke. 'And if she's here, then probably Mrs Fugosi and that geek are here too. Why?'

'Well, it's obvious, isn't it?' Ben stops eating and leans back with his fingertips on the table, the way the General does when he's holding forth. Everyone to whom it isn't obvious looks at him expectantly. 'They're here to convince us what the phoney doctor said is true.'

'Gosh,' chuckles Willis. 'How dumb do they think we are?'

*

Because Nasa Hiko is busy talking to Justice Lissi, Lucia is trapped in conversation with Napoleon and the Top Teens are occupied with each other, there is no one to see Ora leave her room again. She goes no further than the door next to hers. For several seconds she just stands there, on her face the look of a girl who's about to do something she thinks she'll come to regret. *Desperation is the mother of necessity*, she tells herself, and raps on the door.

Because Emiliano has the TV turned up to full volume it isn't until Ora starts pounding with both fists that he realizes there's someone wanting to get in. He flicks the sound down just enough so that he doesn't have to get up and cross the room to be heard. 'Go away!' he shouts. 'Whatever it is, I don't want it!'

Ora leans her head against the door. 'It's me!' she yells. And when this brings no answer says, 'Ora. Remember? I gave you a ride?'

'And?'

Ora scowls. She knew this was a bad idea. Travelling through space and time has obviously done nothing to improve his lousy personality. 'And I want to talk to you.' She can hear him sigh as though she's asked for one of his kidneys. 'Now,' says Ora. 'I want to talk to you now.'

'So come in,' says Emiliano. 'It's not locked.' Though not for want of trying. The locks are operated from Central Control.

Ora steps inside. The room is dark, the curtains drawn against the artificial beach at night, the only light coming from the TV. Emiliano is sprawled on the bed, still wearing the same filthy clothes he had on when she met him, eating an apple. The room looks like a small garbage dump, littered as it is with empty cups and plates and bits of food. There's a ring of forks on top of the bedside lamp. *You can take the boy off the street*, thinks Ora, *but he's going to bring the street inside with him*.

'Turn that down!' she orders. 'I can't hear myself think.'

'No.' He beckons with the apple. 'You come over here.'

Compromise . . . compromise . . . Ora reminds herself. *Make do with what you have*. She slams the door behind her and walks over to the bed.

'Oh my God!' She claps her hand over her nose. 'What's that stink? It smells like you've been burning toxic waste.'

Emiliano takes a bite from his apple. 'Just the sheet.' He chews slowly. 'So what do you want? You come to apologize?'

She glares down at him, her only ally. 'Apologize? Me? What am I supposed to apologize for?'

This he finds highly amusing. 'Oh that's rich. What are *you* supposed to apologize for?' He tosses the apple core through the open bathroom door. 'How about getting us free rooms here in Heartbreak Hotel?'

'Me?' Ora seems to be getting taller with each second that passes. 'How did ending up here get to be *my* fault? You're the one who stopped for Geronimo.'

'And you're the one who went flouncing over to the limo.'

Ora is about to counter with the point that it was he and not she who got involved in trying to fix the car, but as her eyes adjust to the dimness of the room she gets distracted by something she didn't notice at first. She points to the old, handmade blanket nailed to one wall. 'What the hell is that? It looks like someone's occupational therapy project.'

'It's a patchwork quilt,' says Emiliano. 'My old granny made it for me.'

Ora is still staring. 'But what's it doing on the wall?'

'So they can't watch me every minute of the night and day.'

'From the *wall*?' Ora looks at him the way his teachers used to do. 'Criminal paranoia is an ugly thing, Em. You should try to keep it under control.'

Emiliano pretends to laugh, ha ha . . . 'You heard Dr Death. They want to observe us. That means cameras.'

'In the wall,' says Ora, but her voice has lost its scorn. It feels as though something small with a lot of very cold feet is walking up her spine.

'Yeah, in the wall. Where Dr Death gives her daily pep talks. That means it's wired for pictures and sound.' He gives another grin. 'No smoke alarms either.'

Ora looks from him to the shabby patchwork quilt and back to him. It's no less difficult to admit that Emiliano's right than Dr Ramin. 'Are you sure?'

'Positive. That's why I set fire to the sheet. I figured if there was no alarm and they could see me they'd come running. I wanted to make sure the quilt works.'

Ora groans. She's been watched walking around in her underwear. She's been seen staggering to the bathroom with bedhead. She's been observed picking her nose.

As though reading her mind, Emiliano says, 'And they hear you talking to yourself and farting too.' He puts his hands to the sides of his head and flaps them like wings. 'The walls have really big eyes *and* ears. That's why I've got the sound up so high.'

'I suppose the good news is that the Top Teens are almost right. They think we're in a reality TV show.'

She's never seen him smile with delight before. 'You've got to be kidding. In outer space?'

'They don't think we're in outer space. They think we're in LA.'

'Then they haven't tried to open the window.' Emiliano reaches up and raps the solid wall behind the curtain. 'It's not real.'

Forgetting how loathsome – and filthy – he is, Ora sits down on the bed beside him, dropped by gloom.

'Nothing is real. I went downstairs. The whole thing's just an elaborate stage set.' And she tells him about the Kennedy mall and the robots and the significant fact that there are no doors out of the hotel.

Emiliano whistles. 'This place is so creepy I think I'd rather be in jail.'

'Well that's all right then – since we more or less

are.' Ora sighs. 'And I came to ask you to help me get out of here,' she says in a defeated whisper. 'We'd have to be invisible to escape.'

He gives her a look that is an interesting combination of hope and resignation. 'Get out? And where do you think we'd go? This isn't Alcatraz, you know. We can't exactly swim to shore.'

She gives him a look of pure contempt. 'Excuse me, Chief Know-it-all, but I figured we could assume that if ships come in they must go out too. I thought we could stow away.'

'Stow away?' he shakes his head. 'Stow away to where? I haven't gone to expensive schools like you have, but I don't think there are any ships going to India or Mexico from Saint Mona.'

'What does it matter where? At least we wouldn't be here.' Ora grumpily kicks at an apple core that didn't make it to the bathroom. 'Or were you going to spend the rest of your life in this room?'

Since it was beginning to look as though this was exactly what Emiliano was going to do he ignores the question.

'All right, so what's your brilliant plan?'

This, of course, is yet another reason why she wants Emiliano's help. Brilliant plans are a little thin on the ground of Ora's mind at the moment.

'You're the criminal type,' she says. 'I figured you'd come up with one.'

'What? Blind? You may've forgotten, Princess, but I'm not the one who's been downstairs. I wouldn't know where to start. All I know is that I've been over every inch of this room and it's solid – even the ceiling – so I know we're not leaving through here. Whatever this place is used for when it's not pretending to be a hotel, they definitely don't want anyone getting out of it.'

'Well, excuse me for crediting you with more brains than you've got, but I thought I told you everything I saw. There aren't any buttons in the elevator. If you get in on this floor it goes down to the next, and if you get in in the lobby it goes up to here. That's it. And there aren't any exits. Everything leads into everything else.'

'But that's impossible.' Emiliano sits up, his eyes on the foot of the bed. 'We got in here, didn't we? That means there has to be a way out.'

'Unless they beamed us in,' says Ora, only half joking.

He gives her a look, unsure if she's serious or not. 'This ain't a TV show no more, remember? It's the real thing.'

'Oh, really?' Ora reminds him that they were beamed into the spaceship. 'What about that? If they can do that, why couldn't they beam us in here?'

'Because if they did, then there is no way out. Is that what you want? To just give up?'

It strikes Ora as another example of just how irrational people are that not that long ago he was the one ready to give up and she was the one who wanted to fight.

'Of course I don't. I—'

'Anyway, they didn't beam us through walls, did they?' Emiliano's gone back to staring at the foot of the bed. 'And not with all this crap – with restaurants and clothes and exercise bikes and everything.' He shakes his head. 'No, I figure there's got to be at least one door. Somewhere . . .'

Ora's eyes move from one solid wall to another. 'But not up here.'

'Not up here.' He looks over at her. 'It's got to be downstairs, then. Maybe in the mall.'

'That doesn't do us much good, does it?' Ora sighs. I mean we can't exactly go around the hotel tapping on walls or crawling across the floors looking for trap doors, can we?'

Emiliano is still looking at her. 'Maybe not.' He smiles. 'But I think there could be a way for us to do some snooping without making it too obvious.'

'Oh really?' She doesn't sound convinced. 'I suppose we could make ourselves invisible, but I forgot to pack the invisibility machine. You know – because we left in such a hurry.'

'You're just a laugh a line, aren't you?'

'I'm trying to keep up morale.'

'Then you'll be happy to hear that we don't need the machine to make us invisible. We can do it by ourselves.'

Ora sighs. 'And how do we do that?'

Emiliano smiles. She's going to love this one. 'We fall in love.'

'Yeah, right.' Ora smiles too. 'In your fevered dreams.'

'I mean it. If we act like we're really hot for each other we'll be able to check out downstairs without anyone getting wise to what we're doing.'

'Hot.' Oh why did she ever leave home that day? Why didn't she just swim in the pool? Ora's eyes move from his skinny body to his rat's nest hair. 'Is this "hot" as in "really attracted to"?'

'Like a paper clip to a magnet.'

'You have got to be joking. You haven't changed your clothes or even brushed your teeth in days. You can't seriously think I'm going to touch you.'

'I want you to do more than touch me. And I want you to do it with real passion. We have to make it convincing. You can go downstairs and get me some clothes and stuff.'

Ora continues to eye him with suspicion.

Emiliano winks. 'I clean up really well.'

CHAPTER NINETEEN

Ora Sonorious and Emiliano Shuh Make a Spectacle of Themselves

To Ora's surprise, Emiliano was telling the truth: he does clean up well. Washed, if not brushed, and wearing the new jeans, T-shirt and boots that actually fit that Ora got him, he looks almost normal.

'At least you don't look like a threat any more,' says Ora.

'I don't know . . .' Emiliano fidgets as the elevator doors soundlessly close. He tugs at his pants and wiggles his toes. 'It feels really weird.'

'You'll get used to it.' Ora pats his arm. 'We'll have you house-broken in no time.'

The doors slide open.

'Right.' Ora takes a deep breath. 'Here goes nothing.'

He squeezes her hand. 'You can say that again.'

Side by side they leave the elevator, cross the foyer and step through the entrance of the Saint Mona mall.

'Christ.' Emiliano whistles softly. 'It's just like home.'

Ora rolls her eyes. 'Oh dear . . . Did I forget to mention that?'

He scans the concourse. 'And all the salesmen look alike.'

'I guess I forgot to mention that too.'

He puts his arm around her and pulls her closer. 'Don't start sniping, Princess. We're supposed to be in love, remember?'

As if she could forget.

'So now what?' whispers Ora.

'Now we start looking for a token of my undying passion for you.' He steers her towards the neon pink sign that says Born to Walk. 'One store at a time.'

There are two clerks standing silently next to each other in the shoe store. One has dark hair and one has blonde hair, but they have the same smooth features and the same fixed smile. The blonde wears a plastic tag that says: *Hi! My Name is Molly. Have a Nice Day!* The dark clerk's tag says: *Hi! My Name is Cherry. Have a Nice Day!*

They step forward together like synchronized dancers, Molly's blank blue eyes on Ora and Cherry's blank green eyes on Emiliano.

'Can I help you?' they say. 'What would you like?

Dress shoes or casual? Sneakers or slippers? Flats or heels? Boots?'

'Heels,' says Emiliano.

Ora says, 'Flats.'

'Colour?' ask Molly and Cherry. 'Size? Width?' They spread their arms in opposite directions, gesturing towards the racks that line each wall. 'See anything you like?'

'Stereophonic sound,' Emiliano mutters into Ora's ear.

'I'm afraid we don't carry those,' says Cherry.

It's going to be a very long afternoon.

Bethesda's painstakingly lovely face contorts in horror. 'Oh my God! Do you see what I see?'

Kylie and Diane, who, with Bethesda, are recuperating from a hard morning on the massage tables of the health club with a diet soda at Planet Pizza, both turn to look behind them. The geeks are walking towards them down the concourse, their arms wrapped around each other like chains. Every few feet they stop in a doorway to kiss and hug.

'Oh, I don't believe it!' Diane's voice is shrill with indignation. 'I mean, why would they bring *him* to the hotel? He's not even human.'

'It's really too much.' Bethesda snorts in a way more associated with barnyards than designer salons. 'And look at the way they're carrying on. People like that are nothing but animals. I'm very, very tempted to have a word with the management. This isn't what you expect from a hotel like this.'

'I think it's kind of cute,' says Kylie. 'You know, like when you see old people holding hands and stuff. It just goes to show that there really is someone for everyone, doesn't it?'

'Well, I don't think it's cute at all. I think it's totally revolting.' Bethesda gets to her feet. 'I'm out of here. I'm going to do some shopping. Even looking at last season's clothes is better than looking at *them*.'

Diane leaps to her feet as well. 'I'm coming too.'

'And *me*,' says Kylie. 'I'm not staying here by myself. What if they wanted to talk to me?'

'He probably can't talk,' says Diane. 'He probably just grunts.'

Locked in what looks like a passionate clinch, from the corners of their eyes Ora and Emiliano watch the girls gather up their colour-coordinated gym bags and hurry off in the other direction.

'You tried to be friends with *them*?' he whispers. 'What the hell for?'

Ben, Willis and Luke are in the arcade, enjoying perhaps the only accomplishment of the Corporation's science that doesn't do any actual harm, the virtual reality machine. Each boy sits in a large, comfortable chair, wearing a computerized helmet and a tiny monitor over his eyes like glasses.

It is only because Luke, who has been trying his hand at white-water rafting in Colorado – something he would never dare do for real because of his allergies, his migraines and his parents' fear of water – and has just been dumped over a very large falls, decides to take a break and removes his head gear that he sees Emiliano and Ora enter the arcade.

'Hey!' He jabs Willis in the ribs. 'Hey! Look who's here!'

Willis, who is on a date with not one but three gorgeous models, tries to ignore him. 'Lay off,' Willis mutters.

Luke tugs at Willis' headset. 'It's them!' he hisses near Willis' ear. 'It's the geeks.'

Willis pulls the monitors from his eyes and looks. Emiliano and Ora, clutching each other like life preservers, are at the back of the room, leaning against the wall. 'What are *they* doing here?'

'It looks like they're thinking of starting a family,' says Luke.

Willis reaches to his right and shakes Ben's shoulder.

Ben, in the middle of an important peace-keeping mission, is bombing the hell out of a large city and pushes him off.

Willis pushes back.

With the heavy sigh of a general who has just watched his troops go the wrong way, Ben yanks off his headgear. 'What the hell is it? It's not time to eat yet.'

'It's *them*.' Willis nods to the corner of the room now occupied by Ora and Emiliano.

'Geez . . . I forgot all about him.' Ben whistles under his breath. 'Where'd he come from?'

In the hierarchy of the Top Teens, Ben is the Alpha male, Willis the Beta and Luke, because of his non-aggressive nature, is at Zeta – which means that the other two rarely pay any attention to what he says. Nonetheless, Luke clears his throat. 'Do you think maybe we should talk to them?' he asks. The sophistication of the audio-visual system has Luke, alone among the Top Teens, wondering what's really going on. He's never seen anything like it before – not even as theory. He wouldn't mind hearing Ora's ideas on Saint Mona for himself.

'Talk to them?' scoffs Ben. 'Talk to them about what? Drugs and petty crime? They're not even supposed to be here, remember?'

'I just thought—'

'Forget it,' says Willis. 'Ben's right. We have nothing to discuss with the likes of them.'

Luke's a wimp, not a fighter. 'Yeah,' he says. 'I guess you're right.'

Neither Ben nor Willis hears him. They're already back in their games.

Nasa Hiko and her staff meet every day to discuss the progress of her prisoners. Though she doesn't, of course, call them prisoners; she calls them biological resources. 'How are our biological resources today?' she begins each meeting. 'Any new developments?'

Nasa Hiko's staff sits around a large, oval table on

one side of the room, with her at the head. Nasa Hiko's staff consists entirely of AALFs, with the temporary exception of Captain Titanic, who is waiting for the ship that will take her on her next mission – the delivery of new troops to Camelot to await the orders of Napoleon Lissi.

'So . . .' says Nasa Hiko when each AALF has made its report. 'No signs of discontent? No complaints? No questions? No demands?'

'Bethesda isn't happy with the clothes that are available,' says one of the AALFs. 'She says they're very last season.'

Nasa Hiko brushes this aside. It's not as if Bethesda is going to need clothes for very much longer, even if Saint Mona actually had seasons.

'But she does still seem quite content,' says another. 'They all do.'

'The boys haven't been off the virtual reality machines since they discovered them,' says a third.

'And if Kylie and Diane buy any more clothes we'll have to make them another room to keep it all in,' says a fourth.

Nasa Hiko leans back in her chair with a satisfied sigh. 'I think we can safely say that everything's going to plan then, can't we? We should be able to start the core work of the project very shortly. None of them is giving us any trouble at all. Even the old lady has quietened down.'

'She still talks to herself all the time,' says Captain

Titanic. 'Perhaps we should sedate her. I can't believe that's normal.'

'Hormones,' explains Nasa Hiko. 'Humans of that time were at the mercy of their hormones.' Although she has only seen them in pictures, her hand makes the shape of a snake in the air. 'Up . . . down . . . down . . . up . . . Leave her be. I don't want to miss this opportunity to study old-fashioned ageing. It could be very useful.'

'Speaking of hormones,' says Captain Titanic. 'There has been one new development – though not among the Top Teens.' In a less disciplined officer, the set of her mouth might suggest criticism, or even a desire to say *I-told-you-so*. 'The other two have left their rooms. Together.'

'Really?' Nasa Hiko gets up from the meeting table and goes over to the console, followed by Captain Titanic. Monitor 38 shows Ora Sonorious and Emiliano Shuh, pressed together in the dressing room at the back of La Vida Loca. 'Well . . . well . . . well . . . Now this is something I wasn't expecting.'

'It does seem a little ironic that they're the only ones who are showing any interest in procreation,' comments Captain Titanic.

Nasa Hiko smiles at the primitive fumblings on Monitor 38. 'What's that old saying? You never can tell?'

'I still think we should put them in the cells,' insists Captain Titanic. 'We can't let them go on like this.'

Nasa Hiko's smile is now as plump as the butcher's cat once was. 'I don't see any cause for concern. In fact, I'd say that it's no bad thing. It'll keep them distracted – just in case that rebellious streak shows up again.'

'I thought we wanted to *improve* the gene pool,' murmurs Captain Titanic with a certain amount of acidity. 'I shouldn't think we'd want more of them.'

'I wouldn't worry about that.' Nasa Hiko turns from the monitor. 'The old lady will have to leave her room sooner or later. That should keep both her busy and them out of trouble. Kill two birds with one stone as they used to say.'

But Nasa Hiko isn't the only one familiar with archaic sayings.

'Or let loose two cannons,' says Captain Titanic.

For a few brief minutes the day before, Lucia thought she too had a plan.

Nasa Hiko was sitting on the sofa, going through the data of the day on her PCS. Behind her, in the artificial window that fills one wall of the living room, instead of a tropical beach there is a view of the city of London in the twentieth century, which better reflects Nasa Hiko's love of power than a couple of palm trees bending in the wind. Lucia stayed in the doorway for a few seconds, staring at the tower-like clock that rose above her mother's head. It was six o'clock on a summer evening. A helicopter passed by and, below it, a flock of pigeons. Lucia longed to really be there – to see a bird glide through a cloudless blue sky – and it was then that the plan dropped into her mind like an apple falling from a tree. 'Napoleon wants me to ask you a favour,' she announced from the doorway.

Nasa Hiko looked up, gazing back at her as though trying to remember who she was. Finally, speaking to Lucia for the first time since they arrived, Nasa Hiko said, 'Napoleon? Napoleon wants a favour from me? And what would that be?'

Safe from her mother's anger and scorn behind the shield of Napoleon Lissi, Lucia told her about his idea for modelling their wedding after a famous one from the twentieth century.

'Napoleon thought that maybe if I could ask the time travellers some questions we could make sure we got all the details right,' Lucia explained.

'That's a great idea,' said Nasa Hiko, and Lucia felt hope warm her heart like sunshine once warmed bodies on a beach. But not for long. There is no way in the galaxies Nasa Hiko is going to let Lucia talk directly to the past. 'Tell me what you want to know,' she said, 'and I'll ask them myself.'

Defeated once again, Lucia now watches Ora and Emiliano with the attention to detail of someone who is about to be hanged watching the building of the gallows from the window of her cell. So this is kissing; this is what it's about. The thought of being pressed against Napoleon Lissi makes her blood run as cold as those long gone mountain streams of Earth.

And yet she can't turn away. She watches them go in and out of every store in the mall. She watches them wander through every snack bar and coffee shop. She watches them stroll through the gym and the health club, bumping up against the lockers and the climbing wall, their voices never more than whispers she can't make out.

It isn't until they duck into a shower stall attached to the gym that Lucia finally starts to wonder why they didn't just stay in Emiliano's room with its blacked-out screen and its comfortable bed. Why make such a display of themselves? And answers herself with the next thought that comes into her head: because no one's paying them any attention. The Top Teens avoid them as though they really do have some fatal infection and Lucia knows that her mother, seeing this unfamiliar physical demonstration, will only think how primitive they are, wasting energy on emotions, the enemy of the reasoning mind.

They're looking for a way out! thinks Lucia. *They're going to try to escape.*

She sits up straighter, alert and tense. Why didn't she think of that before? There have to be ways out as well as ways in. She doesn't even know how large the medical colony is or how it's laid out; where the spaceport is or her mother's office; where the apartment she's sitting in is or what it connects to. But these are things she can discover – and without having to bump into walls.

Lucia smiles at the screen. Hope has latched itself to her heart once more.

*

By the time Ora and Emiliano return to his room morale is definitely low. They explored every corner of the mall they could – from the shoe store to the gym – but all they have to show for their time and effort is frustration.

'Well, that was a big waste of time.' Emiliano turns on the television, volume up as always to cover their voices, and collapses on the bed. 'You know, I think I'd rather be in Alcatraz – it's a hell of a lot easier to get out of than this place.'

'I take it that's your expert opinion.'

'You don't have to bite into the apple to know that it's rotten.' He's looking straight at her.

Ora drops down beside him. 'I suppose you're right,' she says. 'It's useless. We might as well stay in our rooms till we die.'

But, as ideas go, this one no longer has any appeal for Emiliano. To fight is to live, is what he thinks – and vice versa. 'Oh, we're not beat yet.' Because he has only survived with effort, Emiliano's is a resilient nature.

'We're not?' Ora is no longer gazing at him as though he's the most wonderful boy she ever knew. 'And what do you consider beat? Actually being chained to the wall?'

'I know it's hard for you, but you've got to try to be logical.' He weaves one hand through the air. 'Things enter . . . things leave . . . It makes sense.'

'Oh, thank you for pointing that out.' Ora yanks the pillow out from behind him and flops against it with a weary sigh. 'But things aren't entering or leaving through the shops. Or the gym. Or the health club. Everything's nothing but walls.'

'Well, they get the crap they give away from somewhere. And the food. That stuff's all real.'

'Oh my God . . .' Ora turns to him slowly, her eyes wide. 'That's it. That has to be it.'

Emiliano shakes his head. 'But it isn't. There's only one door into the stores and snack bars. No rear exits. And one in the restaurant.'

'No, you're wrong.' Ora grabs his arm. 'There are two doors into the restaurant.'

'No there—' He stares at her in silence for a second, seeing not a girl with pea-green hair but the elegant restaurant of the Hotel Saint Mona as seen through its sparkling glass doors. 'Jesus Christ. The kitchen. There must be a way out through the kitchen.'

'So does this mean we're dining downstairs tonight?' asks Ora.

CHAPTER TWENTY

After Days of Snuffling, Praying and Worrying Mrs Fugosi Too Decides to Leave Her Room

Due to a combination of boredom, painkillers, illness and despair, Mrs Fugosi spends a lot of the time when she isn't worrying, praying or blowing her nose sound asleep. This afternoon, she has a dream. Mr Fugosi is in the dream, which is not unusual, of course. What is unusual is that she is sitting on her bed in the Hotel Saint Mona when Mr Fugosi strolls through the door. He is in his work clothes, which are grey and covered in grease. Mrs Fugosi is so glad to see him that she doesn't tell him to clean up before he touches anything, as she would have had it not been a dream and he hadn't been dead for so many years.

He sits down beside her on the bed and takes one

of her hands in his. 'Juliana,' says Mr Fugosi, 'what are you doing here?'

Mrs Fugosi starts to tell him about the Top Teens and the spaceship and Dr Nasa Hiko, but Mr Fugosi stops her.

'I know all that,' he says. 'That's not what I meant.'

Mrs Fugosi asks him what he did mean.

'I meant what are you doing *here* – in bed – when you should be looking after those poor children. They need you, Juliana. Now's not the time for you to fall down on the job.'

In all the years they were together, Mr Fugosi never once criticized Mrs Fugosi for falling down on the job.

'But I didn't. I'm not well, Gene. I have a head-ache and a runny nose, and I can barely make a fist.'

'For the love of God, Juliana,' says Mr Fugosi, 'you always have a headache or a cold or aching joints. You're just making excuses. You're frightened, that's all, and you're making excuses.'

'I'm doing no such thing,' argues Mrs Fugosi. 'I'm worried half out of my mind about them – and I'm pray-ing – I pray all the time, but I'm ill, can't you understand that? After all that's happen—'

'It isn't enough for you to pray and worry,' he interrupts her. 'You've got to act, Juliana.' He lets go of her hand and stands up. 'I'm going to get washed up before supper,' he says, 'but you have to understand that those kids need your help. Bad.'

Mrs Fugosi wakes up as soon as Mr Fugosi walks

through the bathroom door. So real was the dream that she jumps out of bed and hurries to the bathroom, just in case Mr Fugosi is really in there, washing up before supper.

He isn't there, of course. But she can still smell him; still see his hairy knuckles and his kind, brown eyes; still hear him saying, *but those kids need your help* . . .

Fully awake now, Mrs Fugosi realizes that everything Mr Fugosi said to her in her dream was true. She's been making excuses. She has fallen down on the job.

With no thought to the state of her hair, her rumpled clothes or even the bedroom slippers on her feet, Mrs Fugosi picks up her bag and marches out the door in search of her charges.

Mrs Fugosi steps out of the elevator and into the lobby with the brisk and efficient air of a person who is used to organizing transport, travel and accommodation, and stands there for a few minutes, taking in her new surroundings. If there is one thing Mrs Fugosi is well acquainted with, it's hotel lobbies. At first glance, the lobby of the Hotel Saint Mona looks very much like every other hotel lobby she's been in. To one side is the entrance to the restaurant and to the other is the entrance to the shopping arcade. In front of her is the reception desk, behind which two young men and a young woman all dressed in immaculate white suits, stand silently, waiting for someone to ask them to do something.

But the longer Mrs Fugosi looks, the more she

frowns. Mrs Fugosi is having another of her bad feelings. Her eyes move from one side of the lobby to the next. It's rather like a game Mrs Fugosi used to play when she was a girl. She'd be given a picture of something completely normal – children having a snowball fight or a family having a picnic – and then be asked to discover what was wrong with the picture. Was there a typewriter in the picnic basket? Was one of the children throwing a baseball? Was everyone wearing only one shoe?

What's wrong with this picture? thinks Mrs Fugosi. No one's parked a truck inside the restaurant. No one's left a large pig at the entrance to the mall. And then Mrs Fugosi laughs, if nervously. Of course! It's the three young people behind the reception desk. They aren't answering telephones or dealing with guests in the busy and purposeful way she's used to. They aren't even chatting among themselves as young people behind reception desks usually do. They're just standing there like mannequins in the window of a clothes store with the same steady smile on each of their faces. And then she realizes that it isn't just their smiles that the three young people at reception share; their builds and features are the same too. *Perhaps they're all related* . . . thinks Mrs Fugosi.

But deciding that the hotel staff all share a gene pool doesn't make the bad feeling go away. It begins to move along her spine.

What's wrong with this picture . . . *? What's wrong with this picture* . . . *?* Mrs Fugosi's eyes take another turn around the lobby – restaurant entrance . . . entrance to shopping mall . . . sofas . . . coffee tables . . . potted plants . . . reception desk . . .

'Good Lord!' she gasps out loud. 'There isn't any door!'

But there must be a door. No one builds a hotel without a door. For God's sake, even prisons have doors. Mrs Fugosi is still looking for the door that she has some-how overlooked when Bethesda, Kylie, Diane, Ben, Willis and Luke come into the lobby and put everything else right out of her head. They are wearing swimsuits and laughing loudly.

'Yoo-hoo!' calls Mrs Fugosi. 'Here I am, kids! Over here.'

At the sound of her voice they all stop and stare, but none of them shows either joy or surprise at the sight of Mrs Fugosi, clutching her oversized handbag, her hair in disarray and the fuzzy pink bunny rabbit slippers that were Mr Fugosi's last gift to her on her feet, bearing down on them across the beige carpet.

'Oh, there you are,' says Bethesda as though Mrs Fugosi is a tube of lipgloss she'd misplaced.

'We were wondering what happened to you,' lies Diane.

'Geez, Mrs Fugoli,' burbles Kylie, 'where've you been? You're missing all the fun.'

'Fugosi,' corrects Mrs Fugosi. Where in tarnation does Kylie think she's been?

Ben and Willis grunt and nod.

Luke says, 'You OK?' which is not a question, of course, but a greeting.

'I'm just dandy,' says Mrs Fugosi. She looks from one to the other. 'But I need to talk to you all.'

Kylie and Diane glance at Bethesda. Bethesda rolls her eyes.

Luke and Willis glance at Ben.

'Sure,' says Ben. He starts to walk on. 'We'll catch you at supper.'

Mrs Fugosi grabs his arm. 'Now.'

The Top Teens, each in his and her way familiar with the erratic, often insane behaviour of adults, exchange wary glances.

Kylie's smile is even sunnier than Florida on a really good day. 'No can do, Mrs F. Di and Beth and I are having waxes this afternoon.'

Mrs Fugosi smiles back, but it is sunshine seen through very dark clouds. 'Surely you can wait a few minutes. Why don't we all get a coffee?'

'I don't really want a coffee,' says Bethesda. 'What I want is to get out of this wet suit.'

'Well, a juice then,' persists Mrs Fugosi. 'Or a tea.'

Diane sighs. 'We've got our waxes booked. We don't have time to sit around and schmooze with you right now.'

Mrs Fugosi's smile disappears completely. 'And what are they going to do if you're late? Give your appointments to someone else?'

'Well, yes.' Bethesda laughs. 'That's exactly what they will do.'

'And who will they give them to?' Mrs Fugosi

gestures to the lobby, empty except for the silent recep-
tionists. 'There's no one else here.'

Kylie pats Mrs Fugosi on the shoulder as the three
girls start to sidle past her. 'We'll catch you later, Mrs F.
At supper.'

Mrs Fugosi watches them sashay towards the elevator, for the first time in many years grateful that she
isn't young. Then she turns her attention back to the
boys.

'What about you?' she demands. 'Do you all have
pressing engagements?'

'I'm really sorry, Mrs Fugosi . . .' Ben shakes his
head sadly. 'But I have to go too. I'm in the middle of an
important bombing campaign.'

'Me too,' says Willis. 'I've got a heavy date this
afternoon.'

Luke rocks back and forth on his heels as Ben and
Willis slide past the old lady. 'We'll see you later,' he
promises. 'At supper.'

'Right,' mumbles Mrs Fugosi. 'Have a nice day.'

CHAPTER
TWENTY-ONE

A Unique Dining Experience

Mrs Fugosi, Bethesda, Ben, Willis, Kylie, Diane and Luke all sit at the round table in the centre of the otherwise diner-free restaurant. The waiters, who are dressed in the same lemon-yellow as the tablecloths and napkins, and who all have the same still features and fixed smile, stand to one side in a silent line, waiting for something to do.

'It's like having dinner on the *Mary Celeste*,' comments Mrs Fugosi as she picks up her menu. On the front of the menu is the outline of a palm tree in gold and beneath it the words, 'A Unique Dining Experience', which Mrs Fugosi can already see is a statement of fact more than a promise.

'What's the *Mary Celeste*?' asks Kylie. 'Some kind of cruise ship?'

'Something like that,' says Mrs Fugosi. Maybe it isn't like dinner on the *Mary Celeste* after all; maybe it's more like dinner on the Ship of Fools.

A waiter soundlessly appears beside them, bringing a tray of water.

At a signal from Ben, another waiter arrives for their orders.

'Good evening,' he says. 'And what would you like from our unique and extensive menu?'

The boys want steak and chicken, two kinds of potatoes and bread. The girls, all of whom have been dieting since they were nine, want salads, dressing on the side.

Mrs Fugosi, who is already finding dining in the restaurant an unsettlingly unique experience, watches the waiter nod as each new item is shouted at him. 'Doesn't he have to write all this down?' she asks.

'Of course not,' says Bethesda. 'That's why we're at a hotel like this, isn't it? He's a trained professional.'

'Isn't it cool?' squeals Kylie. 'They've all got photogenic memories.'

Mrs Fugosi wants to know if the spaghetti sauce is made with meat.

'What kind of meat?' asks the smiling waiter.

'Well I don't know what kind. I thought you'd tell *me*,' says Mrs Fugosi.

'Beef?' asks the waiter. 'Pork? Lamb?'

Mrs Fugosi is flustered. 'Well which is it?'

'Isn't it cool?' coos Kylie. 'You don't even have to order from the menu. You can have whatever you want.'

'But I don't want meat.' Mrs Fugosi can hear that she is bleating. 'I want sauce that *isn't* made with meat.'

'No beef?' asks the waiter. 'No pork? No lamb?' His smile never wavers. 'Chicken? Salmon? Tuna? Shrimp?'

The waiter sidles off to fetch the boys' meals, the girls' salads and Mrs Fugosi's spaghetti with olive oil and garlic. Leaving them alone.

They can't discuss the weather since, as far as any of them knows, there isn't any, so the girls chat about the automatic body-dryer and the health club and the entertainment systems and the boys go on about their virtual reality exploits while Mrs Fugosi listens politely. She is practically comatose with boredom by the time their meals arrive.

They are still being silently served by several waiters when Ora Sonorious and Emiliano Shuh stroll in, holding hands. They don't look at the Top Teens, but very deliberately take a table behind them, noisily pulling out chairs and sitting down.

'Well, bless my soul,' says Mrs Fugosi, who not only forgot all about them in her anxiety over her charges but who can't remember their names and therefore can think of nothing else to say.

'Oh God,' murmurs Diane. 'Dinner with the geeks.'

'They'd never be let in if the General was here,' says Ben.

'Just so long as they don't actually sit with us,' mumbles Willis. 'I wouldn't want anyone to think we're together.'

'It's just like in the Bible, isn't it?' Kylie smiles around the table. 'You know, many are called but not everybody gets chosen.'

Mrs Fugosi, who is still trying to figure out who Willis means by 'anyone', hasn't the slightest idea what Kylie is talking about, but the others, all believing that they have, in fact, been chosen, nod and exchange knowing, congratulatory looks. People who believe they are chosen often behave like this. People who actually have been chosen – Jesus, for example, or Allah, or the Buddha – usually don't.

Bethesda, who believes herself to be far more chosen than anyone else, turns an accusing eye on Mrs Fugosi. 'I really don't understand what *they're* doing here,' she says. 'I certainly can't believe that those cretins are part of the show.'

Mrs Fugosi wonders if it's the discreet lighting, or the recycled air, or the relentlessly anodyne background music that makes her feel so muddled. 'And what show would that be?' she wants to know.

'*What* show?' Like her snort, Bethesda's laugh is remarkably barnyard-like. 'Why the show we're in of course – *Reality Top Teens*.'

Mrs Fugosi can feel that she's smiling just like all the hotel staff – as though her mouth has been glued into shape. '*Reality Top Teens*?' she repeats. 'What's that when it's at home?'

The girls all sigh and the boys chuckle.

'You know,' says Diane. '*The show?*' She spreads her arms wide. 'The one we're on? With the cameras and the audience voting who they like best and all that stuff?'

'You know,' prompts Ben, and quotes the slogan for a programme that features a dozen strangers living in a house they can't leave and constantly squabbling about who didn't do the dishes or left the milk out, 'Life Becomes Entertainment.'

'We're all famous,' says Kylie. 'We'll be on Oprah and Springer and Leno and everything!'

Willis grins, an unattractive proposition given the sliver of meat that is stuck in his teeth. 'We're going to date Hollywood babes and go to the Oscars and everything.'

Mrs Fugosi looks down at her plate as though checking that it's still there, and then back at the six attractive young faces all looking at her as though she's lost her mind. 'Excuse me? Are you saying you think you're on television right now?'

All six heads nod and smile.

Mrs Fugosi doesn't nod and smile in return. 'And what makes you think that exactly?'

'Well, for one thing, there's no such thing as space travel,' says Ben. 'The General would've told me.'

'I've analysed the situation fully,' says Willis, but before he can begin to explain the mechanics of his reasoning Bethesda cuts him off.

'It's the only logical explanation,' says Bethesda. 'You don't have to pretend to us. We know the truth.'

'I'm not pretending anything,' says Mrs Fugosi. 'If we're in a television show this is the first I've heard about it.'

'Wow,' says Willis. 'They didn't even tell you? That's really wild. I guess they had to keep it secret so nobody would beat them to it. It's a really competitive industry. Statistics show—'

'Listen to me,' begs Mrs Fugosi. 'The reason *they* didn't tell me about it is because there is no reality TV show. And, as far as the truth goes, I believe what Dr Hiko told us.'

Bethesda smirks. 'You are a . . . a mature woman, Mrs Fugosi. You can't believe we're on another planet, can you? With little green men?'

'With people who are just like us.' Which is a far more frightening prospect in Mrs Fugosi's opinion. Just like us – the people who brought you the crucifixion, the Crusades, the Spanish Inquisition, the pogroms, slavery, the genocide of millions upon millions of people all over the Earth, constant war and the atomic bomb. How comforting is that supposed to be? She smiles thinly. 'And possibly only one person just like us, since as far as I can tell everyone except that doctor is some kind of robot.'

'Oh puhleese . . .' shrieks Diane. 'Have you been listening to that green-headed freak?'

'No . . .' Mrs Fugosi's voice is as hard and cold as an ice cap. 'I haven't been listening to anyone. I've been looking around. In the mall . . . in reception . . . *here* . . . The staff all look alike – and they don't act like people—'

'What are you talking about?' asks Kylie. 'They smile, don't they?'

The devil smiles . . . thinks Mrs Fugosi. Aloud she says, 'But they don't talk. They don't busy themselves when one of us isn't asking for something. They don't think, they just do what they're told.'

'That's because they're highly trained professionals,' says Willis.

'Like soldiers,' puts in Ben.

'Or like robots,' says Mrs Fugosi.

The Top Teens turn their attention to their plates.

Mrs Fugosi watches the boys stuff hunks of meat into their mouths and the girls shred lettuce leaves for a few seconds, her own meal untouched. 'And what about the fact that we can't leave the hotel?' she finally explodes. 'Don't you think that's suspicious? Don't you think it's odd that there are no other guests here? That the windows are all dummies and there aren't any doors? Have any of you noticed that? That there's no way out of here?'

Bethesda looks at the others and rolls her eyes. 'Um duh . . . Mrs Fugosi, are you on medication or something? That's what we tried to tell you. Of course we can't get out. Of course there aren't any other guests. **Because we're on reality TV**.'

Willis laughs so hard that he nearly chokes, but Mrs Fugosi makes no move to slap him on the back, as she would normally do. She folds her arms across her stomach in a way that the late Mr Fugosi would have recognized meant there was no way he was going fishing when he promised he'd fix the screen door.

'Or we're not on reality TV, we're imprisoned on a strange planet in the future.'

'You know what my gran always says, Mrs F?' asks Kylie.

'No,' says Mrs Fugosi, looking not at Kylie but at the waiters lined up against one wall like bottles. 'I don't think I do.'

Kylie mistakenly takes this as a desire to know. 'My gran always says that it has to be one heck of a storm for no one to get anything good out of it.' She shakes her fork in Mrs Fugosi's direction. 'So I think what you should do is stop getting so wound up because we can't leave the hotel and think of all the cool things we do have.'

'That's right,' says Ben. 'The gym is state of the art.'

'And what about the health club and the shops?' asks Diane.

'And the TV's got hundreds of channels,' says Luke, 'and the clearest picture I've ever seen.'

'Plus the virtual reality thing is totally mind-blowing,' adds Willis. 'I've never seen anything like it before. It beats the pants off of PSP.'

Ben nods enthusiastically. 'I've been in practically every war there ever was already. Just wait till the General hears about this. It could revolutionize military training.'

'You see?' Kylie smiles like a cherub on a Christmas card. 'This place isn't so bad, is it? I mean, really, it's like heaven here. Or do I mean paradise? I always get them mixed up.'

'It's nothing like heaven,' says Mrs Fugosi. 'Or paradise either, for that matter. And as for having everything you could want, what I want is an exit. That's what I want.'

Diane stops sipping her diet soda and gives Mrs Fugosi one of her best cheerleader smiles. 'Is this negativity part of the show? Are you just trying to rattle our cages to see what we do?'

Mrs Fugosi stares at Diane's teeth. She would certainly like to rattle something.

'Relax, Mrs Fugosi,' advises Ben. 'You've done a good job. You know, in fooling us and everything.'

'And we're happy,' says Diane.

'Except for the clothes,' Bethesda cuts in. 'The styles are so passé.' She smiles sweetly over a slice of carrot. 'I really think you should have a word with the producers, Mrs F. You know, get us some decent things. I'm really not happy about being seen by the world in last season's styles.'

'It's not a problem for me,' says Kylie. 'I mean, everything's free!'

'Nothing in the history of mankind has ever been free,' replies Mrs Fugosi. She sighs hopelessly. It isn't easy to help people who refuse to see that they need help. 'Don't you understand that none of this is real? Not any of it.' She pushes her untouched plate away. 'I'm not even sure that this is real food . . .'

Ben spears a piece of steak with his fork and flashes the boyish grin that won over the *Top Teens* scout. 'It sure tastes like real food to me.'

Mrs Fugosi's expression does a fairly good job of defining the word 'aghast'.

'Have you all lost your minds?' This is not, of course, the way Mrs Fugosi would normally speak to *Top Teens* contestants. She's supposed to treat them as though they're royalty and she's just a serf, but right now losing her job is the least of her problems. 'Can't you get it through your heads that this *is not* a television show? And it isn't a free vacation either. You mark my words, there's something very sinister going on here.'

'Excuse me, Mrs Fugosi,' says Bethesda, 'and I don't want you to take this the wrong way, but, personally, I think you're the one who's nuts.'

'Bethesda's right,' says Diane. 'I mean, not that you're nuts, but that you're really over the top. I mean, it's not like anyone's going to kill us or anything, is it?'

'Have any of you heard a word I've said?' demands Mrs Fugosi. 'Don't you understand? We're in danger. We can't just sit here having dinner until these people or whatever they are decide to evaporate us the way they did the car. We have to do something. We have to get out of here.'

Diane smiles at Mrs Fugosi as though she's a small and not particularly bright child. 'There are worse places than this,' says Diane.

Luke, whose home is one of them, nods emphatically. 'Too true.'

'Don't you ever watch the news?' asks Willis, who is also thinking of home.

Kylie puts on a sad face. 'Poor Mrs F,' she murmurs. 'Is it the menopause? Are your hormones bothering you?'

Ben, whose own mother is prone to crying jags and hurling small objects around, puts down his fork and lays a comforting hand on Mrs Fugosi's shoulder. 'There's nothing to worry about,' he tells her. 'I know martial arts. I'll make sure nothing happens to you.'

God help me, thinks Mrs Fugosi. *I'm lost in space with a bunch of airheads.*

'Thank you, Ben,' says Mrs Fugosi. 'I can't tell you how much better that makes me feel.'

Mrs Fugosi watches the Top Teens leave the restaurant with a heart so heavy it might be made of solid gold. But she isn't ready to give up yet. Although, so far, her prayers have gone unanswered – and possibly not even heard – she still has faith. Faith is always rewarded.

And so it is that, alone at the large round table in the centre of the elegant dining room of the Hotel Saint Mona, Mrs Fugosi clasps her hands and bows her head.

'Dear Lord,' Mrs Fugosi silently prays, 'I know I'm not the best person you ever created – He was nailed to a cross – but I'm not the worst either. And I know that I can't hope to understand the way you work, but I really don't believe that you intended me to end my days like this. Please,' she pleads, 'all I'm asking for is a little help.'

Mrs Fugosi's prayers are finally answered, though not by God.

She raises her head to find Emiliano Shuh and Ora Sonorious standing on either side of her. Emiliano leans down so that his mouth is beside her ear. 'Mrs Fugosi,' he whispers, 'I have an idea.'

In Mrs Fugosi's other ear Ora whispers, 'He means *I* have an idea.'

And Mrs Fugosi hears Mr Fugosi say *those kids need your help* again – and for the first time wonders which kids he meant.

Because Nasa Hiko is busy preparing everything for the medical tests soon to be carried out on the time travellers, it is Captain Titanic who watches the scene in the restaurant on monitor 43.

As an example of how much less reliable humans – even well-trained and disciplined humans – are than AALFs, if an AALF had witnessed Mrs Fugosi's unique dining experience, it would have reported it to Nasa Hiko in flat facts. It would not embroider them or leave anything out because it doesn't react but only responds.

Captain Titanic, however, is not an AALF. When she hears Mrs Fugosi trying to incite a riot among the Top Teens and when she sees Ora and Emiliano approach the old lady and whisper in her ear, she immediately thinks: *I told you so! Didn't I say those three are trouble?* And then, being well-trained and disciplined and knowing she would probably spend the rest of her career in the wilds of the outer galaxies if she actually said those words to the great Dr Nasa Hiko, she immediately buries them. But the further back she pushes the words *I told you so!* the more resentful and angry she becomes at the way the great Dr Nasa Hiko treats her – constantly dismissing her opinion and ignoring her good advice. As though the great Dr Nasa Hiko is omniscient and infallible and Captain Titanic is no more than a glorified machine to be ordered around, do all the difficult and dangerous work and take all the risks. Captain Titanic doesn't think it's fair. Having seen for herself how humans used to live a thousand years ago with all their bright clothes and bright possessions and barbecues and walks in the rain and breathable air, buried even deeper than her words of insubordination, something has begun to stir. It is the sense that her life serves no other purpose than to keep the Corporation powerful and rich. There's nothing in it for her – no snappy sports car, no frivolous clothes, no Frank Sinatra, no potato chips and certainly no joy.

Which is why when Nasa Hiko does ask her how the evening's monitoring went Captain Titanic doesn't report anything out of the ordinary. 'Everything normal,' says Captain Titanic.

Fate again.

CHAPTER TWENTY-TWO

Desperate Measures and Desperate Times

'Good evening to all our honoured guests.'

The honoured guests of the Hotel Saint Mona, having just returned to their rooms for the evening, all look around to see the face of Dr Nasa Hiko, beautiful as a glacier, smiling at them from the walls of their rooms. Mrs Fugosi looks too.

'I have some good news for you tonight,' Nasa Hiko informs them. 'To begin with, on behalf of the Corporation, I'd like to congratulate you on the intelligence and resilience you've shown in adjusting to your new environment. You've done yourselves proud.'

The six honoured guests all smile.

Mrs Fugosi presses her lips together and pulls her blue bathrobe more tightly around her.

'But the real announcement I want to make,' continues Nasa Hiko, 'is that I am delighted to be able to tell you that your period of quarantine is almost over. None of you has shown any sign of illness since your arrival, so we are confident that you are well and that you bear no foreign diseases that might infect our citizens. Naturally, we will need to do a routine medical examination on each of you before you can go out to see the marvels of our planet – just to be certain – but this is a mere formality.'

'I just hope the marvels of her planet include the new season's clothes,' says Bethesda.

Kylie and Diane laugh.

Ben and Willis punch each other in the shoulder.

Luke smiles, but in his head he's asking himself how this fits into the TV show.

'The examinations will begin in three days,' says Nasa Hiko. 'After they are over, I would like to invite you all to a gala dinner at my private apartment to meet the other important people on Saint Mona.'

'Cool!' crows Kylie. 'It seems like ions since I went to a party.'

Diane and Bethesda are both thinking of what they will wear and remain silent.

'You think there'll be some hot babes?' asks Willis.

Ben says, 'Definite, man. If that's what the adults look like here think of what the teenage girls must look like.'

Luke, still trying to figure out how this fits into the TV show, says nothing.

'I'll speak to you in the morning,' promises Nasa Hiko, and the walls go blank.

In Nasa Hiko's private apartment, Lucia, who has been listening to her mother's message on her PCS, looks up at the living room window. It is night in London and winter. The top of the tall clock is dusted with snow. She watches the large black hands move slowly to a new hour. Time is running out.

On the other side of the complex, Mrs Fugosi gets to her feet.

Satisfied with her little speech and with the progress she has already made, Nasa Hiko takes one last look over Captain Titanic's shoulder before returning to her lab. Mrs Fugosi, in her blue robe and her bunny slippers, has left her room and is knocking on Kylie, Bethesda and Diane's door. Nasa Hiko sighs. Why can't this woman ever behave normally and do what she's supposed to do? Right now, for instance, she's supposed to go to bed.

'Now what's she doing?' demands Nasa Hiko.

'She's saying good night to the Top Teens,' explains Captain Titanic, who, because of all the years spent on her mission, is well acquainted with the customs and rituals of the past.

'Good night?' echoes the great Dr Nasa Hiko. 'Whatever for?'

'It's what mothers in the twentieth century did,' explains the captain. 'Say good night. When the children are young they tuck them in bed and read them stories as well.'

'Thank the Corporation that we have Personal Communications Systems and don't have to waste time with that nonsense any more,' says Nasa Hiko.

They watch Mrs Fugosi enter the girls' room. Bethesda's lying on her back, her headset on and her face covered with a blue cream that's supposed to retard the signs of ageing, even though Bethesda is far too young to actually have any yet. Kylie's watching a music video while she paints her toenails pink and orange. Diane's wrapping her hair around dozens of tiny tubes to make it curly like Bethesda's.

'I just wanted to say good night,' says Mrs Fugosi.

Without so much as glancing at her Diane, Kylie and Bethesda all say, 'Good night.'

The room looks like a tornado's passed through it. There are clothes piled everywhere; make-up spread over every available surface; empty boxes, cartons, bags and cans of diet soda overflowing from the wastebaskets.

'Why don't I just tidy things up a little before I go?' asks Mrs Fugosi.

'What does she think the AALFs are for?' snaps Nasa Hiko.

'She's primitive,' replies Captain Titanic. 'She still likes to do things for herself.'

After she manages to clear a path through the room Mrs Fugosi moves on to Willis, Luke and Ben.

The boys are all watching a horror movie.

'Night, Mrs F,' says Ben.

'Night,' says Luke.

'Have a good one,' says Willis.

'Don't tell me she's going to clean up after them too,' groans Nasa Hiko. She straightens up. 'I've had enough. I'm going back to work. And you should get some rest. You've got a big flight coming up.'

Captain Titanic and Dr Nasa Hiko are already leaving Central Control as Mrs Fugosi steps though the door of Emiliano's room.

Ora sits cross-legged beside Emiliano on his bed. 'I don't like the sound of those medical examinations,' Ora is whispering beneath the blaring television. 'I think something's up.'

Emiliano nods. 'Me too. If we're going to do something we better do it pretty fast.'

Mrs Fugosi, who, because of her arthritis, is not sitting cross-legged but is sitting primly on one side of the bed, says, 'So, what's your plan exactly?'

'Well, you know . . .' Emiliano shrugs. 'First we see if there is an exit through the kitchen. That's where you come in. We need to create a distraction.'

Mrs Fugosi frowns. 'But what about the cameras? Even if the waiters are all distracted by me, the cameras will still catch you going into the kitchen.'

'We just have to hope that they don't,' says Ora.

'Hope that they don't?' Mrs Fugosi continues to frown. 'I don't want to dampen your enthusiasm, but I'm afraid that doesn't sound like much of a plan to me.'

'I figure there's a chance that whoever's monitoring them will be watching you, and not me,' says Emiliano. 'If everything works out the way we want it to, we'll be long gone before they think of checking.'

It is, of course, the only chance they have.

'Um hum . . .' murmurs Mrs Fugosi. It's a thoughtful and far from carefree sound. 'But what happens once you're in the kitchen? Surely you'll be stopped immediately.'

Emiliano would be the first to admit that, like most people, there are a lot of things he doesn't know – and probably even more that he doesn't know that he doesn't know. Professional kitchens, however, are not among them. He spent last summer working as a busboy and dishwasher in a beach restaurant for two meals a day and a bed.

'That won't be a problem,' he assures Mrs Fugosi. 'Everybody'll be busy.' Having lived by his wits almost forever, Emiliano's good at slipping past people unnoticed. 'And if they do clock me, I've got surprise on my side.'

'And then once Em's found a way out he'll come back for us and we'll find where the spaceships leave from,' says Ora. 'There's bound to be one that's getting out of here that we can stow away on.'

'I see.' Mrs Fugosi's hands are folded in front of her, very much as though she's praying, but what she's doing in fact is thinking fast and hard. As plans go, Ora and Emiliano's is not the best she has ever heard. The idea of going west instead of east to reach India is perfect in comparison. The idea of starting a world religion with a few fishermen to help you is foolproof in contrast. Mrs Fugosi has never been a particularly adventurous person. The most exciting thing she's ever done was ride down a river in a rubber raft, and that was a small river and she was wearing a life preserver and at least knew where she was supposed to end up. Indeed, Mrs Fugosi has always been the kind of person who pays her bills on time; who insures everything that can be insured; who books her vacations months in advance. And she has always known where she thought she would end up. She would marry Mr Fugosi, they'd have a family, and when the kids were grown and Mr Fugosi retired they'd buy an old Airstream trailer and travel around the country until they died. But, thinks Mrs Fugosi, where have all these plans and precautions gotten her? All on her own and billions of light years away from where any of her insurance policies can do her any good, that's where.

'Well . . .' Mrs Fugosi shrugs. 'I guess it's worth a try.'

'Really?' Emiliano and Ora don't dare smile. 'You mean you will help us?'

'Of course I'll help you.' And, echoing the words of one of the greatest poets who ever lived, adds, 'It's not as if I have anything to lose, is it?' She smiles at them the way their mothers never have. 'I want you to know that I think you're both very brave,' says Mrs Fugosi.

Emiliano smiles back. 'Maybe we're just nuts.'

'Speak for yourself,' says Ora.

CHAPTER TWENTY-THREE

Mrs Fugosi Makes Her Acting Debut

At breakfast the next morning, Ben, Bethesda, Diane, Kylie and Willis all talk excitedly about the gala dinner party being held in their honour in Dr Nasa Hiko's private apartment after their medical examinations are done.

'The doctor didn't say if it was formal or dress casual,' Kylie is saying.

'Oh, it'll be formal,' decides Diane. 'It's for all the bigwigs, isn't it?'

'I just hope we can get outside to do some shopping,' says Bethesda. 'I am not going to something this important in a dress no one with an ounce of taste has worn since December. Not on national television.'

Luke has been eating his cornflakes in silence but

now he puts down his spoon and says, 'You know, I wanted to ask you about that.'

Ben pushes the empty plate that held his bacon and eggs away and starts on a stack of pancakes. 'Shoot.'

'Well . . .' Luke summons all his courage. He has been so trained to do and say only what's expected of him that he might as well be throwing himself out of a plane without a parachute rather than merely speaking his mind. 'It's just that . . . well . . .'

Diane yawns. 'Oh, for God's sake, what is it?'

'I was just wondering.' He lowers his voice so that the others have to lean towards him to catch what he's saying – just in case his parents really are watching and he's about to disappoint them. 'If this is a reality TV show, then how come there haven't been any eliminations?'

'Because *Top Teens* doesn't work that way, does it?' says Ben. 'It's who's got the highest score at the end.'

Luke continues to look painfully puzzled. 'But then why do we have to have check-ups? And where do we go when they let us out of the hotel?'

There's an old saying that Luke is unaware of but that the other Top Teens are about to illustrate perfectly. This is the saying: A man sees what he wants to see and ignores what he doesn't want to see.

'I thought there were academic criteria for this programme,' moans Bethesda. 'I don't see how you ever got through middle school.'

Willis, who of course has a 4.0 grade point

average, laughs. 'Don't you get it? It's all just part of the set-up. The party's where they announce the winners.'

'Oh,' says Luke, sounding less than convinced but so relieved that he got his concerns off his chest that he doesn't really care.

'It's like when my mom threw a surprise party for the General for his fiftieth birthday,' says Ben. 'She told him she was taking him out to dinner and when they got to the restaurant practically every officer from the base was there.'

'I bet my mom's got her fingers *and* her toes crossed by now,' says Kylie. And she gives an enormous smile over the breakfast dishes to show her mother how much she appreciates her support.

Bethesda pushes back her chair. 'I have to go. I've got an appointment to get my hair done.'

'I'll go with you,' says Diane. 'I was thinking of getting highlights for the party.'

'Me too,' says Kylie. 'I thought I'd have something really special done to my nails.'

Ben and Willis, having finished their breakfasts, and Luke, having said his piece without being struck down by lightning, follow the girls out.

Two tables away, Mrs Fugosi, who sits by herself with her one cup of coffee and a plate of toast, sighs with relief. *Praise the Lord* . . . She thought they'd never leave.

Mrs Fugosi once saw a man have a heart attack in front of the ice cream freezer in her local supermarket, and it is this memory that she uses as her model to create the diversion that will allow Emiliano to slip into the kitchen, hopefully unnoticed if not actually unseen.

Mrs Fugosi finishes her coffee, picks up her handbag and, taking a deep breath and saying a brief prayer ('Please, Lord, you know I don't like to badger you, but if you're ever going to help me, help me now'), gets to her feet. She waddles slowly towards the door, her breathing heavy and her steps hesitant. Halfway across the elegant restaurant, Mrs Fugosi suddenly cries out in pain, dropping her handbag as she clutches her chest. She staggers rather dramatically against a table for two, bringing it with her as she crashes to the ground. Mrs Fugosi would not only have made an excellent mother, she would have made a very good method actor as well.

Ora, who has been sitting at the table nearest the kitchen with Emiliano, jumps up immediately and rushes to Mrs Fugosi's aid.

'Mrs Fugosi!' shrieks Ora. 'Oh my God! Oh my God! Mrs Fugosi, are you all right?' Ora is also a pretty good actor. Indeed, she throws herself so completely into her role that it looks as though she might be having a heart attack too.

Emiliano also gets up, as though he is going to run after Ora. 'Get a doctor!' he shouts to the waiters. 'Get a doctor, quick!'

The waiters, of course, are programmed to serve. The advertising shout-line used to sell AALFs is *We're Here for YOU!* But it's food and drinks they get, not medics. Although these AALFs can fetch and carry, can change orders and apologize if your meal isn't to your liking, they aren't programmed for heart attacks. Nor can they actually understand what's happening, having no hearts or minds of their own. It therefore takes several minutes of Mrs Fugosi moaning and gasping, Ora shrieking and flailing about, and Emiliano shouting, 'Emergency! Emergency! For God's sake get a doctor!' before they finally grasp the similarity between what is happening and the kind of emergency they are programmed for – asteroidal impact or violent revolution. They draw the weapons hidden beneath their jackets, and all charge towards Mrs Fugosi and Ora like a herd of armed, stampeding bison.

His concerned eyes on the stricken figures on the floor of the elegant restaurant, Emiliano moves swiftly backwards.

'Call a doctor!' he shouts again. 'Can't you see they need a doctor? It's a medical emergency!'

At last the waiters register the problem.

'Get a doctor!' says one.

'It's a medical emergency!' says another.

'I'm contacting the hospital now,' says a third.

His eyes still on Ora Sonorious and Mrs Fugosi, Emiliano slips backwards through the kitchen door.

CHAPTER
TWENTY-FOUR

Emiliano Finds Himself in Several Books He's Never Read

Emiliano takes one step inside the kitchen and stops.

How is it that things are always so much more difficult than you think they're going to be? His plan was to leave the dining room by the door through which the waiters come with their laden trays of food and step into the kitchen – just like that.

But this looks less like a kitchen than the room he just left.

There are no stoves or counters or refrigerators or freezers or chopping boards or sinks. There are no shelves of foodstuff, and no pots and pans or utensils, either. It is just a small room, no wider than an average corridor. On one side is a wall of tall, narrow, chrome cupboards; on the other is a wall of metal compartments with heavy glass doors and panels of coloured buttons, which make it look more like mission control than a place where meals are prepared. Across from where Emiliano stands with his back to the door is only a blank wall.

This can't be the kitchen. His eyes move slowly from side to side. Can it? In Emiliano's experience, limited as it may be, you can't run the smallest restaurant without at least one cook, a saucepan, a refrigerator and a grill. But not only are there are no cooks and no saucepans in sight, the room is so clean and so empty that it doesn't look as though anyone's ever been in it before, never mind grilled a burger or fried a potato here. At least the dining room has tables and plates of food.

It doesn't make sense. He knows that burgers have been grilled and potatoes fried in this room. He's seen them; he's eaten them. But in this, of course, Emiliano is wrong. There have been no burgers grilled or potatoes fried in this room, no matter what he's seen or eaten. For, as difficult as it might be for someone who's just breakfasted on blueberry pancakes, sausages and hash browns to believe, the food that is served in the restaurant of the hotel is just another illusion. Here in the kingdom of science, music hall magic is more common than weeds used to be.

Forget it, he tells himself. There isn't time to work it out now. And anyway he's not here to make lunch, he's here to find an exit.

Emiliano strides down the length of the room till

he reaches the end wall. He taps it methodically, starting on one side and working his way up and around, as he did in his room. And, like the walls in his room, this one has the same solid sound.

In fact, this is just another illusion because, solid-sounding or not, this is indeed a door – and one that can be opened easily if you know where the microscopic sensor is, are tall enough to reach it and have the chip needed to operate it.

Ignorant, short and chipless, Emiliano abandons the false wall and turns his attention to the cabinets on his right.

Inside the first one are shelves of dishes, cups, glasses and bowls.

Inside the next is a large, waist-high plastic container full of what looks like dry dog food and a plastic scoop, and bags of something labelled KZ2X on the shelves above it. Emiliano gives the contents of the container a sniff. It smells like his burnt sheet.

This doesn't make any sense to him either, of course, but that's because he doesn't realize what a miracle of technology KZ2X is. It isn't dog food at all. Indeed, what it is, is the basic, chemically produced protein substance that feeds the empire, and its honoured guests. From this unlikely source come the capsules eaten by the citizens of the Corporation – and the pancakes, salads, steaks and chocolate brownies eaten by the Top Teens and their fellow travellers as well.

The other cabinets yield the same sparkling dinnerware and the same oversized containers of kibble with the same aroma of toxic waste, and what he correctly guesses are dishwashers and waste disposal units.

Emiliano turns around and studies the bank of compartments on his left. The coloured buttons are marked with complex numbers and mathematical symbols that are meaningless to someone who never got past the five times table.

He opens one of the heavy glass doors. Inside it, too, smells like his burnt sheet. He stares at the metal sides of the compartment for several seconds; there is no exit back there. He turns back to the wall of cupboards.

The fictional detective Sherlock Holmes often said that once you'd eliminated the impossible whatever remained, however improbable, must be the truth. Emiliano has never read any of the Sherlock Holmes stories, but he is nevertheless in agreement with Mr Holmes' words. If there's a way out of the kitchen – which there must be – then it has to be behind the shelves of dishes and KZ2X.

Like Mr Holmes, Emiliano is methodical as well as logical. He starts at the far end of the room, and tests the wall behind each shelf. It takes a long time.

Although he doesn't realize just how long until he hears a high, bubbly female voice in the dining room say, 'I don't know about you two, but going to the beauty parlour always makes me really hungry. I could eat a moose.'

Christ, lunch already.

He hears the scraping of chairs and the mono- tonic murmuring of the waiters. The voices of the other girls join Kylie's, wondering what they should eat to nourish their bodies after a strenuous morning of having their hair done.

Waiters will soon come through the door to fill the orders of the Top Teens. Which makes this a pretty good time to hide.

Emiliano has been through enough of the cabinets by now to know that there are few hiding places for any creature larger than a mouse.

He opens the nearest stores cupboard and wedges himself in beside the bin of kibble, closing the door with a touch. Emiliano sighs with relief, but, as so often happens in life, it is not a relief that lasts for long. It immediately occurs to him that if one of the waiters decides to open his hiding place, it's likely that even a robot will be able to tell the difference between empty space and Emiliano Shuh.

The options on hiding places being down to one, he hastily squeezes himself into the space between the bin and the back of the cabinet. It's just as well that he's small and not accustomed to regular meals.

This time he doesn't get so much as a nano-second in which to feel relieved. No sooner has he wedged himself behind the bin than the pressure of his body on the back of the cabinet causes it to slide silently open.

What happens next is very similar to what happened to the heroine in another book Emiliano has never read. Just as poor Alice fell through the rabbit hole,

Emiliano falls back into darkness, stopping only when he hits the opposite wall.

Surprised but not hurt, Emiliano gets quickly to his feet. His shoulders touch the walls on either side of him and it's so dark that he can't see his hand when he holds it in front of his face. Reaching into the backpack that never leaves his side, he takes out the flashlight he liberated from the Grumps' cabin a lifetime ago, and turns it on.

Alice stumbled into Wonderland, but Emiliano has stumbled into a narrow alley. The door he fell through has closed behind him, but now that he knows that it's there he can see its faint outline in the wall. It is taller than he and taller than the depth of the unit he was in, so it was obviously there before the kitchen was put together. Which makes this alley what?

He gives a silent laugh. Which makes this alley a secret passage. He wanted a way out, and instead he's found a way in.

The beam shimmers down the passageway and straight into darkness.

What Emiliano has lacked in advantages, opportunities and luck he has made up for in courage. He was always the boy to take the dare; always the one to go on when everyone else turned back. There is only one way to find out what lies at the end of this tunnel, and that is to walk into the darkness himself.

What the hell . . . he thinks – and starts to walk.

He moves stealthily, one foot after the other, his ears straining to hear even the slightest sound, hardly daring to breathe as he pushes the darkness ahead of him inch by inch.

The passageway snakes along through the complex like a trail through a forest. The doors are few and far between. Each time he comes to one, he stops and listens, trying to guess what lies on the other side. But he passes each one by. He wants to know where this tunnel begins, not where it goes.

This is like the story from another book Emiliano's never read. The one where the hero has to choose between more than one closed door. Will the door he chooses have a waiting princess behind it, or a three-headed monster with teeth the size of samurai swords?

The one thing Emiliano is very certain of is that he has never been fortune's favourite son. He is so unlucky that he is likely to choose the one that will lead right to the room where the great Dr Nasa Hiko sits at her desk.

Emiliano sighs. Well, if he does – he does.

Hi, he'll say, *I was in the neighbourhood so I thought I'd drop by*.

CHAPTER TWENTY-FIVE

Ora and Mrs Fugosi Find Out More Than They Wanted to Know About the Future

There are, in fact, several exits from the illusion that is the Hotel Saint Mona besides the one that Emiliano fails to find in the kitchen and the one that he does find in the cupboard.

For example, there is a door in what seems to be the solid wall behind the reception desk that leads directly to the Phoenix Wing of the vast and rambling medical complex. It is through this door that the paramedic AALFs who attend Mrs Fugosi and Ora come; and through this door that Mrs Fugosi and Ora are removed from the hotel, although, since they are both sedated as soon as the paramedics arrive, they don't know this, of course.

All Ora and Mrs Fugosi know is that one minute

they're on the floor of the restaurant, surrounded by a mirror of waiters and the next they're in a sharply bright room, surrounded by bare white walls.

Mrs Fugosi wakes up woozy, and for a few seconds lies there, trying to remember what happened. The last clear memory she has is of two identical young men in white uniforms suddenly striding through the doors of the restaurant, each of them guiding a silver-coloured hospital trolley. One of the young men knelt beside her and put his hand on her arm. Thinking she must still be on the floor of the restaurant, Mrs Fugosi now opens her eyes. But it's a blank ceiling, not the blank faces of the waiters or the paramedics, that gazes down at her. Mrs Fugosi raises herself on one elbow. An arm's length away, on a narrow bed like the one she's in, is Ora.

'Ora?' whispers Mrs Fugosi. 'Ora, are you awake?'

'I think so.' Ora sits up, rubbing her eyes. 'What happened? Did we faint?'

'I guess we must have. For a minute or two.'

Neither of them is aware that they've been unconscious for most of the day.

Ora looks around. 'Where are we?' The answer is that they are in a small, rectangular room, unfurnished except for their beds, and free of any distractions such as windows. It's like waking up and finding yourself inside a shoe box. She looks over at Mrs Fugosi. 'Do you think this is some kind of morgue?'

It's not a bad guess. Where they are is more or less a morgue for the undead.

Once upon a time in the history of humanity the man who cut your hair and shaved your beard was also the man who drained you of bad blood and hacked off damaged limbs. Thousands of years later, here in Saint Mona's technologically sophisticated medical complex, there isn't a barber in sight – or a surgeon. Indeed, there is not so much as a thermometer or a bandage in sight, either – nothing that would suggest that they are in a resting room of the Phoenix Wing of the hospital, where the bodies of REPs wait to be transferred to a life-support shelf. That's progress for you.

'Of course it's not a morgue,' Mrs Fugosi assures her. 'We're alive, aren't we? My guess is we're probably in a pantry off the kitchen.'

Mrs Fugosi couldn't be more wrong if she'd suggested they might be in Dublin, of course, but Ora is happy to think that she's probably right, and quickly slides off the narrow bed. The room looks enough like a morgue to her for Ora to want to leave it as quickly as she can. 'Then let's get out of here. We've got to get back to our rooms in case Em's looking for us.'

Mrs Fugosi, who is finding an appetite for fearless adventure that she never knew she had, hooks her handbag over her arm like a warrior grasping her shield and follows Ora to the door. 'I hope they haven't locked it,' she whispers.

There is no fear of that. There are no locks in the Phoenix Wing for the simple reason that no one who has come into it has ever been able to walk out again before.

Hardly daring to breathe, Ora touches the door

and it slides open. Pressed against each other, she and Mrs Fugosi cautiously peer around the frame. Half expecting to see pots and pans and possibly a chef or two, they are slightly taken aback to find themselves looking down a glaringly bright and immaculate hallway, lined on both sides by narrow doors like the one to the room they're in.

'This isn't the kitchen,' says Ora.

'Then we must be behind the kitchen,' reasons Mrs Fugosi. 'You and Em were right. This must be the way out of the hotel.'

Since this is the first good news either of them has had in what seems like a very long time, Ora doesn't hesitate to consider even fleetingly what else it might be.

'Come on!' And she steps into the silent corridor, and looks up and down as though she might see a sign that says EXIT. 'I wonder which of these doors gets us out of here . . .'

The sad truth, of course, is that the answer to Ora's question is: none of them. The way out of the corridor they're in is actually through the resting room itself, which is connected to the management area by its back wall.

Ora puts an ear to the first door they come to. It's silent as a grave. She glances over her shoulder at Mrs Fugosi. 'I don't hear anything.'

The new, brave and adventurous Juliana Fugosi doesn't hesitate either. 'Let's try it then.'

When Ora was little, her parents gave her several tapes of fairy tales to listen to at bedtime. So Ora, as much as anyone, should know about the dangers of opening a box – or a door – but she seems to have forgotten. The door slides open at Ora's tentative touch.

The room in front of them is little more than a cubicle, airless and dark, a fact that they can sense if not actually see. They step over the threshold, but the contrast between the glaring brightness of the corridor and the lightlessness of the chamber behind the door makes them virtually blind.

Ora reaches into the gloom and touches what she assumes must be a wall.

'Do you hear breathing?' asks Mrs Fugosi. 'I think I hear breathing.'

Ora shakes her head. 'You can't hear breathing,' she says. 'This is just some kind of closet. There isn't enough room for anyone in here.'

Mr Fugosi always complained about the amount of junk Mrs Fugosi carries around in her handbag. 'No wonder you can never find your keys,' he used to grumble. 'You've got everything in there but the kitchen sink.' Mrs Fugosi argued that you never knew what was going to come in handy – a can opener, a roll of tape, a fork – but this is one of the few times that something has. It's unfortunate that Mr Fugosi isn't here to witness this historic occasion. Mrs Fugosi reaches into her bag and fishes out a small flashlight. She turns it on.

The room is, indeed, not much larger than the closet in Ora's bedroom back home. Built into the far wall, the length of Ora's arm from where they stand, are a dozen narrow cubicles enclosed in glass.

Ora squints into the gloom. 'It looks like fish tanks,' she whispers.

But there are no fish.

Mrs Fugosi moves her light across the cubicles. It may be a small flashlight but its beam is bright for its size. Bright enough for them to see the still, human figures behind the glass, and the tubes and small machines fitted to them; bright enough for them to see that many of the still figures are missing a limb or an eye or even an ear.

Several seconds pass before Ora can force herself to speak.

'What is this place?'

'I'm not sure,' answers Mrs Fugosi, 'but I think it could be hell.'

CHAPTER TWENTY-SIX

Emiliano Finds Something a Lot Better Than a Closet Full of Mutilated Zombies

People used to pray.

They prayed to the sun and to the moon. They prayed to mountains and to rivers. They prayed to Zeus and Yahweh, to Quetzalcoatl and to Shiva, to Allah and to Agni and to Jesus. They prayed all the time.

People once had corn gods and bird gods and gods with antlers. They had gods with severe personality disorders who were vengeful and cruel; gods who were gentle, understanding and kind; gods with a good sense of humour who liked to play jokes and cause mischief; gods who liked to dance and sing. They had gods with dark natures who demanded human sacrifice to keep the sun shining and the rivers flowing and themselves in a good mood. They had gods so depressed by the way humans carried on that they were willing to sacrifice themselves just to get people to behave.

Now that the only god is science no one prays any more, of course. To whom would you send your entreaties? To Justice Lissi? To Nasa Hiko? To the computer that runs everything on Henry Kissinger?

Like everyone else in this time, Lucia knows that religion is no more than superstition. Hocus-pocus and gobbledegook, as her mother would say. Science, her mother also would say, is based on reason, but religion is based on fear – a point of view that could be argued, though no one ever does. Despite all of this, Lucia is praying pretty hard right now. Not Mrs Fugosi's 'Dear Lord' prayers to a benign old man somewhere above the clouds, but more general pleas for help from anyone who might happen to be listening.

Please . . . please . . . Lucia silently begs as she touches every millimetre of the room that she can reach. She watched the scene in the restaurant with rising excitement – watched Mrs Fugosi stagger and fall; watched Ora race to help her; watched Emiliano slip through the kitchen door. The time is now – they're attempting their escape. *Please . . . please . . . please . . .*

Ever since she hacked into the blueprints for the medical colony of Saint Mona and discovered that there's a door hidden behind the back wall of Nasa Hiko's study that leads to a network of secret corridors that connect to every section of the complex, Lucia has been searching for a way to open it. Ora and Emiliano aren't the only ones with a plan. The time travellers want to escape and so does Lucia; it makes sense to her that they should escape together. All she has to do is reach the spaceport at the same time they do, and she can do that through the hidden passageways. If, that is, she could get to them.

Please . . . please . . . please . . . pleads Lucia. The mechanism to open the door has to be here somewhere.

At the moment she has temporarily given up.

Lucia sits in front of the far wall in her mother's study, staring at the artificial window as though she might be able to will it to reveal its secret. The window in Nasa Hiko's study shows the garden of Eleanore Patterson's cottage in Cape Moon, Massachusetts, on a summer morning in 1801, an image that was originally painted in watercolours by Eleanore Patterson herself and that Nasa Hiko found in the vaults of Camelot. Nasa Hiko chose the painting, not because it is so endear-ingly quaint and touching, but because it shows just how far mankind has come – like a stone bracelet found in a neolithic grave.

Lucia watches the sunlight fall lazily across the climbing roses and the butterflies and birds dart in and out, free as the air.

Please . . . she pleads. *Please . . . please . . . please . . .*

It is then that her prayers, just as Mrs Fugosi's were, are answered at last. And, remarkably enough, by the same person.

The door that leads from Nasa Hiko's study to the rest of the complex suddenly opens and Emiliano Shuh walks through the vegetable patch on the right side of Eleanore Patterson's garden – and into the study of the great geneticist and saviour of mankind.

'Hi!' says Emiliano. 'I was in the neighbourhood so I thought I'd drop by.'

Emiliano has been wandering Nasa Hiko's secret passageways for several hours now. Which makes it a rather stunning example of how his luck isn't always bad that the exit he finally chose is the one through Eleanore Patterson's garden. Of course, he isn't aware of how many seriously worse places there are on Saint Mona where he could have ended up than the great doctor's study, but, his eyes on the most beautiful girl he has ever imagined, never mind seen, he thinks that luck has finally decided to be his pal.

Lucia can hardly believe that the boy with the hammer and nails is actually standing in front of her. Up until now the only boy she's ever known is Napoleon – and this boy is nothing like he is. They don't even seem of the same species. And then Emiliano smiles. Apparently she has never seen a smile before either.

'Are you real?' asks Emiliano. She doesn't look real. Not in the world he comes from.

'Of course I'm real.'

'I mean really real. A human – not an android.'

Lucia doesn't know what an android is.

'You must know,' says Emiliano. 'Robots. Machines that look like people.' The puzzled expression stays on her impossibly perfect face. 'Like everybody else in this hole except you and the doctor.'

Lucia's eyes light up with understanding, which makes them a truly spectacular shade of aquamarine. 'Oh, you mean the AALFs.' She shakes her head. 'But they're not really machines, they're Almost Artificial Life Forms – modified people. They have human bodies but their minds are controlled by computers.'

Emiliano whistles. Flesh and chips. 'Just when I thought things couldn't get any better.' He crosses over to Lucia. 'Maybe I better introduce myself.' He extends his hand. 'Emiliano Shuh.'

'I know who you are,' says Lucia. 'I've been watching you . . . you and the others.' And, seeing that this information makes him stop before his hand touches her, adds, 'I wasn't really spying on you. It's just that I've always been interested in your century.'

The wariness doesn't leave his eyes. 'And you are?'

Lucia has given this moment – when the time travellers ask her who she is – a lot of thought. She knows what they think of Nasa Hiko and though she hates to lie she's afraid that they won't trust her if she tells them the whole truth. Lucia has learned from her movies that trust is important in friendships. Later, when they're far from here, she can tell them exactly who her mother is. 'I'm Lucia.'

He takes a step forward. 'Does Dr Death know you're here?'

Lucia is so accustomed to hearing her mother

spoken of with awe and respect rather than sarcasm and horror that she's surprised into a laugh. 'If you mean Nasa Hiko, I think she considers herself Dr Life,' says Lucia. 'That's what Project Infinite Future's all about. Making life.'

Sometimes, days – even weeks – go by where nothing much happens; and other times so much happens so quickly that it's difficult to keep up.

'Project what?'

'Project Infinite Future.' Lucia hesitates, wondering how much to tell him – then decides that if she wants him to trust her she should tell him what she knows. 'That's why Nasa Hiko brought the Top Teens to Saint Mona. That's why she's here.'

'To do what exactly? Keep them living forever?' Now there's a thought.

'No, not exactly.' Lucia laughs again. 'Nasa Hiko's a great scientist, but even she hasn't been able to do that. She's brought them here to breed them.'

Like many people, Emiliano used to wish that he could travel in time. He thought the future would be better than the here and now. He thought it probably had to be. It is now that Emiliano remembers Agosto Vega. Emiliano met him in a store doorway in LA. Agosto had once had a wife, two little girls, a good job, a house, a car and two cats named Cisco and Pancho. Through a series of events far beyond Agosto's control, he lost his wife, his two little girls, his good job, his house and his car. One of the cats was crushed by an SUV, and the other ran away. After he finished telling Emiliano the tragic story of his life, Agosto gave him what Emiliano can now see was the only sound piece of advice he's ever received. 'What you gotta remember,' said Agosto, 'is that things can always get worse.'

'She brought them here for what?'

'To breed them,' Lucia repeats.

'You mean like cows? Why does she want to do that?'

'She's saving mankind.'

'From who?'

Lucia shrugs. 'From itself, I guess. We have some problems with our gene pool.'

It's all he can do not to laugh out loud. *Some problems?* What kind of problems could you have that a bunch of spoiled brats like the Top Teens would be the solution to?

'You mean you've wiped out all the really stupid, selfish genes?'

Lucia smiles. She doesn't care for the Top Teens either. They may not give the human species as bad a name as Nasa Hiko does, but they don't give it a good one. 'No, that's not it. We've just sort of wiped out a lot of genes in general. Genetically speaking, we're bankrupt. My . . . Nasa Hiko's hoping to enlarge the pool.'

'So I guess that means this isn't really a terrific planet with fantastic sightseeing opportunities.'

'It's a medical colony. It's used for research and breeding – things like that. There aren't any humans here except Nasa Hiko and Captain Titanic.'

'And you,' says Emiliano.

Lucia nods. 'And me.'

Emiliano frowns. 'So what are you doing here?'

Lucia has thought about this question too. This time she tells the truth. 'I ran away.'

'Really?' Emiliano grins. The first time he ran away he took a bus to LA and thought that was pretty daring. 'What'd you run away from?'

'It's a long story,' says Lucia, who is not about to go into too many of its details right now. With quite a lot of luck there will be plenty of time for that later. 'My mother wants me to marry someone I don't want to marry.'

'An *arranged* marriage?' Guaranteed that if anyone arranged a marriage for him it wouldn't be with someone who looks like Lucia. 'What century is this? Have I gone forward in time or back?'

'My mother doesn't have many old-fashioned ideas,' says Lucia, 'but that's one of them.'

'He must be pretty bad if you'd come here to get away from him.'

'He has his downside,' understates Lucia.

'And what about me? You going to turn me in to Dr Death?'

'No,' says Lucia. 'I'm going to help you escape – on one condition.'

Emiliano's smile turns slightly sour. There's always a catch.

'And what's that?'

'That you take me with you.'

'Take you with me?' He couldn't possibly have

heard her right. 'Why would you want to come with me?'

'Because Nasa Hiko's going to send me back home.'

No one knows better than Emiliano that adults always stick together. 'That figures.' He nods. 'All right, you've got a deal. Now what do we do?'

'Do you have a gun?'

'A gun? Why would I have a gun?'

Lucia removes a small object, very much like the one Captain Titanic used to evaporate the stretch limousine so many lifetimes ago, from a compartment in the arm of the chair. 'There are a couple more in that desk.' Lucia points to the top drawer. 'They could come in handy.'

'No.' He shakes his head. 'I don't do guns.'

'But you have to have a gun. We don't know where we're going. There's a lot of rebellion in the empire – and at least three wars. We have to be able to protect ourselves.'

'Not like that,' says Emiliano. 'I don't believe in guns.' Guns kill things you can never get back.

Lucia gives him a puzzled smile. Guns play a big part in many, if not most, of the movies she's watched. 'Are you sure you're from the Earth in the twentieth century?'

'Positive. Not all of us are armed.'

'Well . . . if you're sure . . .' This time she points to the opening in Eleanore Patterson's garden. 'We have to go back the way you came.' She removes another small object from the compartment in her chair, but this time it's not an instrument of death. 'I've got the blueprints for the complex and the flight schedule in here. We shouldn't have any trouble finding the spaceport.'

'There's one other thing, though,' says Emiliano. 'First we have to get my friends.'

'Oh, right,' says Lucia. She had forgotten about his friends.

CHAPTER
TWENTY-SEVEN

Emiliano Shuh Isn't the Only One Who Feels a Little Disappointed in the Future

Mrs Fugosi and Ora stare at the blank wall of the resting room, rather like crash victims sitting by the side of the road with blankets around their shoulders while the wreckage of their car with the wrapped Christmas presents visible in the rear window smoulders just a few feet away.

'Maybe we're wrong about what we think we saw,' Ora is saying. She isn't sure whether she's trying to cheer up herself or Mrs Fugosi, but the discovery of the closets full of zombies on life-support systems definitely requires that someone be cheered. 'Maybe this is just a regular hospital. You know, maybe this is just the intensive care unit or something.'

'*Or something?*' echoes Mrs Fugosi. 'Or

something like what?' Mrs Fugosi doesn't see the wall her eyes are fixed on. What she sees are the rows of narrow bunks enclosed in glass, stacked one upon the other like the compartments of sandwiches and slices of pie in the automat she loved to go to when she was a child. Which is seeming much longer ago than it did an hour before. 'There must be hundreds of bo— of people in those rooms. Maybe thousands . . .' Behind every door they opened was the same grisly sight. She turns her frozen gaze to Ora. 'Did you see their skin? Their eyes? They looked like battery hens.' Battery hens that had been hacked apart and kept alive – possibly to be hacked apart again another day. *I have seen the future* . . . thinks Mrs Fugosi . . . *and it really stinks* . . .

Ora, of course, saw exactly what Mrs Fugosi saw – it's not something she's ever likely to forget. Nonetheless, she summons every bit of advice about having a positive attitude that Dr Ramin ever gave her and tries again.

'Well, maybe there was some mega disaster,' Ora suggests. 'Maybe they were hit by an asteroid, or there was some plague.'

'Um . . .' hums Mrs Fugosi. 'I suppose there is that possibility.' But it's not one she really believes. Mrs Fugosi has seen plague victims and earthquake victims and the victims of hurricanes and tidal waves on the news. She has also seen several documentaries about concentration camps and a programme on the forced march of the Cheyenne. She will never forget the picture of that little girl who'd been set on fire by Agent Orange in Vietnam. She can tell the difference between a natural disaster and one created by man.

'Or maybe there was a nuclear war,' suggests Ora. 'It could be that, couldn't it?'

'But they don't look burned, do they?' she says to Ora. 'Wouldn't they look burned if there'd been a nuclear war?'

'I guess so,' says Ora.

Mrs Fugosi sighs. 'I always thought we'd eventually wise up,' she says. 'Try to save ourselves and the planet before we destroyed everything. I always thought the future would be better.' Which is the problem with hope; it leads you on against all reason.

'Well, at least we know we're right to want to get out of here.' Ora is truly doing Dr Ramin proud. Though not for much longer. She looks around at the four white walls and the white ceiling and the white floor, thinking of the corridor with its narrow doors to misery. 'Not that we *can* get out of here,' she adds. 'Now we really might as well be in jail.'

Mrs Fugosi puts an arm around her shoulders and gives her a hug. 'Don't you worry,' says Mrs Fugosi. 'Em strikes me as a very resourceful young man. He'll find us. I'd bet my life on it.'

Ora doesn't point out that that's exactly what she is betting. 'And how's he going to do that?' she snaps. 'He's only a homeless teenager, Mrs Fugosi. Just because he dresses in doorways doesn't make him Superman. He can't do anything we can't do. If he could get in here then we should be able to get out.'

'You'll see.' Mrs Fugosi gives her another squeeze. 'We'll just have to be patient.'

As Dr Ramin could have told Mrs Fugosi, patience is not one of Ora's strengths.

'And what if they've caught him?' demands Ora. 'For all we know they've drugged him up and stuck him in one of those death cells.'

'Just put your faith in God,' says Mrs Fugosi. 'I'm sure He'll help us.'

'He hasn't helped us so far.' And Ora swings at the wall with her highly trained foot in rage and frustration.

Mrs Fugosi says, 'Do that again.'

Ora looks at her. 'Do what?'

'Kick the wall.'

'Are you serious?'

'Watch the ceiling as you do it,' orders Mrs Fugosi.

Ora gives another kick, hard and fast as she learned to do in her qui quong classes.

The ceiling shudders. Just as the ceiling in their finished basement at home shuddered when she had her punching bag hanging there. Because it's a false ceiling to hide the pipes that run underneath the floor above.

'It shouldn't do that, should it?' asks Mrs Fugosi.

'It's not solid,' says Ora, already climbing on to one of the narrow beds. 'It's just a panel.'

'Be careful!' urges Mrs Fugosi.

Ora pushes at the ceiling. Not only is it not solid, it's remarkably light – which makes at least one thing she has to thank the technology of the future for.

'Give me the flashlight.'

The thought running through Mrs Fugosi's mind is this: *God helps those who help themselves.*

'Wait a minute,' says Mrs Fugosi. 'Let me give you a hand.' And she hauls herself on to the bed beside Ora and holds the ceiling open so that Ora can slip through.

The cavity above the resting room is dark and humming softly with the gentle sounds made by thousands of life-support machines. Through it run not the copper pipes of the Sonoriouses' recreation room but the intricate electronic system that forms the arteries and veins of the medical complex. Ora cautiously moves through the gloom along the struts – heading in the opposite direction to the door.

What am I doing? she asks herself. *Where do I think I'm going?*

And then, hearing voices, she stops.

She flattens herself along the beam and puts her ear to the durable, flexible and light panel of the ceiling below her.

'I am Lucia Hiko,' says a strong, clear, female voice. 'My mother wants me to check on the condition of the time travellers who were brought here this morning. If they're out of danger I'm to bring them back to their rooms.'

'I haven't received any instructions about that,' says a flat, male voice.

'We haven't received any instructions at all,' says another.

'I'm giving you all the instructions you need,' the

girl informs them. 'My mother's far too busy to see to every little thing. Now let me see them or she'll want to know the reason why.'

Her heart pounding, Ora scrabbles back to warn Mrs Fugosi that Dr Death's daughter is on her way.

'What is it? What happened?' asks Mrs Fugosi, as Ora drops through the ceiling with a nimbleness and alacrity that would reassure her parents that the thousands of dollars they spent on her gymnastic lessons was also money well spent.

'You're not going to believe this,' gasps Ora.

But she doesn't get the chance to tell Mrs Fugosi what it is she isn't going to believe, for at that moment the back wall parts and the most perfectly beautiful human either of them has ever seen wheels herself into the room.

'I'm Lucia,' she says. 'Emiliano sent me to get you.'

CHAPTER TWENTY-EIGHT

Some Differences of Opinion

Ora lets Lucia lead her and Mrs Fugosi to the hidden passageway where Emiliano is waiting for them without any argument. What's the point? If it's a trap, she can easily overpower the crippled girl and take her hostage.

But Emiliano is there as promised.

Ora lets him explain about what he found in the kitchen and how he discovered the secret passageway and, eventually, Lucia, and about her offer to help them escape without interrupting even once.

It isn't until he finishes with a pleased smile as though he's solved all their problems and expects to be congratulated that Ora scowls and says, 'I don't like it.'

The smile vanishes. 'What do you mean you don't like it? What's not to like?'

Aware that Mrs Fugosi and Lucia are staring at her in the same astonished way, Ora keeps her eyes on Emiliano. 'How do we know we can trust her?'

'Of course you can trust me,' Lucia answers. 'I want to get out of here as much as you do.'

'Too right,' says Emiliano. 'Why the hell wouldn't you trust her?'

It is Ora's turn to smile and she takes full advantage of the bitter-sweetness of the moment. 'Because she's Nasa Hiko's daughter, that's why.'

The stares of astonishment move from Ora to Lucia.

'You what?' mutters Emiliano.

'Oh, dear,' murmurs Mrs Fugosi.

'I heard her,' says Ora. 'I heard her say she's Lucia Hiko.' And now she looks challengingly at the girl in the wheelchair.

But it isn't to Ora that Lucia replies. 'It's true,' she tells Emiliano. 'I didn't tell you because I didn't want to make things more complicated. But it doesn't mean you can't trust me. If anything you can trust me more. No one knows better than I do what my mother's like.' She smiles ruefully. 'And no one has more reason to want to get away from her.'

'Oh, dear,' Mrs Fugosi murmurs again.

Emiliano recovers quickly from his surprise. There's nothing he understands better than wanting to get away from your parents. If he hadn't fled his own he wouldn't be here now – he would probably already be dead. And he understands that deception is often a necessity. If he were the daughter of Nasa Hiko he wouldn't have told him either.

'I don't have any problem with that,' he says. What he wants to do now is not waste time arguing. 'And anyway,' he says to Ora, 'I don't see that we have any choice but to trust her. Unless you have a better idea.'

As it happens, Ora doesn't have a better idea, but she isn't about to let that sway her. 'But she's Dr Death's daughter. It's *her* mother who brought us all here.'

'And how does that get to be her fault?' Emiliano demands. 'For your information, Little-Miss-Can't-Be-Wrong, Lucia stowed away to get here because her mother's making her marry someone she doesn't like.'

'Oh, and isn't that heartbreaking?' hisses Ora. 'Of all the disgusting things that are going on in this cesspool that's definitely the one that gets my tears.'

'Will you two please stop bickering?' pleads Mrs Fugosi. 'It seems to me that you're missing a pretty important point.'

Ora looks sulkily at Mrs Fugosi. 'And what's that?'

'The point,' says Mrs Fugosi gently but firmly, 'is that we're not going to get out of here, no matter what.' Mrs Fugosi once saw a film about a flock of chickens that escaped from a battery farm, but it was a cartoon, not a documentary. No chicken in history ever escaped from a battery farm in real life. 'Do you have any idea what this place is?' she asks Emiliano. 'Do you know what they do here?'

He nods. 'Yeah, I do. They breed people.'

If Mrs Fugosi had had the opportunity Emiliano

had to talk with Agosto Vega she might not be so shocked by every new horror she discovers about Saint Mona.

'Breed people? Breed people for what? To hack them up like hunks of meat? Because that's what Ora and I saw. People hacked up like hunks of meat.'

'That'll be the REPs,' says Lucia.

'REPs?' repeats Mrs Fugosi.

'Replicant Life Forms,' Lucia explains. 'This is the Phoenix Wing. It's where the REPs are kept.' Seeing that this information brings no look of enlightenment on the faces of her companions she adds, 'REPS are created to be spare parts for repairing members of the government who get ill or shot or have some kind of accident.'

'Spare parts?' Ora's voice is like an echo from a deep, dark cave. 'You use people for spare parts?' There seems to be no end to the unpleasant surprises the future has in store. She'd rather have been transported back in time. She'd much rather take her chances with a woolly mammoth or barbarian hoards any day.

Lucia nods. As slavery was just a matter of fact to George Washington and his friends, so this is just a matter of fact to her. 'My mother says it's an important tool of medical science. So people can live for at least a hundred years. The rest of the complex is used to breed them – them and the AALFs.'

Mrs Fugosi's voice has joined Ora's in that deep, dark cave. 'AALFs? What in the name of God are AALFs?'

'AALFs are what they call the robots,' explains Emiliano. 'Only they're not really robots, they're people whose brains have been replaced by computers.'

'Good Lord . . .' moans Mrs Fugosi. 'Is there any crime against God and humanity that we haven't thought of?'

Lucia inadvertently answers her question. 'But now some of the complex will be used to breed—'

Ora cuts her off. 'Don't tell me, let me guess. Could it be Top Teens?'

Mrs Fugosi looks from Lucia to Emiliano. 'Is that why they brought them here? To breed them like cattle?'

'It's called Project Infinite Future,' says Emiliano.

Lucia says, 'My mother's the saviour of mankind.'

'Oh, really?' Mrs Fugosi's smile is thin as a communion wafer. 'No offence intended, dear, but in that case I can only hope that she ends up crucified.'

'We're the ones who are going to end up crucified if we don't get out of here,' Emiliano reminds them. 'Do you think we could continue the conversation later? We really should get going.'

Ora snickers. 'And just where is it we're supposed to be going, if that's not too much to ask?'

'To the spaceport.' Lucia holds up her PCS, an object smaller than the postcards Kylie bought in the gift shop and no thicker. 'I've put a map of the complex on this. According to the command centre log there are three ships leaving Saint Mona tonight. Two of them are medical personnel carriers and the other's a transport ship. That's our best bet, since it should only have a one-person crew.'

The producers of *Top Teens* were right to hire Mrs

Fugosi; in a crisis her practical side always comes to the fore. 'And where is it going?'

Lucia shrugs. 'All it says in the log is that it leaves at 23.23.23.'

'I see . . .' Mrs Fugosi continues being practical. 'And what about guards?'

'Oh, there'll be guards,' Lucia assures her. 'Everything in the Corporation has to be guarded.'

'Uneasy is the head that bears the crown,' murmurs Mrs Fugosi. She smiles at Lucia. 'And just how do you plan to get past these guards?'

'There won't be anyone in the secret passageways – only my mother uses those. It's not until we actually reach the spaceport that we have to go into the public corridors.'

'I see . . .' says Mrs Fugosi. 'And what happens then?'

'Well . . .' Lucia glances at Emiliano. 'We kind of thought we could figure that out once we're there. But I did bring these – just in case.' And she removes a clutch of small metal objects from the compartment in the arm of her chair.

Mrs Fugosi takes a step backwards. 'Guns?'

Ora turns an accusing eye on Emiliano. 'I suppose the guns are your idea.'

'Oh, do you? Well, it just so happens that I'm totally against using guns.'

'So am I,' says Mrs Fugosi. 'I really can't see that they'll do us any good.'

'But the guards are armed,' argues Lucia. 'We have to be able to resist them.'

'There's more than one way to resist,' says Mrs Fugosi. 'Have you ever heard of Mohandas Gandhi or Martin Luther King?'

Emiliano has heard about Mr Gandhi and Dr King, and Ora has seen the movies made of their lives, but both men are considered so dangerous and subversive that the Corporation has erased every mention of them even from its own archives so Lucia has no idea about whom she's talking.

'They were two of the greatest revolutionaries who ever lived,' explains Mrs Fugosi. She takes the guns from Lucia and returns them to the arm of the chair. 'Let's hope we have a long and peaceful voyage ahead of us so I can tell you all about them.'

'We're not going to have any kind of voyage ahead of us if we don't get going,' cuts in Emiliano. 'They shut the cargo hold ten minutes before take-off.'

'That doesn't exactly give us much time,' says Ora.

'It's enough,' cuts in Emiliano. 'Especially if we'd started five minutes ago.'

Mrs Fugosi adjusts her bag over her wrist. 'Well, then we'd better shake a leg, hadn't we? I'll just go and get the Top Teens and we can be on our way.'

'What?' say Ora and Emiliano together.

Lucia say, 'Oh, I'm afraid that's impossible. My mother . . . the project . . .'

'I'm not trying to be difficult,' says Mrs Fugosi,

who is therefore managing to be extremely difficult without trying at all, 'but I can't possibly go without them. They were put into my care, and care for them I will. I can't leave them here.'

Emiliano sighs. Don't they have enough things to worry about?

Ora can think of only one thing worse then hurtling through space with no idea of where you're going and that is to do it with the Top Teens in tow.

'But Mrs Fugosi,' argues Ora, 'they like it here. They don't want to go. They're happy. I think if they're happy we should leave them where they are.'

'Me too,' says Emiliano. 'They're as happy as racoons at the dump. It'd be practically a crime to take them away.'

Mrs Fugosi stands a little bit straighter. 'They're only happy because they're stupid and don't understand the situation,' she says. 'It doesn't matter what your personal feelings are. We can't abandon them – not knowing what we know.'

'But Mrs Fugosi,' Emiliano pleads, 'you have to be reasonable. We don't have time to go back for them.'

'Em's right,' says Ora. 'The cameras will see you. It's too risky.'

'So what if they see me?' Mrs Fugosi shrugs. 'They're not going to have the police out looking for us. We went to the hospital, not to jail. I'd be surprised if they even know that we've been gone. I'll just act normal and no one will be the wiser.'

Ora remains sceptical. 'I still think it could be

dangerous. What if you do manage to convince the Top Teens? Someone's bound to notice you all leaving together.'

'Well, we'll just have to try to do it discreetly, won't we?' Mrs Fugosi shrugs. 'On the other hand, I certainly don't want to put you in any more danger than you're already in. So if you really feel that strongly I'll just have to stay here with them.'

'Don't be ridiculous.' Ora has no intention of leaving Mrs Fugosi on Saint Mona – not after all that they've been through together. 'Even if we told the Top Teens everything they wouldn't come – they wouldn't believe us. You'd be sacrificing yourself for nothing.'

'If they won't come even after they know the truth, then that's their decision,' answers Mrs Fugosi. 'But it's a decision they have to be allowed to make.'

'All right . . . all right . . .' Emiliano has no intention of leaving Mrs Fugosi either. He's got enough bad memories haunting him like ghosts; he's not adding leaving Mrs Fugosi on Saint Mona to them. 'Talk to the brats. But I'm going with you. There's no way you're going alone.'

'Oh no, I didn't mean—'

'No, I'll go,' says Ora. She doesn't particularly want to be left alone with Dr Death's daughter, no matter what the others think of her. 'And I'm not going to argue about it,' she adds, fixing Mrs Fugosi with a look as stubborn as her own.

'Then you're going to need this.' Lucia holds out her PCS. 'It's set on the map programme. This moves the cursor. This zooms in. This zooms out. This turns the page. This accesses the details of any area. This switches you to blueprint mode so you can see where the electrics and air conductors run.' She looks at Ora. 'Got it?'

Ora almost failed her computer class because of an impressive lack of interest, but now she nods confidently. Trying to stay alive has definitely sharpened her ability to concentrate. 'Got it.'

'Good.' Lucia taps the pad and a light begins to flash. 'That green light shows you where we are now.' A blue light joins the green one. 'That's the entrance to the hotel.' She taps again and a purple dot begins to pulsate. 'And that's where we'll meet, just behind the spaceport.'

'But what about you two?' asks Mrs Fugosi. 'How will you get there if we have the map?'

'We have this.' Lucia pulls a second PCS from her chair. The guns weren't the only things she took from Nasa Hiko's desk. 'It's my mother's, so it's got limitless access. But if you're not on time we can't wait. We'll have to go without you. You've got no more than half an hour.'

'Which is far longer than any of us would want to hang,' says Mrs Fugosi.

CHAPTER
TWENTY-NINE

Mice Aren't the Only Ones Whose Plans Often Go Belly up

One of the reasons Nasa Hiko prefers working with AALFs to ordinary humans is that besides being easy to manipulate, not talking back and not asking questions, AALFs don't panic. The AALFs in charge of the restaurant didn't panic when Mrs Fugosi fell on the floor, and they didn't panic when they lost track of Emiliano. In each case, they tried to identify the problem and deal with it as they were programmed to in a swift, efficient and unhysterical way. They called for the paramedics for the old lady and never gave a thought to what happened to the boy, since thinking isn't something that they're programmed to do.

Which partially explains why it takes so much longer for Nasa Hiko to realize that there's a treacherous snake of a problem loose on Saint Mona than it should have taken.

Indeed, it isn't until the chief medical attendant of the Phoenix Ward calls Nasa Hiko to tell her the test results on Mrs Fugosi and Ora that she has any inkling that anything unusual has happened.

Nasa Hiko is watching the Top Teens enjoying their afternoon on the monitor and amusing herself by playing a genetic guessing game based on which of them will produce the best children, when her PCS starts to flash. She snaps it on, her eyes still watching Kylie, Diane and Bethesda cycling to nowhere on the exercise bikes in the gym on the monitor, her mind fixed on her own glory.

Like many great people, Nasa Hiko hates to be interrupted by the mundane concerns of underlings. 'What?' she snaps. 'What did you say?'

'The test results are all normal,' the chief medical attendant repeats. 'Do you want me to release the specimens?'

'Release whom from where?'

'The old lady and the girl with the green hair. From the hospital,' the AALF replies. 'There was a medical emergency.'

Nasa Hiko snorts with irritation. 'A medical emergency? What kind of medical emergency? Why wasn't I informed?'

This is, of course, an unreasonable question. Nasa Hiko has made it very clear exactly what things she expects to be informed of, and an old lady and girl with green hair screaming and rolling around on the ground appear nowhere on that list.

'I'm informing you now,' says the chief medical attendant, which, since an AALF wouldn't recognize an unreasonable question if it held up a sign, is not a sarcastic retort but a statement of fact.

'It's a good thing I'm here then with nothing else to do, isn't it?' mutters the great Nasa Hiko, and she pushes her chair back from the console and gets to her feet.

She's annoyed, but she isn't yet worried. No warning bells ring in the recesses of Nasa Hiko's intelligent mind or unused heart. Like the species of which she is such an outstanding example, Nasa Hiko has gotten to where she is today not merely through her brains but through her overwhelming self-confidence and arrogance as well. She never expects to be thwarted, unless it's by her daughter. She always assumes that she will win; that she should win; that she must.

It's almost a shame that Nasa Hiko considers poetry too frivolous and unfunctional for someone of her soaring intellect.

If she were interested in poetry, Nasa Hiko might know that over a thousand years before this fateful day a farmer in a country called Scotland ran his plough into a mouse's nest and wrote a poem about it. 'The best-laid schemes o' Mice an' Men Gang aft a-gley' is how this particular poet summed it up. Which means that things often go wrong, no matter how well you've planned them or how smart you think you are.

Nasa Hiko has never read this poem – and she wouldn't think it applied to her if she had.

But this potential for disaster is, of course, something she has in common with mice. Nasa Hiko may be able to design life, but she can't control the universe. Despite her great brain and all of its reason and logic, Nasa Hiko's plans are starting to gang a-gley with a vengeance.

CHAPTER THIRTY

Ben, Luke and Willis All Think that Ora Sonorious Is Nuts – but Diane, Kylie and Bethesda Don't Think at All

Mrs Fugosi's confidence that they wouldn't have any trouble getting back into the hotel turns out to have been well founded. She and Ora slip back into the complex through the concealed door at the rear of the La Vida Loca boutique. The clerks are standing smiling blankly by the counter just as they were when Ora came in with Emiliano and, because they never expect the unexpected, don't notice Ora and Mrs Fugosi until they reach the middle of the shop, talking about sneakers. The AALFs aren't programmed for either curiosity or suspicion, of course, and so aren't troubled by their sudden appearance. It is only humans who can ask 'How?' or 'Why?' or 'What if?' – which makes it something of a shame that they don't do it as much as they should.

'So far so good,' Mrs Fugosi whispers as they leave the store by the front door.

Mrs Fugosi and Ora stroll down the concourse as though there is nothing more in their minds than shopping.

'Oh, look at that,' cries Ora.

'Oh, look at this,' cries Mrs Fugosi.

Mrs Fugosi finally catches sight of Ben, Luke and Willis in the virtual reality arcade. Mrs Fugosi can tell from the expression of rapture on their fresh, young faces that they're so absorbed in their games it's unlikely that they'd notice if the room was suddenly vaporized around them.

'You go talk to the boys,' decides Mrs Fugosi. A pretty young woman has more chance of catching their attention than an old one with the looks of a pleasant root vegetable. 'I'll deal with the girls.'

'That's fine with me,' says Ora. After her last attempt to talk to Diane, Bethesda and Kylie she'd rather try to reason with Satan.

Ora strolls casually into the arcade, and positions herself between Ben and Willis, leaning against Ben's chair as though she's watching him play cards.

'Ben,' she says. 'Ben, I really have to talk to you.'

Ben is playing a game called Compassion for Canada, which is based on a real military campaign that happened on the Earth, though it won't take place until Ben is in his fifties, and, since it's unlikely that he'll be on the Earth then, he'll probably never have the chance to turn Toronto into a pile of rubble for real. It's a very exciting game.

'Over here, damn it! Over here!' Ben shouts through his radio to the pilot of the rescue helicopter. 'Over here!'

'Ben!' she gives him a gentle shake.

Ben gives a yelp of pain. 'It's all right,' he gasps. 'It's only a flesh wound.'

Ora slides smoothly over to Willis' chair. 'Willis,' she says. 'Willis, I have to talk to you. It's really important.'

Willis is on a date with his favourite movie star. He is just opening the door of a candy-pink Porsche for her and, like Ben, is oblivious to the fact that Ora is trying to get his attention.

Ora puts her hands on Willis' shoulders and squeezes hard. 'Willis!' she hisses. 'Willis! Take off that stupid contraption and listen to me.'

'No pictures!' yells Willis, and pushes her away.

This time Ora tries Luke. She leans over him, her head next to his. 'This is important! I have to talk to you!'

At that very instant Luke is at Disneyland, a place his parents refused to take him when he was little because of the germs. Luke is having his photograph taken with his arms around Goofy.

Luke thinks that Ora is his mother, come to ruin his day. 'Oh, not now,' mutters Luke. 'Can't it wait?'

'No,' answers Ora. 'It could be a matter of life and death!'

'Oh, for Pete's sake,' Luke moans. 'There's no such thing as death in Disneyland.'

Dr Ramin always told Ora that, just as the shortest distance between two points is a straight line, the best solution to a problem is often the simplest, but like most of the things Dr Ramin told her Ora didn't believe it, of course. It is only now, as she stands beside Luke trying to look innocent and wondering how to get the boys' attention without attracting the attention of whoever is manning the monitors as well, that Ora realizes Dr Ramin was right about this too. She leans forward and gives the power button in the control panel of Luke's chair a tap.

'Oh for Pete's sake, now what?' Even when his parents aren't around he can't have any fun. Luke yanks off his helmet – and then nearly drops it when he sees Ora standing beside him. 'What are *you* doing here? I thought you were dead.'

'Excuse me?'

'We saw them taking you and Mrs Fugosi out of the restaurant,' Luke explains. 'We thought you were dead.'

'No,' says Ora. 'No, we're not dead yet.'

Ben, Willis and Luke all sip their latte grandes in silence as they listen to Ora's whispered account of why she's come back from the dead to rescue them – an account that includes AALFs and REPs, the Phoenix Wing and Project Infinite Future, the Corporation's special plans for them, Lucia Hiko and what she believes is the most powerful argument of all, the fact that they've been eating something that looks like dog food.

No one says anything for several seconds after Ora finishes, and then Ben says, 'You're nuts. You're completely out of your mind.'

Willis laughs but Luke just nods.

'You can't expect us to believe any of that,' says Ben. 'It's like something out of a movie.'

'You're like something out a movie,' mumbles Ora.

Luke says, 'OK, just for the sake of argument, let's say that you're right and we aren't on reality TV – we really were taken into the future. Then this has got to be an incredibly advanced civilization. They wouldn't need to bring us here in order to expand their gene pool. They have science.' Science, Luke has been taught, can do no wrong.

'Didn't you hear me? It's science that's gotten them into this mess,' hisses Ora.

'Then science would get them out,' pronounces Willis. 'It'd be a lot easier than going back in time to get us.'

'Then why did they go back in time to get you?' demands Ora. 'So you can play games all day? What kind of sense does that make?'

'Well, no,' says Ben. 'I mean, if we're accepting that we are in the future, then what Dr Hiko told us is the reason, isn't it? They brought us here so they can get back to their roots.'

Ora has never been so close to being driven to

tears by exasperation before. 'How can you believe that after all I've told you?'

Luke gives her a sympathetic smile. 'Well, you don't actually have any proof that what you say is true, do you?'

'But I do have this.' And Ora takes Lucia's PCS from her pocket and slips it to him under the table.

If he hadn't been pressured into being Top Teen material by his parents, Luke could have been the sort of computer nerd that makes the head of the FBI lie awake at night, worrying about security. He surreptitiously studies the tiny computer for several seconds, then starts tapping the keys.

'What'd you say this project's called?' asks Luke.

Kylie, Diane and Bethesda are talking about getting new outfits to improve their tennis games when Mrs Fugosi finally spots them huddled in front of the sports store like cats watching a mouse in the grass.

'I mean, as long as we have this incredible, professional court we might as well take advantage of it,' Kylie is saying, 'and look profess—' she breaks off as she sees a familiar short, plump figure waddling towards them at an impressive speed. 'Sugar lumps,' says Kylie. 'The old bag's back.'

Diane and Bethesda glance over their shoulders.

'I don't believe it,' whispers Diane. 'I thought she was dead or something.'

'Turn around, quick,' orders Bethesda. 'Pretend you don't see her.'

Mrs Fugosi knows that they saw her from the way their heads all spun around like revolving doors, and – knowing that time is racing on pretty much without her – decides to dispense with the usual conversational niceties. She marches straight up to them, summoning all the authority someone her size and shape could be expected to muster. 'Girls,' she says, 'your lives are in terrible danger. You have to come with me. Now!'

Diane points to a short-sleeved white shirt with a tiny lizard the colour of cheap peach ice cream on the breast pocket. 'What do you think? Do you think it's me? Or is it a little *old*?'

'I think it's cool,' says Kylie. 'I like the lizard.'

'Classic but still individualistic,' judges Bethesda.

Mrs Fugosi says, 'Didn't you hear me? We don't have time for this nonsense. We've discovered what's really going on here. We have to escape while we can.'

'Do you think sweatbands are really passé or do you think they might be coming back?' asks Bethesda.

'There's a ship leaving very soon,' says Mrs Fugosi, 'and we have to be on it.'

'I think I could use some new make-up too,' murmurs Kylie. 'Something that makes me look . . .'

Mrs Fugosi doesn't grab hold of Diane or Bethesda's shoulders and shake them hard as she would like to do, but digs her nails into the palms of her hands to keep herself calm. 'What's wrong with all of you?' Her voice, though low, is shrill as a siren. 'Have you been drugged?'

But after the annoyance and tedium that was the

previous day's dinner with Mrs Fugosi – or the old bag as they prefer to call her – the girls have decided that they don't need her – and they certainly don't want her. They carry on as though she isn't there.

'I'm talking to you,' hisses Mrs Fugosi. 'We have got to get out of here.'

It is Bethesda who gives in and turns around. 'Look, Mrs Fugosi, we don't want to be rude, but we really don't want you hanging around, nagging us all the time. We're sort of like on vacation? And working too. You know, working in the show? So if you don't leave us alone I'll call someone and have you thrown out.'

There are no limits to the ability of human behaviour to bedazzle and surprise.

'I don't believe this,' gasps Mrs Fugosi. 'I'm trying to help you. How dare you talk to me like that. Don't you even want to know what's going on?'

'Mrs F,' says Diane, 'we know what's going on. We're in—'

'You're in no such thing,' snaps Mrs Fugosi. 'You're on another planet, in another time, and they've brought you here to breed you. Like sheep.'

Bethesda finally looks Mrs Fugosi in the eyes. '*Breed us like sheep?*' she splutters. 'I think they released you from the hospital too soon, Mrs Fugosi. You're obviously not well.'

'I'm in a lot better shape than you'll be in if you don't listen to me.'

'You really have to get a grip on things, Mrs F,'

advises Kylie. 'These are really nice people. Look at all the cool stuff they've given us.'

Look at all the cool stuff the white men gave the indigenous of the Americas . . . thinks Mrs Fugosi. Aloud she says, 'Just because someone showers you with gifts doesn't mean their intentions are good. In fact, I'd say it's usually quite the opposite.'

Having decided that this latest assault by the old bag is a test to see how patient and understanding the contestants are, Bethesda suddenly changes tack and puts a solicitous hand on Mrs Fugosi's arm. 'You know, I'm getting very worried about you, Mrs F,' she says. 'I think we better call the management to get you back to your room. You really need to rest.'

Mr Fugosi used to joke that Mrs Fugosi fell asleep talking and woke up talking, but this last exchange has left her speechless. She opens her mouth and shuts it again.

'Oh my God . . . now what?' says Diane. 'Look who's with the guys.'

Ben, Willis and Luke are strolling towards the boutique with Ora Sonorious.

'Good grief,' gasps Kylie. 'What are they doing with *her*?'

'Assuming that they have a lot more sense than you do they're getting out of here,' says Mrs Fugosi.

CHAPTER THIRTY-ONE

The Difference Between Compliance and Infallibility

Despite the fact that this visit isn't in her schedule, Nasa Hiko is in a pretty good mood as she strides into the Phoenix Wing. Now that she's past her initial irritation, she can see that whatever it was that happened to the old lady and Ora Sonorious has actually done her a favour. Now she has the perfect excuse to examine them herself without the risk of riling them or having to use force. Nasa Hiko is especially interested in examining Mrs Fugosi since she has never known anyone her age who still possessed all their original body parts.

Humming the anthem of the Corporation under her breath, the saviour of mankind uses the entrance that connects to a passage from her office, coming in the back way and avoiding the main desk, heading directly to corridor 120.

Nasa Hiko walks purposefully past the dozens of 'maintenance' cells, past the doors that lead to the operating theatres and past the hallway that leads to the breeding wing until she reaches the second rest room, the last door on the left.

She holds herself straight and puts on her best smile, malnourished by decades of disuse, ready to be both comforting and cordial. Already starting the little speech she's prepared, she opens the door.

The words 'I can't tell you how concerned I was when I heard you weren't well, perhaps it has something to do with our artificial environment' fall into empty space and clatter to the ground. The two narrow beds in the room are empty.

Nasa Hiko hits the management area like an asteroid. 'Where in the cosmos are they?' she roars. 'Why didn't anyone tell me that they'd gone?'

The reason no one told her is obvious; she never asked, which illustrates yet another disadvantage of AALFs over humans. But since she has now asked, the chief medical attendant gives her the answer.

'Your daughter came for them,' it says.

'My daughter?' Nasa Hiko looks so baffled by this information that you'd think she didn't know she has a daughter. 'My daughter came for them?'

The chief medical attendant nods. 'I thought you knew.'

'*Thought?* You *thought* I knew? You don't think.

Your brain's an electronic chip. How could *you* possibly have thought anything?'

The chief medical attendant isn't thrown by this attack as a true human would be. It doesn't get defensive or start making feeble excuses.

'Yes,' it says, 'I thought you knew. Your daughter said you sent her.'

Like many important and powerful people, Nasa Hiko is well-protected from even the smallest shard of objectivity. Lucia, like the time travellers, doesn't even feature on the long list of those who might possibly present a threat to her. A girl in a wheelchair? Primitive humans? It's enough to make even Nasa Hiko laugh. Indeed, what she thinks is that Lucia, true to her habit of being wilful and stubborn, has decided to ask Napoleon's question about white weddings herself. So certain is Nasa Hiko that this is no more than the petulant behaviour she has come to expect from her child that it doesn't even occur to her to wonder how Lucia knew where Mrs Fugosi and Ora Sonorious were or why she chose them to ask. So although she is certainly annoyed she isn't worried or fearful or thinking that any treacherous plot is afoot. It wouldn't occur to her that they might be trying to escape, for the simple reason that there is nowhere to escape to. Nowhere to hide. Every centimetre under the environmental dome that covers Saint Mona is controlled by Nasa Hiko and patrolled by the Elite Guard; outside of the dome the colony is even more of a hell, especially if you depend on oxygen to breathe.

'What do you want me to do?' asks the chief medical attendant in its mathematically logical way.

'Nothing, you've already done enough,' says Nasa Hiko.

CHAPTER THIRTY-TWO

Mrs Fugosi, Ora, Luke, Willis, Kylie, Ben, Diane and Bethesda Discover Some of the Things That Have Made the Corporation Prosper and Thrive

Bethesda, Diane and Kylie, all of whom have been raised to think of men as the natural leaders and figures of authority, are finally persuaded to try to escape because Ben tells them to.

'We've got to get out of here,' says Ben. 'We're not in a reality TV show like we thought. We're prisoners of some psycho from the future. Luke checked it out.'

There isn't even enough time for Diane to cry or for Kylie to look on the bright side, but Bethesda does manage a brief grumble.

'And exactly how are we supposed to get out?' Bethesda would like to know. 'You going to call the marines?'

'They'd come if they could,' says Ben. 'But since they can't, Ora here has a plan.'

Bethesda sighs. 'Oh that's great. Geek girl's got a plan.'

Kylie chews her bottom lip, an indication that she is trying to think. 'I don't know . . . I mean, look at her – she isn't really what you think of as a leader, is she? Maybe if we talked to that nice doctor . . .'

'We can't talk to her,' says Ben. 'She's the enemy.'

'God . . .' moans Diane.

'Just when you think things can't get any worse, right?' grumbles Bethesda.

Luke surprises even himself by coming to Ora's defence. 'Why don't you shut up for a change?' he suggests. 'Because if you don't have a better idea, then this one's worth a try.'

Bethesda folds her arms across her chest with a look of disgusted resignation. 'Whatever,' says Bethesda. 'But if this doesn't work, I'm holding *you* and geek girl responsible. Got it?'

Luke nods. 'Got it.'

'Ooh,' mutters Ora. 'We're really scared.'

It is the door at the back of the boutique that, as Ben would say, is their objective.

Mrs Fugosi, Ora and the Top Teens all saunter into La Vida Loca as though they're on a group outing. They fill the small store with more activity and noise than the two sales clerks have ever seen before. If they were human, their stress levels would be through the roof; not being human they bustle in all directions, trying to take care of everyone at once in their usual empty and efficient way.

The girls chat as they search through the racks of clothes near the rear of the store. The boys hover behind them, shuffling in place, and occasionally grunting, 'Yeah' and 'OK' when asked their opinion on a top or a skirt.

Mrs Fugosi involves herself in looking through the baskets of accessories on the counter. She throws several woven belts over her shoulder. 'How pretty . . .' she murmurs. She examines a handful of brooches. 'Oh, aren't they sweet . . . ?' she coos. She fingers a pair of leg warmers. 'I didn't realize these things had made a comeback . . .' she chuckles. At last she removes a silk change purse decorated with beads from one of the baskets and holds it up. 'Do you have this in green?' she wants to know.

The others comb through the racks, looking at this and looking at that, but can't seem to find anything they really like.

Ben holds up a long, red party dress for Bethesda's approval. 'What about this? This looks like you.'

'It looks more like *you*,' snaps Bethesda.

Only Ora has any success. She fills her arms with several skirts and scarves, and goes into the dressing room. After a few minutes she sticks her head through the door. 'Excuse me,' calls Ora to the clerk who isn't kneeling at the storage cupboard under the counter, looking for a green silk change purse. 'But could some-body help me, please? The zipper's stuck and I'm afraid of tearing the skirt.'

In Ora's personal experience, human salespersons are often grumpy and disgruntled and reluctant to give any extra help, but this, of course, is not a problem with AALFs.

'Let me take a look at that,' says the clerk, and steps into the cubicle.

This is Ben's signal to act. It is not the moment Ben's been waiting for all his life – that moment, gradu-ating with honours from West Point, may of course never happen now – but it will do. With all the agility, cunning and ruthlessness of a crack Green Beret he moves behind the counter and drops the long, red party dress over the head of the searching salesgirl.

'You don't mess with the United States Army,' he whispers, as Mrs Fugosi hands him the belts, and then the brooches and foot warmers to secure their captive since government issue rope isn't available at the moment.

In the dressing room, Ora, despite her lack of military ambition, performs a similar procedure. It's almost unfortunate that Mr and Mrs Sonorious aren't here to witness their daughter in action and see what a good idea Ora's classes in oriental martial arts were. As soon as the clerk takes the skirt and starts fiddling with the zipper, Ora overpowers her so quickly and effi-ciently that she might have been specially trained in disabling enemy agents, instead of simply watching a lot of action movies when there was nothing else on TV. Ora ties up the clerk with La Vida Loca's best scarves.

Luke is waiting outside when Ora emerges from the dressing room.

'Mission accomplished out here,' says Luke.

'Right,' says Ora. 'Time to go.'

Justice Lissi is justifiably proud of the ruthless efficiency with which the Corporation rules its empire. There are procedures; there are routines; there are rules. It is through these procedures, routines and rules that the Corporation has maintained its power and control for so many centuries. That it is through these procedures, routines and rules that the Corporation has also caused so much destruction isn't something that would concern him, of course.

And so it is that, following these procedures, routines and rules, Nasa Hiko requests guards to retrieve Ora Sonorious, Mrs Fugosi and Lucia. 'I don't think they're any threat,' she tells them. 'I just want them put back where they belong. But if they give you any trouble, then do what you must to subdue them.'

No alarm bells ring; no sirens wail. Indeed, since there are no external signs that anyone might be looking for them, Ora and Mrs Fugosi are feeling pretty pleased with themselves as they lead the others from the hotel.

'Now all we have to do is get here,' says Ora, pointing to the purple light.

'I just hope you really are right about this,' mutters Bethesda. 'I had an algae wrap booked for later.'

'Ora's right,' says Ben, with the decisiveness that would have done him so well in his military career. 'We told you, Luke found Project Infinite Future on that little computer. It's exactly like she says.'

Ora says, 'Shh! I'm trying to concentrate.' She studies the map on the PCS, plotting their route. 'It doesn't look too difficult,' she says to Mrs Fugosi. 'We can go left up here, then left again at the third inter-section . . . then right at the fifth . . . then right at the fourth . . . left at the seventh . . . and straight on from there.'

Luke reaches out for the computer. 'You want me to have a look?'

One of the reasons Mr Fugosi always got lost tak-ing his shortcuts was that he would never let Mrs Fugosi navigate. If she said turn right, Mr Fugosi would turn left. If she said go through the park, Mr Fugosi would follow the first cab he saw because, he reasoned, cab drivers always knew where they were going. The time they drove to Mexico from Los Angeles they wound up going via Seattle. To avoid any delay like that happening now, Mrs Fugosi steps between Luke and Ora before he can snatch the computer out of her hands.

'Lead the way, Ora,' orders Mrs Fugosi. She smiles at Luke. 'We're right behind you.'

They take the first left, and at the third intersection they go left again.

'Sugar lumps,' mutters Kylie. 'Now I've gone and broken a nail.'

Willis' stomach growls, as though aware that it is about to miss several meals.

Mrs Fugosi and Ora silently count the turnings as they make their way up the hall, one . . . two . . . three . . . four . . . five . . .

'Not long now . . .' whispers Mrs Fugosi.

In this she is more hopeful than accurate.

As they take the first right Ora and Mrs Fugosi – and, of course, the Top Teens – discover just how efficient the Corporation really is.

'Uh oh.' Ora jumps back, treading on Mrs Fugosi, who steps on Luke.

'I knew I should've led,' says Ben.

'I told you to let me see the map,' says Luke.

Mrs Fugosi presses herself against the wall and the others all follow suit. 'What is it?'

Ora flattens herself beside her. 'It looks like Darth Vader.'

Ben sighs. The General's right; women have no place in the army. 'Yeah, right . . .' he mutters, and slides in front of Ora to peer around the corner, but he pops back so fast you'd thing he was on springs. 'It does look like Darth Vader,' he whispers.

Kylie's still fiddling with her nail. 'I always felt kind of sorry for Darth Vader,' she comments. 'I don't think he got enough love as a child.'

Mrs Fugosi looks nervously at her watch. 'I should've done this alone . . .' she says. 'We've got less than eight minutes to reach the ship.'

Having just learned the first rule of diplomacy,

Luke peers over Ora's shoulder at the electronic map. 'What if we double back and take the hall before this one?'

Also having learned the first rule of diplomacy, Ora nods. 'That should work. It's not as direct but it'll get us there.'

The only problem with the new route is the Darth Vader lookalike patrolling this hall as well.

'We're trapped,' announces Mrs Fugosi. 'We'll never get to the spaceport in time.'

'You see?' wails Bethesda. 'At least if we'd stayed where we were I could've had my wrap. Now I'm going to be arrested.'

Luke points out that she's already in jail.

'Anyway, they'll probably shoot us before they arrest us,' says Ben.

Ora is staring at the PCS again, trying very hard to prove Mrs Fugosi wrong. Stress, however, is not always an effective memory enhancer. Ora can't remember what she's supposed to tap to zoom out or turn the page, functions that might be useful at the moment, and hesitates with a finger over the keys. At which point Luke forgets all he's learned about diplomacy and reaches over her.

'Just let me have a look,' says Luke.

Startled, Ora hits a key. It is not, of course, the one she wanted.

'What's that?' asks Mrs Fugosi.

'It looks like the blueprint of the whole complex,' says Ora.

Luke studies the image on the screen. 'There seems to be a hatch into the ventilation system in every corridor.'

Mrs Fugosi raises her eyes from the drawing on the monitor to the chrome-coloured panels above them. 'Maybe if we could get into the ceiling, we could get to the exit through that.'

'Climb *through* the ceiling?' Kylie glances at her nails.

Ora looks up. Mrs Fugosi's idea is not a bad one; but it's not a good one either. The ceiling is a good six feet over their heads. The thought of hoisting the roundness of Mrs Fugosi through it is a daunting one.

'We can get you all up there,' says Ben, confidently.

Ora, however, is shaking her head. 'There isn't time.' Not if they're taking the fragile Kylie, Bethesda and Diane as well. And then she notices another series of hatches, these in the walls and less frequent than the ones in the ceiling.

It's Willis who points out that they don't lead anywhere. 'They look like ordinary fuse boxes.'

'That's it!' cries Luke. 'If we knock out some of the power it'll give Darth Vader something to do besides look for us.'

'Well . . .' says Ora.

'Well . . .' says Willis.

'Did you see that in a movie?' asks Ben.

Mrs Fugosi says, 'Um . . .'

'Of course,' Luke continues, 'If we knock out the power we won't be able to see where we're going.'

'Oh, that's not a problem,' says Mrs Fugosi. She opens her pocketbook. 'I have a flashlight.'

CHAPTER THIRTY-THREE

Luke's Plan Isn't One Hundred Per Cent Successful

Lucia and Emiliano have been waiting at the door behind the spaceport for some time now.

'Less than eight minutes to go,' says Lucia.

Emiliano crosses his fingers, something he hasn't done since he was four, when he realized how useless it was as a means of protection. 'They'll be here.'

That's when a siren starts to wail.

'Shit.' Emiliano looks to Lucia. 'What's that?'

'Power failure somewhere,' answers Lucia. 'It's probably just an asteroid.' She doesn't sound worried. 'It happens all the time.'

Emiliano watches another minute vanish. 'Maybe the power failure'll delay take-off,' he suggests.

Lucia shakes her head. 'No way. It's coming from

the medical centre, not the spaceport. And anyway, everything's automated and the spaceport should have several back-up power systems. The ship will leave when it's programmed to go even if we're hit by a hundred asteroids.'

A second alarm vibrates through the walls, and then a third.

'It looks like we are being hit by a hundred asteroids,' says Emiliano.

A fourth alarm goes off.

'It's not asteroids.' Now Lucia does sound worried. 'It's not random. Each one's closer than the last and in a clear sequence.'

'It must be Ora and Mrs Fugosi.' He tenses, ready to run as soon as they arrive. 'They must be covering themselves by knocking out the lights.'

'Then they must've seen a guard.' Or two, or four.

The next alarm is so close they both jump.

'But they're not just covering themselves,' says Lucia. 'They're laying a trail that the AALFs can easily follow. The soldiers will be right behind them.'

Emiliano laughs. 'Unless you've got X-ray vision you can't be sure of that.'

'Yes, I can,' whispers Lucia. 'I can hear them. Listen.'

Lucia's hearing – which owes quite a lot to a hunter who's been dead for over ten thousand years – is considerably better than Emiliano's, of course, but by concentrating harder than he's ever done before he can just make out a sound that is either a distant waterfall or quite a few booted feet moving quite quickly.

'So now what?'

Lucia takes out her gun, slips it between her hip and the wheelchair, and cracks open the door. 'The guards are all rushing off to block the main entrance. This is our chance to make a dash for the ship.' She looks back at Emiliano. He hasn't budged. 'Now.'

The next alarm can't be more than a corridor away. The lights above them go out.

'Just a few more seconds,' he pleads.

Lucia doesn't argue, but she does take him literally. 'O-one . . .' she counts. 'O-two . . . O—'

A small and fragile dot of light appears at the end of the hall. Emiliano can see a large, irregular shadow behind it that he assumes to be Ora and Mrs Fugosi.

Relief makes him laugh out loud. 'What'd I tell you?'

Behind Ora, Mrs Fugosi, the Top Teens and Mrs Fugosi's pocket flashlight is a larger, brighter light – and a good number of AALF guards.

'What'd *I* tell you?' asks Lucia.

CHAPTER THIRTY-FOUR

Lucia Demonstrates That She Understands More About Passive Resistance Than Mrs Fugosi Gave Her Credit for

Because the Corporation is run on procedures, routines and rules, Ora, Mrs Fugosi and the Top Teens have managed to keep ahead of the ever-increasing number of soldiers now following like hounds behind them by the simple expedient of doing the unexpected and weaving through the corridors in a twisting, uneven route.

But the corridor where Emiliano and Lucia have been waiting is straight as a tube and, like a tube, has an exit on either end.

As they finally come in sight of Emiliano and Lucia, the Elite Guards of the Corporation are only seconds behind them

'Stop, or we'll disable you!' warns the most elite of the Elite.

Because of these instructions – and because they have, in fact, reached Emiliano and Lucia Hiko – Mrs Fugosi and Ora stop, and the Top Teens, of course, stop too.

This is the first time since they started running through the corridors, yanking out circuit boards, that any of them have had a chance to see what's behind them.

'Sugar lumps,' whispers Kylie.

'Now look what you've done,' say Diane and Bethesda.

'God, but I want to go home,' mutters Willis.

Ora and Luke just breathe.

Ora is looking accusingly at Emiliano. 'So now what are we supposed to do?' she wants to know.

'You all go on,' orders Lucia. 'You've got about a minute and a half to get on the ship.' She places her hand over the control panel on the arm of her chair. 'I'll hold them off.'

'What did I tell you about guns?' hisses Mrs Fugosi. 'I don't care if they're not fully human, I will not have any violence.' She puts a hand on Lucia's shoulder. 'Besides,' she adds, 'you might get hurt.'

'Don't worry,' says Lucia. 'I'm trying to get you out of here, not get you disabled so you have to stay.'

Emiliano grabs hold of the chair. 'I'm not going without you. We can't—'

'I'll be fine,' says Lucia. She pushes his hand away. 'Now go!'

Emiliano has no further chance to argue. Not only

are Mrs Fugosi and Ora dragging him towards the door and the crush of Top Teens blocking him from behind, but the wheelchair suddenly shoots forward, Lucia screaming, 'Help me! Help me! I'm Dr Hiko's daughter and I've been kidnapped!' as she hurtles towards the troops.

Caught off guard, the AALF soldiers immediately halt, waiting for their computer brains to tell them what to do. They are still waiting when Lucia and her wheelchair plough into them.

CHAPTER
THIRTY-FIVE

Captain Titanic Leaves Saint Mona With a Certain Amount of Relief – and Possibly Guided by Fate

Captain Titanic stands beside her ship, watching the last of the coffin-like crates marked *Building Supplies* being loaded aboard. The crates do not, of course, contain building supplies. What they contain are destruction supplies, in the form of comatose AALF soldiers being smuggled into the outpost of Camelot under the nose of the rebel army. The AALFs won't be activated until Napoleon Lissi's assault on the troubled Earth several months from now.

While she oversees the loading, Captain Titanic is talking to Nasa Hiko on her PCS. That is, Nasa Hiko is talking, and Captain Titanic is listening.

Blahblahblah this important mission . . . Blahblahblah the glory of the empire . . . Blahblahblah the survival of civilization . . . Blahblahblah democracy and freedom.

And then Nasa Hiko says, 'Blahblahblah if anything should happen you can rest assured that the Corporation will give you a hero's funeral and name a planet after you.'

Captain Titanic would much rather have her life and a bag of potato chips than a planet named after her. She interrupts the saviour of mankind's monologue to ask, 'But what could happen? It's a secret mission. There isn't even a crew. No one knows it's taking place.'

'Nothing,' replies Nasa Hiko. 'I didn't say something would happen. I was just saying *if* it did. It's just an expression.'

Captain Titanic has been in the service of the Corporation for a good long time – long enough to know that this means that Nasa Hiko knows something that Captain Titanic doesn't know. That Camelot is under siege by the rebels. Or that the Earth itself has finally reached the stage of total environmental meltdown. Or that, because of the degenerative damage to its atmosphere, it is experiencing such cosmic storms that entry is dicey indeed. Captain Titanic has heard reassurances like Nasa Hiko's before. In the history of the Corporation, not a single mission has been sent off to almost certain doom without official assurances that everything was going to be all right and there was nothing to worry about.

'Oh, of course.' Captain Titanic nods. 'It's just an expression.'

'I have to go now,' says Nasa Hiko. 'Contact me when you arrive.'

Captain Titanic nods again. 'Right. I'll do that.' *If she arrives.*

Because of her conversation with Nasa Hiko, Captain Titanic leaves the overseeing of the rest of the loading to an AALF and goes on board her ship. Once she's in her seat, she removes something from the storage compartment in the arm. It's the brochure for the Hotel Caribe that she took from Ora's mother's car. Captain Titanic gazes at the pictures of sandy white beaches, swaying palm trees, turquoise seas, wide blue skies and golden suns. There are people sitting on the beaches and swimming in the water, and most of them are smiling. Captain Titanic knows about such things – about the warmth of the sun when there was still an atmosphere to stop it from frying you and the colours of the sea and skies before they turned to sludge – because she has been on the Earth in better times than now.

Outside the ship, the AALF Captain Titanic left in charge looks up towards the helm, waiting with the patience of a robot for the command to shut the hold.

Captain Titanic is now picturing herself sitting outside one of the 'delightful cottages with an authentic native feel' of the Hotel Caribe, sipping fruit punch actually made from fruit and eating potato chips. Captain Titanic sighs. Even if she isn't blown out of the air or incinerated by the Earth's atmosphere or pulverized by showers of asteroids, there will be no gentle breezes or attractive cabins or fruit punch waiting for her when she reaches the Earth. And once more the thought comes into her mind: *it isn't fair*. Why should she run what is very likely a suicide mission when she could be sitting on a terrace overlooking a sea that sparkles like stars with sand between her toes? Which is when another, more treacherous, thought occurs to her: *why indeed?*

Captain Titanic puts the brochure back from where she took it, and finally gives the command to close the hold.

'Hold closed,' the AALF on the ground informs her.

Captain Titanic fastens her seatbelt. 'Prepare for take-off,' Captain Titanic says to the ship.

'All systems ready,' it replies.

Captain Titanic leans back in her seat. 'Fire engines one through six,' she orders.

One by one the engines kick in, and Captain Titanic smiles as she has never smiled before.

Captain Titanic, of course, believes herself to be the only human on board. Just as she has no idea that, while she slowly rises through the roof of the spaceport, not far away a patrol of Elite Guards is disentangling itself from Lucia Hiko and the wheels of her chair, she has no idea that deep in the belly of the transporter nine humans from the twentieth century are bracing themselves against the coffin-like containers that fill the cargo hold as the ship shudders off the ground.

This is something she won't find out until it's way too late for her to do anything about it.

For which she has the great Dr Nasa Hiko to thank.

If Nasa Hiko hadn't made Lucia so quick-witted and intelligent, Captain Titanic would be told about her passengers before she left the orbit of Saint Mona.

But Lucia is quick-witted and intelligent – and not a bad actor either – so it will be days before the truth of what happened to Ora Sonorious, Emiliano Shuh, Mrs Fugosi and the Top Teens is discovered by Nasa Hiko.

Which pretty much serves the saviour of mankind right.

CHAPTER THIRTY-SIX

Mrs Fugosi, Emiliano, Ora and the Top Teens All Leave Saint Mona too – Lucia Doesn't

Ora plays the tiny flashlight over the boxes that surround them. 'Building Materials,' she reads. 'Destination: Camelot, the Earth.'

'Wow, how cool is that?' Kylie's ponytails bob with enthusiasm. 'Camelot! I always wanted to go there.' Kylie played Queen Guinevere in her high school's production of the musical of the same name and was very taken by it.

Freed from the necessity of being nice by reality, Bethesda groans and rolls her eyes. 'Oh, for God's sake, you flake. Camelot's not a real place.'

'Actually,' says Willis, 'that's not strictly true. There are several Camelots in the United States alone.'

He pulls his eyebrows together in concentration. 'In Texas . . . Nevada . . . Californ—'

Diane interrupts the flow. 'Well, thank God for that.'

'Thank you, God,' says Kylie with impressive solemnity. 'We knew you wouldn't let us down.'

Diane leans back against the crate behind her. 'I, for one, can't wait to get home. I don't even care what state we wind up in as long as there's a phone.'

'You said it,' says Ben. 'Wait'll I tell the General about this. You can bet some heads are going to roll.'

Luke looks at his watch, which shows the same time it did when the limo went off the road so many light years ago. 'I wonder how long it'll take to get there.'

'You know what I'm going to do after we get home,' says Kylie. 'I mean, after I hug my mom and dad and stuff like that?'

'I'm going shopping, that's what I'm going to do,' says Bethesda. 'I need some serious retail therapy to help me get over all this trauma.'

'I'm going to get an agent,' says Diane. 'There's got to be movie and book rights in this story. I mean, forget *being* on talk shows. After this, I should be able to get my own.'

Kylie's ponytails shake back and forth. 'Not me. I'm going to seriously dedicate myself to world peace. You know, like all those Miss Americas do? I've always been inspired by them, but after this . . .'

'I'm going to have the biggest meal in history,

that's what I'm going to do,' says Willis. 'Real food – a steak that bleeds and stuff like that.'

Ben's mouth begins to water at the thought. 'Me too. As soon as I've been debriefed.'

But after what he saw on his quick trawl through Nasa Hiko's PCS, the trauma that has Bethesda rushing to the stores and Diane starting her talk-show career has made Luke resolute. 'I'll tell you what I'm *not* going to do. I'm not going into genetics, no matter what my parents say. I think Kylie's got a point. Now that we know what happens in the future, we should try to prevent it. That's why I'm going into environmental science and do what I can to save the planet.'

All the while the Top Teens have been talking, Ora, Emiliano and Mrs Fugosi have all been lost in their own thoughts.

Emiliano's thoughts have largely concerned Lucia. The first thing he's going to do when he reaches the Earth is find a way back to Saint Mona to get her.

Ora is looking forward to firing Dr Ramin, now that she doesn't need him or his Reasons to Be Cheerful any more. Having seen the future – and realized the horrific depths to which human selfishness, greed and stupidity can lead – Ora is glad just to be alive. She feels that she finally understands life's meaning – and it isn't to have small bones or a popular boyfriend or a platinum credit card. It's just to be alive in a world where you can sit by the ocean and watch the waves.

Mrs Fugosi, however, has been thinking of the address on the crates. Camelot, the Earth. What's 'Camelot, the Earth' supposed to mean? If there are as many Camelots on the Earth as Willis says, then surely it should say Camelot, Nevada, or Camelot, Norway, or Camelot, Great Britain. Camelot, the Earth strikes her as pretty vague.

'I wouldn't start making any big plans,' she says now. 'We may not be out of the woods yet.'

'Oh, you're such a worrier, Mrs F,' Kylie laughs. 'I mean, all's well that ends, right? You'll see. It's like my gran always says. You know, things always work out, don't they?'

Mrs Fugosi stifles a sigh. Kylie could bring out the maternal instincts of Stalin, never mind a pushover like Juliana Fugosi. She forces herself to smile. 'Of course they do, dear,' says Mrs Fugosi. 'Everything's going to be perfect.'

Very much like a medieval princess imprisoned in a tower, Lucia Hiko stares forlornly into the distance. In her case, of course, she is not staring out of a tiny window at the ferocious forest that lies below, but at the more fearsome sight of Napoleon Lissi's handsome face, so very far away but still so hard and cold.

'I'm fine,' Lucia is saying. 'Really. I'm fine.'

'We were so upset when we heard what happened,' Napoleon tells her yet again. 'If they hurt one hair on your head I'll—'

'I told you before,' cuts in Lucia, who has told him several times, in fact. 'They didn't hurt me. They didn't even have guns.'

'Well, they'll wish they had guns when I get hold of them,' promises Napoleon. 'I'm going to make them wish they'd never been born.'

'I bet they already wish that,' says Lucia.

She certainly knows that she does.

'Don't worry,' Napoleon reassures her. 'Our wedding will make you forget all about this. It's going to be perfect.'

'Of course it will be,' Lucia automatically agrees – but she isn't really listening. Her mind and heart are elsewhere, shooting through the stars.

DOUGLAS ADAMS

THE HITCHHIKER'S GUIDE TO THE GALAXY

Losing your planet isn't the end of the world.

Earth is about to get unexpectedly demolished to make way
for a hyperspace bypass. It's the final straw for Arthur Dent
– he's already had his house bulldozed this morning. But
for Arthur, that is only the beginning . . .

In the seconds before global obliteration, Arthur is plucked
from the planet by his friend Ford Prefect – and together the
pair ventures out across the galaxy on the craziest, strangest
road trip of all time.

The Hitchhiker's Guide to the Galaxy is a best-selling cult
classic – and the funniest adventure-in-space you will
ever read.

JULIE BERTAGNA

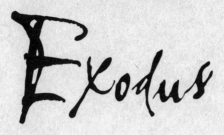

As the waters rise, the old world is lost. But a new world waits to be found . . .

Mara's island home is drowning, slowly but surely, beneath storm-tossed waves. As the mighty icecaps melt, the Earth is giving up its land to the ocean – and a community, a way of life, is going to die.

But Mara has seen something extraordinary – hints of a New World, rising from the sea and reaching into the sky. Cities where desperate refugees can surely find safety.

In a desperate bid for survival, Mara and her friends set sail in the ultimate exodus. But Mara's quest will become something even greater – a journey into humanity's capacity for good and evil. And a heart-wrenching story of love and loss . . .

LIAN HEARN

The Otori Trilogy

Across the Nightingale Floor
Grass for His Pillow
Brilliance of the Moon

In a remote mountain village high in the lands of the Three Countries lives Takeo, a boy with the exceptional skills of the deadly Tribe – preternatural hearing, the ability to be in two places at once and invisibility. But brought up among the peaceful Hidden, Takeo has yet to discover the dangerous potential of his own abilities. When his life is saved by the mysterious Lord Otori Shigeru, Takeo begins the journey that will lead him to his destiny.

As Takeo grows from boy to man he must find a path through the complex loyalties that bind him to warring clans, the ruthless Tribe and the shadowy Hidden. At the same time, Kaede, a young heiress, must also find her way, using her intelligence and exquisite beauty to assert herself in a world of all-powerful men.

For both it is a journey of revenge and treachery, honour and loyalty, beauty and magic and the overwhelming passion of love.

A selected list of titles available from Macmillan Children's Books

The prices shown below are correct at the time of going to press. However, Macmillan Publishers reserves the right to show new retail prices on covers which may differ from those previously advertised.

Douglas Adams

| The Hitchhiker's Guide to the Galaxy | 0 330 43895 6 | £6.99 |

Julie Bertagna

| Exodus | 0 330 39908 X | £5.99 |

Lian Hearn

Across the Nightingale Floor	0 330 41528 X	£6.99
Grass for His Pillow	0 330 41526 3	£6.99
Brilliance of the Moon	0 330 41350 3	£6.99

D. M. Quintano

| Perfect | 0 330 42062 3 | £4.99 |

All Pan Macmillan titles can be ordered from our website,
www.panmacmillan.com, or from your local bookshop
and are also available by post from:

Bookpost, PO Box 29, Douglas, Isle of Man IM99 1BQ
Credit cards accepted. For details:
Telephone: 01624 677237
Fax: 01624 670923
Email: bookshop@enterprise.net
www.bookpost.co.uk

Free postage and packing in the United Kingdom